The Wandering

Children of the Light Series©
Book One

Pirate Ship

Mary Schmal

by Mary I. Schmal
Illustrated by Leanne R. Ross

Leanne Ross

ISBN 978-1-64140-189-0 (paperback)
ISBN 978-1-64140-191-3 (hardcover)
ISBN 978-1-64140-190-6 (digital)

Christian Faith Publishing, Inc.
832 Park Avenue
Meadville, PA 16335
www.christianfaithpublishing.com

Printed in the United States of America

Dedicated to the following who live in the Light:

My grandma, Emma A. Zabel
My dad, Professor Carl J. Lawrenz
My mom, Irene A. Lawrenz
Duane R. Weaver
Edward A. Schmal
Michael E. Schmal
Jeri-Lynn Betts
My godfather, Professor Frederic Blume, and godmother, Norma Hoenecke
My beloved uncles and aunts and my three grandparents whom I've never met but someday will

And to Dan, Andrew, Tammy, Jacob, Shelly, Autumn, Natalie, and Savannah who know and understand my passion for lighthouses and my even greater passion for them.

Lillian Elisabeth Bates (12)

(-twins-)

Luke Stephen Paul Bates (12)

Florence (Dellie) Delight Werde (10)

-cousins- of the Bates

Garrett De Elbert Werde (12)

The Children of the Light

Julia Rose Bates (11)

Thomas Silas Charles Bates (9)

Gabriel Merritt Bates (8)

Paulina Anne Bates (10)

(-twins-)

Madeleine Kathryn Bates (8)

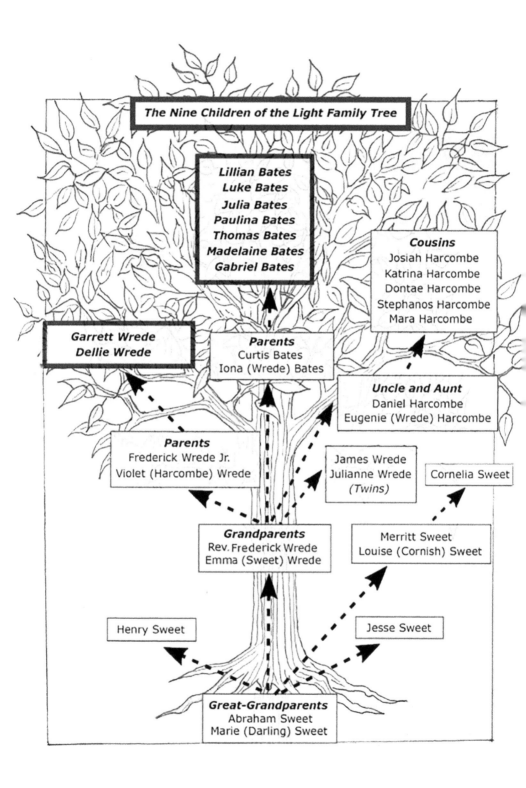

The Nine Children of the Light Family Tree

Lillian Bates
Luke Bates
Julia Bates
Paulina Bates
Thomas Bates
Madelaine Bates
Gabriel Bates

Cousins
Josiah Harcombe
Katrina Harcombe
Dontae Harcombe
Stephanos Harcombe
Mara Harcombe

Garrett Wrede
Dellie Wrede

Parents
Curtis Bates
Iona (Wrede) Bates

Uncle and Aunt
Daniel Harcombe
Eugenie (Wrede) Harcombe

Parents
Frederick Wrede Jr.
Violet (Harcombe) Wrede

James Wrede
Julianne Wrede
(Twins)

Cornelia Sweet

Grandparents
Rev. Frederick Wrede
Emma (Sweet) Wrede

Merritt Sweet
Louise (Cornish) Sweet

Henry Sweet

Jesse Sweet

Great-Grandparents
Abraham Sweet
Marie (Darling) Sweet

Contents

Foreword

On the northernmost tip of an island in Wisconsin, seven children live together at Cobblestone Lighthouse. Two visiting cousins make the group nine. As with children everywhere, each is different and special. Each struggles. Each wishes to discover. And each has a particular need. To understand love. To find joy and peace. To learn long-suffering (patience) and gentleness. To know goodness and meekness (kindness). To exercise temperance (self-control) and to follow faith (faithfulness). In short, to understand God's free spiritual gifts.

Over the course of approximately a year, these nine children have learned to understand who they are as "Children of the Light." They long to be loved, to find contentment, to experience approval, and to have fun—as children of lighthouse keepers in 1884 to 1885. They also learn their importance as children of an even greater Light.

The Wandering Pirate Ship shows the struggle and discovery of Lillian Bates. She is twelve years old at the time of her adventure. She is guided in her journey against the darkness of hatred to understand love. Guided by family and friends and us. This is her story.

E. C., A. C., S. C.

But the fruit of the Spirit is love . . .

—Galatians 5:22

Prologue

With quick feverish strokes, Lillian swam toward the small boat. Her long skirt and high cloth boots slowed her down, but she had neither time nor strength to remove them. At the very least, they kept her warm in the chilled waters of Lake Michigan. *Will I make it? Swim faster, faster!* Through blurred vision, Lillian forced her eyes to close and her body to push ahead.

Her conscience tormented her. *It's all your fault, Lillian. This horrible situation is because of you!* "Hold on!" she shouted although no one heard.

One more stroke. Lillian's thoughts raced faster than her arms could propel her forward. *Then one more. A few more and I'll be there!* Finding herself far from land in the middle of Lake Michigan, she felt destined to finish what she had begun. *I have to do this!* The vessel from which she had jumped lagged in the distance as she swam closer to the rowboat. If her rescue failed, no one could save her, but she didn't care. Her body felt numb as she struggled to fight against the cold. Then suddenly, her shivering limbs relaxed.

Warm water, its color looking distinctly red, seemed to surround her as she felt an instant thaw. Lifting herself from the mysterious surrounding warmth, the contrasting cool air blowing against her body, she shivered without losing a second of focus.

She threw one arm, then another over the weathered sides of the tiny craft, her momentary joy turning to rage.

"Leave him alone, you monster! Pick on someone your own size, you big brute!" Then without warning, long hateful arms grabbed Lillian's chilled flesh, pulled her upward, and slammed her to the floor of the rocking boat.

Acknowledgments

Special thanks is extended to Shelly Fink for her logo design; Scott Lawrenz for his letter transcriptions from the Rhoda Rohn family; Lori (Betts) Lawrenz and the late Jeri-Lynn Betts for numerous newspaper articles relating to Betts family history; *The Door County Advocate*, Washington Island, Wisconsin; Bob Wilson (Traverse City Historical Society, Traverse City), Michigan; Captain Arvon Byla and Crewman Richard Powell of the schooner *Madeline*; Paul King (Rock Island State Park and Recreational Staff, Rock Island, Wisconsin); Barbara Elafson (Washington Island Historical Society, Washington, Island, Wisconsin); the late William H. Olson (Jackson Harbor Press, Washington Island, Wisconsin) for a copy of William C. Betts's Lighthouse Log from Rock Island, Wisconsin; and Terri (Nova Scotia Live Chat); Janet Lindemann, Laura Lindemann, Kenneth Kremer, Roy and Ruth Breiling, Nancy Lohr, Rowena Kuo, Will Ross, Ella Ross, Deb Uecker, Tamara DeLonge, Shelly Fink, Leanne Ross, Jeannette Windle, Susan Smith, and especially Erin Kogler for their editing expertise and/or encouragements in preparing this manuscript; Kathy Weaver for her help with the intense, fun research; the late Irene Lawrenz for her exemplary proofreading insight, wisdom, and worthy suggestions; Dr. John C. Lawrenz for his biblical insights; and to Dan Schmal for his technical talents and unwavering encouragement and love.

Chapter 1

The Very Beginning

Three weeks earlier on a Sunday in May 1884
Late evening on Cobblestone Island in Lake Michigan, Lakeshore
County, Wisconsin

As always, Lillian had a plan. And Lillian was determined to win. The smart, quick-thinking, cunning girl of twelve was not to be outwitted by her pesky little brother. He was nine. Nine. Earlier in the day, Thomas had insisted on helping her lug water up from the lake. She was happy with his offer to help, but trouble was, he also insisted on doing the job *his* way, which he said was far better than *her* way. He even called her clumsy. Lillian never claimed to be perfect, but one thing she was sure of: she was *not* the least bit clumsy. In fact, her father continually praised her for being quick and athletic about her help with lighthouse duties. *Thomas* was the clumsy one, not her.

What did Thomas know . . . about life . . . or anything? Had she been honest, she would have said the same about herself. *She* knew nothing about life . . . or anything because she knew nothing of love. All she knew was her present mission: to rid her *talented* little brother of his assorted annoying antics. His bothersome behavior needed to be unwound, unstrung, and uncovered, for in Lillian's eyes and certainly in her heart, Thomas was *not* the brilliant child every-one seemed to think he was. And she was *done* with him pointing out his cleverness to everyone in the family, and especially to *her*, the oldest of the Bates children.

Lillian peeked around the corner, survival fixed in her mind. *Her* survival. Not his. Her eyes glowed with madness caused by burning sibling rivalry. Her father was up in the lantern room, so she and her mother would have to determine how to straighten out Thomas. When it came to disputes among the children, *she*, Lillian Elisabeth Bates, should be the one in charge, *not* Thomas. Perhaps her demand could be put into writing. Her mother could record the fate of Thomas in the lighthouse logbook. That would certainly make the necessary Who Is To Be In Charge law a lasting record for now and the future. Certainly, her mother would side with her, the firstborn.

As she thought about how to get her point across quickly, she fought another annoyance. Her long thick tresses would not stay in place. With a grunt, she swept her long hair to the back of her neck but then stopped suddenly, letting one strand dangle in her face. She smiled as a new thought formulated in her steaming brain. *If I state the situation simply, then Mother will agree with my plan. Either Thomas will be put in his place or . . . or . . .* She had trouble coming up with the "or else."

Lillian frowned, not pleased as her plans were disrupted by what she saw around the corner. *Mother should be putting away dishes or sweeping the floor or doing something I can more easily interrupt. I am not used to seeing Mother like this. After her kitchen tasks, before going to bed, Mother always goes upstairs to check whether Father needs help with lighthouse duties. What on earth is she doing?*

The flickering light from a kerosene lamp cast eerie shadows about the room. Lillian's percolating anger subsided just a bit as she saw strain painted across her mother's face. Thoughts of their recent disagreement washed over her. *Maybe I should just apologize for laying into Thomas earlier today and hope she then lays into Thomas tomorrow. That might be the better plan.* Lillian bit her lip, wondering what to do. She leaned forward but was stopped short. *She's praying! Mother is praying at the kitchen table. She usually does that in bed before she turns down the light of her bedside lamp.*

Lillian's mother pushed back stray strands of hair from a weary face. The strong and capable woman looked unusually pale. Iona Bates was the wife of Cobblestone Island Lighthouse Keeper Curtis

William Bates, the mother of seven, their schoolteacher, and the assistant lighthouse keeper besides. *Mother never looks pale. She can't afford to look pale. She's simply too busy! But Mother looks weak!*

Lillian sighed as she again drew back long strands of her thick dark locks she had just brushed during her bedtime ritual. As she bent over, her curls fell forward into her face, blinding her attempt to get a closer glance into the kitchen. She fumbled in her pocket for hairpins, finally managing to tie her mop back.

"And guard and keep the children," she heard her mother whisper. "Especially watch over Lillian."

Of course. Single me out, Mother.

Her mother sat transfixed at the large kitchen table of the lighthouse. *What is she doing?*

"Keep all nine of them in your loving care."

Nine? Oh, of course. Nine. With my two cousins, there are nine of us here at the lighthouse this summer. Suddenly, Lillian realized that additional members of the household meant her mother had more work to do. A blanket of guilt smothered her thoughts. *I shouldn't have argued with her. She was not happy with how I treated Thomas. But he was treating me worse!*

"Keep them out of danger and help Lillian be more understanding of the children from Village Galena . . ."

Lillian's teeth clamped shut as she sighed. *The kids from Galena are truly mean and senseless and wicked. Especially to us Bates kids. And especially Lucinda Lynda Pinda Schma-linda. I hate her—I hate them all.* Another sigh, this one openmouthed, replaced Lillian's furrowed brow—for sure, a distinct longing. *But I want what they have. I want to do what they do.* She stomped one foot in fury, but her mother seemed too absorbed to notice.

On the great oaken table lay the well-worn leather-covered book that her father and mother kept in their room. The huge volume, clasped with brass, was fun to open when they brought it out for family devotions in the parlor. Lillian had never seen her mother read it at the kitchen table.

Lillian watched slender fingers flip open the tarnished hinge as her mother shuffled through the Book's many pages. She seemed to search for something in particular. Lillian jumped back and out of sight as her mother suddenly picked up the Book and pressed it close to her heart, reciting from memory, "The angel of the Lord encampeth round about them that fear him." She managed to smile faintly before finishing, "and delivereth them."

She's crying! Mother is crying!

"I do believe this," Lillian's mother spoke again, this time barely above a whisper. Brushing away heartfelt tears, she finished with a soft pleading, "I *ask* for this. Thank you in advance, Lord. Thank you. Amen."

Ditching plans to present her demand or even apologize, which Lillian didn't *want* to do but felt she *should* do, the young girl took a totally different course of action. As determined as she had been to make her mother stop her little brother from being so aggravating, she now made up her mind not to interrupt. The arrest warrant to stop the taunts and tones of Chieftain Thomas could wait until morning.

Lillian tiptoed down the hallway from the kitchen to the stairway leading to her upstairs bedroom. As she climbed, she tossed a thick strand of hair that had once again fallen into her face. She glanced down toward the kitchen. *Mother was praying and asked for something. Something special. I could sense it. I'm sure of it. She believes in prayer—and knows she'll get an answer. I wonder what she asked for.*

But most of all, I wonder if I'll get to do what I want! They all do it in Galena, so why can't I do it too!

Chapter 2

The Escape

About two weeks later. Sunday, June 8, 1884
Late morning on Cobblestone Island in Lake Michigan, Lakeshore County, Wisconsin

An embankment of limestone cobbles sloping down toward the water glistened white hot in the summer sun. Lillian stepped over the jumbled assortment of stones, burning the bottoms of her bare feet. Reaching the water's edge, she cooled herself, the water around her ankles intoxicating her with a freshness that flushed her cheeks. The cold made her shriek with pleasure, and the scorching sun no longer held her in its intense grip. She lifted her long skirt and adjusted the dangling shoes that hung from one shoulder. Were she from Village Galena, she would have immediately plunged in. But she was not. She was the oldest daughter of the seven Bates children who lived at Cobblestone Lighthouse. Too many duties had prevented her from learning to swim at the island's only beach a mile from the lighthouse. Mad though it seemed, she could not and did not swim. It was a ridiculous fact.

The small arrowhead-shaped Cobblestone Island measured approximately four thousand acres, its natural beauty captured by surrounding rocky shorelines, stony white cliffs, and rustic forest interiors. On the northern tip of the island where Lillian lived at Cobblestone Lighthouse, the lake frontage below the cliff discouraged swimming. Jagged and slippery rocks lined the shore, and their mother constantly warned them to stay clear, especially considering what disaster had befallen Soren, the little brother of Lillian's best friend, Kari. Swimming in the rock-studded waters at the base of the lighthouse cliff was dangerous. The thought of swimming there was as foreign to Lillian as letting the lard cool on its way to the lantern room in the old days before Cobblestone Lighthouse used mineral oil. Unthinkable.

But lately, Lillian thought about swimming all the time. This tall, slender, athletic twelve-year-old wanted what she wanted. She did acknowledge that her parents had had no time during her growing years to take her all the way to Galena's beach, dragging along younger siblings. But she also resented her parents for not figuring out a way to make such trips possible. Lillian had never learned to swim and bitterly resented the children of Galena on the south side of the island because they had and did, often. Throughout the spring after the Bates family returned to the lighthouse from wintering on their mainland farm, her spite had risen to an all-time high. Her feelings of anger were like a sea squall ready to destroy any disagreement poised in her path. Ever since the family had left their winter home on Washburn Island for the new spring and summer season at Cobblestone Lighthouse, she and her mother had argued over this matter of swimming.

Lillian knew it was not in her mother's plans to comply with her wishes. Lillian's more pleasant side felt awful about the arguments, so she tried to dismiss her longings—but her disagreeable side seemed ready to take over and face whatever battle lay ahead.

In fact, that very morning she had fought violently with her little brother over the very matter of swimming and had been sent away to cool her temper. *Imagine! Thomas thinking I'm not able to swim! Why, I am far more athletic than he is, and that's why he's envious. He knows he couldn't swim if he tried. I positively know I can do it. I just need the chance to try.* She thought about her siblings and cousins and how different redheaded Thomas was from all of them.

Paulina has a tint of red in her hair but just a tint that makes her look nice like Mother. But Mother is mostly blond with pretty reddish streaks. Thomas doesn't take after her at all. Not at all. And he certainly doesn't take after Father like I do.

Lillian, Luke, and Julia did take after their handsome father, Keeper Curtis William Bates. All three had thick dark hair and deep-set brown eyes. Gabriel was the next closest in looks, but his hair was not as dark, and he had soft hazel eyes. The Wrede influence in him was clear. Paulina looked most like their mother. She was blue eyed and blond with reddish highlights that gleamed in the sunlight. Paulina also resembled cousins Dellie and Garrett who all seemed to have inherited a significant dose of fair Wrede German blood.

And then there was Madelaine. Her look was unique. Her thick golden hair had natural curl, and her large brown eyes prompted people to stare or take second glances. She would be a beauty someday, but luckily, Madelaine was oblivious to her own looks. At eight, she took no stock in her appearance. She did take stock in people though and freely showed an interest in different personalities. She loved people, but at the same time, she was more than content to be alone. Unlike many her age, she was comfortable with herself. Madelaine was particularly devoted to Gabriel. Although he was as "all boy" as she was "all girl," they shared a bond, not so much because they were twins but because they shared similar sensitivities.

Then there was Thomas, an island unto himself. In Lillian's opinion, he neither took after their mother nor father. He was Thomas Silas Charles, an alien in the family. Not only did his red hair set him apart. He had the most unusual green eyes. They were conniving eyes that always tried to set Lillian straight as if *she* was wrong and *he* was right. She hated him for making her feel inferior.

Lillian determined that Thomas did not fit nicely into the family. Or perhaps she was reluctant to understand how he was actually quite special. Thankfully, however, her ponderings were interrupted by a familiar voice.

"Why not enjoy the plunge, Lillie?"

"Miss Garnet! How wonderful to see you!" Lillian responded excitedly. "You think I should swim? Really?"

"Why not?" Miss Garnet's brilliant eyes, clear and blue, matched the cloudless sky. Fixed in place was the ample figure of an older woman standing above a short sloping embankment of limestone cobbles, rocks worn smooth from the relentless action of Lake Michigan. The woman stood like a hovering melody, unmoving yet a kaleidoscope of unheard sounds that Lillian seemed to taste more than hear. Somehow, Lillian knew Miss Garnet was privy to her passionate thoughts and felt no reserve to enter into a discussion she felt would surely go her way. Lillian returned an unforced smile. Anxious to approach her older woman friend, she teetered forward on the hot cobbles below.

Miss Garnet met Lillian straight on with a challenge: "Take the plunge then!"

"Wonderful idea!" Lillian shouted back, catching her left hand on the rocks as she floundered in excitement. "Miss Garnet, you have no idea that I was just thinking about swimming." Lillian's expression turned from delight at seeing Miss Garnet to an intent urge to explain her complete train of thoughts. "And I had to get away from my little brother Thomas." Lillian deepened her scorn. "He rubbed me the wrong way once too often this morning. He really gets on my nerves. His comments annoy me so much!" A profusion of bitterness erupted from within and blew from her heart like dandelion puffs scattered by a warm autumn breeze.

"Oh?" Miss Garnet simply smiled.

"And Mother sent me away—to think."

"To think?"

"Yes, she questions my love for Thomas."

"Do you love Thomas?"

"He's my brother, Miss Garnet! Of course, I *love* him but . . ."

"Love should hold no buts, Lillian."

Lillian's sudden irritation sensed an impending lecture, and she cautiously drove the conversation onto a new path. "I . . . I'm glad to see you," she hesitated. "Where are the others?"

"At home," Miss Garnet's dazzling grin gave answer. The silver white of her hair matched the intense glow of the beach cobbles bathed in late morning sunlight. The skin on her aged face also matched the smooth whiteness of the stones. Several fat seagulls flew in and out of the scene, and a soft breeze blew in a freshness that belied spring. "Have you never swum before?" the woman countered quickly. She wished to continue the topic only because she was genuinely interested. "Perhaps I've come to watch your first try." Her smile matched the vim of her voice.

Immediately, Lillian's uneasiness righted itself. She smiled back at her friend who lived just above the water on a nearby hill. The day, a rare one for Lillian, had her surprisingly craving solitude. She usually wanted to be with people but not on this day. Even so, the young girl welcomed Miss Garnet as a pleasant diversion from her anxious morning thoughts, her sudden longing to swim, and a strong inbred caution against what Miss Garnet had called "taking the plunge."

Encouragement to do precisely what she wished to do but failed to accomplish bothered Lillian, and she wasn't exactly sure why. For all her dozen years, she had never felt such an intense urge to swim—and wondered whether the recent taunts of the island children had mercilessly stoked her anger and roused her spite. When she thought about her past, which she wasn't exactly unhappy about, she simply reasoned that her family was too busy living at the lighthouse to teach her something as frivolous as swimming. Swimming was a luxury that time, household duties, and the involvement with small children could not permit. Previously, she had been okay with knowing that, but the children of Galena fueled her determination to swim. They called her odd and strange and weird because *everybody on an island swims and she does not.* Before this time, she had not given that obvious fact a moment's thought. But they were right. Dead right. And she was at the age when feeling odd felt uncomfortable. A strong temptation tugged at her will. She felt she had the right to do what every other child on the island did.

The children of Galena routinely romped and laughed on the nearby beach at the southern shore of the island. This Lillian observed and scorned. As the unusually warm days of late spring began to heat up even more, so did the jeers from this swimming crowd when they saw her pass by without a thought to join them in the cool water. With her head held high as she passed by, her eyes secretly scanned the crowd, her ears attending to their delightful dunks in the water. Lillian detested the beach group all the more for what they had and what she lacked. Perhaps she showed disgust in her demeanor that they collectively misinterpreted as pride and detachment on her part and not theirs. Because so many things Lillian observed about the children from Galena were inconsistent with how she had been brought up at the lighthouse, she perceived all the time they spent fluttering about in the water was somehow wrong as well. And this made her battle against a desire to swim that, in all honestly, she couldn't admit was as bad or wrong as she imagined.

Why do I feel this way? Mother doesn't want me to swim, but maybe it's because the rocky shoreline at home really is as dangerous as she says. Should I run over to the beach and swim there now? It's sandy and clean and full of too many people to be dangerous. Plus, the very idea that Miss Garnet approves of my "taking the plunge" must mean it's safe to swim here rather than at home. Miss Garnet would never steer me into danger. Lillian smiled, knowing her desire was winning over her caution. She knew it was a matter of time before she would indulge. In fact, her longing to do something on her own was never greater than at that very moment. Whether right or wrong, she would swim and swim and swim.

Lillian closed her eyes. Momentarily, she pushed from her thoughts all household duties and the growing annoyances over Thomas. She imagined herself escaping to an unknown world, floating toward an island shore where smooth cobblestones lay submerged below cool shallow waters. She drank deeply of this image, letting the smooth contours of the moment sink into her soul. Silently, she thanked Miss Garnet for interrupting her jumbled thoughts of her disagreeable life at home to usher in more pleasant desires.

"No, Miss Garnet. We never swim." Lillian looked away from Miss Garnet in an attempt to collect her thoughts and to think through why she and her siblings had never learned to swim. "There are seven of us at the lighthouse," Lillian attempted to explain, "and

Mother has been too busy to teach us such things. With two sets of twins and three children in between, there just hasn't been the chance to learn or to let us older kids go so far alone with the younger ones."

I'm old enough now. Lillian's thought was accompanied by a resentful frown.

"And, and the swimming beach is a whole mile away from the lighthouse," she continued in defense, feeling the need to cover for her parents. "Mother and Father could hardly take that much time away from their official duties to teach us to swim. There are too many of us, and we were always too young to, to . . ."

"You sound defensive, Lillian." Miss Garnet paused. "Now here is *their* defense. They have taught you other things, haven't they? Things of far greater importance than learning to swim?" Miss Garnet's intent gaze bore holes straight into the pupils of Lillian's dark eyes. Lillian felt ashamed. The answer was obvious, but the answer that came out was more self-defense.

"Well, yes, of course," she shot back, searching in her mind for another reason to cover for her parents being too busy. "And now that my two cousins, Garrett and Dellie, are staying with us . . . my mother has even more children to cook for and keep track of."

"Do you not keep track of yourself? You *are* twelve years old."

"Yes, I *am* twelve and old enough to learn how to swim on my own. I've watched the swimmers many times at Galena Beach." Yes, beneath her cool detachment toward them, she had indeed observed how they swam.

Miss Garnet smiled knowingly. From behind her gray skirt that fluttered in a gentle breeze as she stood on the grassy landing above, she produced a single piece of odd-looking woolen clothing. Miss Garnet handed over the blue-gray wad. Knowing this was a gift, Lillian directed her slender body upward across the embankment of cobbles until she reached level ground. Just as she reached for the balled-up garment of wool from Miss Garnet's outstretched hand, Lillian noted a motion to her left, toward the northern hill. Her sister Julia came racing somewhat clumsily forward, her long skirt flowing. Julia's dark straight hair trailed in the wind. How Lillian loved this sister who was slightly younger, slightly less agile, definitely less aggressive, but infinitely lovelier, at least to Lillian's way of thinking.

"Lillie! Lillie! Mother said we could meet Kari at the meadow to pick wildflowers. And the boys are coming along to watch a schooner load up with stone."

Ordinarily, Lillian would thrill for a chance to see Kari, her best friend on Washburn Island, but not now. Disappointment welled from within as she turned back to seek further wisdom from Miss Garnet. But Miss Garnet had disappeared. Now her frustration formed a new dilemma. What should she do with the funny-looking bathing garment crumpled in her hand? And would Thomas be along? He wasn't "one of the boys," but he might come tagging along. Lillie quickly threw the woolen wad into her satchel before Julia could ask ten thousand questions. *I will swim.* With this firm resolve, she released herself from the nagging fear that she probably should not.

Lillian did not hesitate to accept Julia's invitation to ride across to Washburn Island to meet dear Kari. *Someday I will swim! I will come to know the feeling the children of Galena know as they swim all summer long.* She determined to find another break from her duties in life to come back to this spot. And she *would* swim and swim and swim *and possibly never stop.*

"Yes, Julia. Let's go. I see the yawl is in the dock."

"Good! Mother gave me a coin for both of us and for the boys to cross too."

"Does Mother want new flowers?" Lillian asked in wonder over this opportunity to get away.

But Julia did not have to answer because their mother always wanted new flowers to put on the large kitchen table at the lighthouse. Lillian reasoned that their mother was obviously ahead in her daily work to have let her, and now Julia and the boys, take the mile-long walk to the water and let them cross to Washburn Island.

What had Mother said earlier that morning? Lillian, you need to take a long walk. To get away. To think things through. To dwell on the meaning of love. Sure, I love my little brother, but do I always have to give in to annoying "master" Thomas Silas Charles's every want and need? Whatever other reason lay behind this sacred released time, Lillian was sure she had followed her mother's direction to learn something about love.

She *loved* being as far away from Thomas as possible. At age nine, Thomas seemed to be the most intellectually gifted of the children, the very reason Lillian despised him so. She was the oldest, and in her mind, she should be in charge. It didn't matter that Thomas was different, unusual, and special. To Lillian, he was the ever present, ever annoying sibling she could very well live without. She would dearly *love* her mother for keeping Thomas at home for once. While *loving* her new determination to "take the plunge" as Miss Garnet had encouraged, she somehow felt Thomas would get in the way. He would surely tell her to do it *his* way.

Oh please, please, please. No Thomas. Please. She smiled broadly when "the boys" appeared over the grassy hill without Master and Commander Sir Thomas Silas Charles Bates.

Lillian and her eleven-year-old sister Julia; Lillian's twin brother, Luke; and their twelve-year-old cousin, Garrett, sailed off to Washburn Island. Fun-loving brother Gabriel came along too. At eight years old, Gabriel was the youngest in the family and also twin to beautiful dark-eyed Madelaine who had stayed home with nine-year-old Thomas. And so had ten-year-old Paulina, another sister who wanted to dream up some artful play with Garrett's sister, their creative cousin, Dellie, also aged ten.

Paulina and Dellie will have their own adventure at home—drawing or creating a playhouse in the woods, Lillian thought. *They can do their girlie-girl thing at home, but I prefer adventure, without Thomas!*

Lillian smiled a beautiful yet conniving smile in anticipation over what might be in store for them on Washburn Island.

So four Children of the Light stayed at home on this sunny summerlike afternoon in 1884 while the remaining adventurous five took off in a yawl boat, steered by an able captain.

Larger than Cobblestone, Washburn Island lay a brisk ten minutes south when the wind was right. Lillian patted the sack that held her new swimsuit treasure. Plotting in her head, she bit her lip and narrowed her eyes, wondering how and where she could quickly change in order to swim across to Washburn Island while the others sailed alongside.

But before she could finalize her plans, Julia whizzed past in a whirlwind, snatching away Lillian's bulging satchel. Floundering ahead with her arms flailing to steady herself on the uneven sloped surface, Julia left behind her dazed sister still standing on the sun-baked cobbles. Julia stopped to turn, just long enough to tease back a playful shout, "Beat you to the yawl, sis!"

Chapter 3

Watching the Sadie Thompson

Immediately following that Sunday on Washburn Island

Lillian sulked the whole way across to Washburn Island. The boys hadn't noticed, and Julia figured Lillian's sullen mood was simply because she had been beaten in a race to the ferry sailboat. Lillian liked to win. Julia smiled as she tried to reason out the situation. With her sister being fiercely competitive, Julia considered how losing was probably good for Lillie's humility. She didn't have to win *every* time. Besides, once on the island, Lillian would be happy to meet up with Kari whom she hadn't seen in quite a while. But for the whole ride over, Lillian seemed lost in thought.

Kari Hansen met the girls at the dock, swinging a large but empty straw basket across her left arm. Kari had inherited her mother's love for flowers and seemed to keep her mother's spirit alive by tending the "dooryard garden" that her departed young mother had left behind in front of their small house on Washburn Island. Kari now lived alone with her father. Their tiny log house that had once housed four now seemed spacious for only two.

Kari's father, Christopher Hansen, a spirited and popular

individual, reigned as Washburn Island's sole blacksmith, a man also known for making locks and keys. Kari, his flower-tending tomboy daughter, flashed her friends an excited grin that made her freckles spread across her cheeks. Her anticipation for adventure took away any trace of Lillie's lingering annoyance, and the girls locked arms. Excited to be together, the three pranced off to pick wildflowers.

Meanwhile, the boys jumped off the two-masted fisherman's yawl and headed to where the schooner *Sadie Thompson* lay docked at Morrison Harbor.

Sadie Thompson stood stately in the water.

"Look at that!" shouted Gabriel. "I wonder how big she is."

A sailor on board let a line of rope slide through his hands as he slackened a sail and tied the rope expertly as if he had done it many times before. He brushed a dirty left hand against his right cheek as he glanced down at the three boys. "She be ninety-two feet long with a sixteen-foot beam. And you know what else? Her gross tonnage is fifty tons, boys. She kin take a mighty cargo of rock in her hold, by jingo! She be the pride and joy of Mr. Peter Thompson, her master from Whitefish Harbor, if you have to know. She be a good sailing vessel too." The sailor grinned exposing a dark, somewhat toothless mouth.

Gabriel's innocent eyes sparkled at the information, but Luke gave his little brother a strong elbow nudge. "Hush up, Gabriel. Let them work."

"I'm not bothering anyone."

"She was built two years ago in '82 down in Maney-tee-wash and got a magnet on board," the scruffy sailor continued. The second time he showed his toothless cavern made Gabriel shudder.

Then Ross, another sailor on board the *Sadie Thompson*, gave his partner a shove. "Charley, we have work to do. Enough of your lecturing for the kiddies."

"I'm proud of this here schooner, Ross, and I mean to say so," Charley continued.

Ross waved him off as a hopeless chatterbox and went back to work, shoveling assorted sizes of limestone cobbles into the center hull.

Then as the three boys were approached by Charley, they instinctively backed up just a little on the pier.

"Want you to know sumpin'? Want you to know sumpin' real speciallike?"

Gabriel wasn't sure about this man, but he loved seeing a new schooner, especially in an age when iron-hulled steamers were over-taking sailing ships on the Great Lakes. Gabriel loved anything powered by wind. The workings of sails and ropes intrigued him, so he brightened in anticipation of learning something new about schooners. A good step ahead of his brother and cousin, he met Charley face-to-face with determination. "Aye, aye, sir. I want to know." Gabriel saluted the sailor with the innocence of an eight-year-old.

Charley let out a yelp and added a hearty laugh. "This here schooner helps shipwrecks, see? She's got a magnet on board." Charley had already said that, so losing his courage to befriend this giant old man, Gabriel stepped back one pace, thinking this sailor was either forgetful or not entirely in his right mind. He was definitely not the brightest lamp in the tower.

"This here magnet kin find anchors an' chains an' boiler parts an' engine pieces, see? In a wreck, see?"

In his excitement over the power of the magnet, spit sprayed from his mouth and landed on Gabriel's nose. Gabriel gulped in horror, thinking Charley for sure would delight in finding a wreck that very afternoon just to salvage parts. Only Gabriel was not sure if he wanted to be in that adventure. He thought Charley might even cause a wreck just to see the magnet do its job.

"She kin carry her cargo good enough, but she kin load up real good with junk from ships that be blasted to pieces in a storm," he said ominously, trying purposefully to make Gabriel's eyes grow wide with fear. Seeing his success, he continued, "She's first one out in spring and always one of the last to lay herself up when the leaves turn ta or-ange." He pronounced orange as two distinct syllables, which Gabriel found fascinating. Losing his fear to fascination, he was beginning to like this peculiar old guy.

Gabriel looked over the two-masted schooner. He wondered about the name but was still somewhat afraid to continue the conversation.

Eerily, as if the sailor were not only a wretched old seaman but a mind reader as well, Charley spilled out, "And do ya want to know about her name? Well, ya see, Sadie be the name of the wife of the master, Peter." He waited until he was sure he had the boys' rapt attention before he continued slowly and deliberately, "Until the wife drowned in the Channel 'O Destruction!" And with that, he let out the same raucous yelp that had startled the boys seconds before. This time, all three stepped back.

Charley called, "I'm a comin', Ross Clow. I just give them strappin' boys a lecture to learn them a thing or two about shipping." And he yelped another good one. In disdain, Luke rolled his eyes and pulled Gabriel away to end any further conversation with this Charley fellow.

"Charley's kinda strange, Luke, but I like him. I don't like the other guy, Ross Clow, though. He's not friendly," sputtered Gabriel.

"C'mon, Gabe. Let's go around the other side of the pier and watch this Ross guy load in the cobbles. I don't care if he's not friendly. I don't plan on taking him home with us or even talking to him anyways."

For a long time, Luke, Gabriel, and their cousin Garrett sat on the grassy bank and watched the bulging muscles of Charley Skruggs, Ross Clow, and two other nameless crewmen as they shoveled and loaded *Sadie Thompson* with rock cargo bound for Milwaukee.

Meanwhile, the girls were off picking wildflowers in nearby Kari's Meadow, a special area near the dock that Kari had once discovered and proclaimed as her and her friends' own. Lillian had kept an eye on her brothers, wondering exactly what kind of mischief they were getting into. She watched Gabriel's interaction with Charley although she wasn't close enough to make out what they were saying.

Fresh breezes and a changing surf added interest to the girls' special meadow hideaway. Nearby, amidst the wildflowers, stood a serviceable building meant to preserve fish for the fishermen. This rugged ice house standing north of the pier was the only intrusion

upon the natural scenery. The girls felt peaceful in their meadow. Lillian stood on the level cobbles that lined the land and adjoined the water on the outer edge of Morrison Harbor. As a cool northeast wind blew, she reached to pull a strand of hair out of her mouth. She was careful to keep her distance from the water since she now wore shoes. Stretching ahead, she saw beautiful Cobblestone Island. A thin line of brilliant white outlined the western shoreline. Sunlight illuminated the distant cobble rows where moments ago she had dipped her feet and contemplated her first swim. Her longings returned, but she felt helpless to act upon them.

Graceful seagulls flew in and out of the scene, taunting one another in playful calls as if engrossed in some kind of competitive game. A single blue heron stood on one leg, and red dragonflies chased each other across the rushes. The sandy mud of the pond bottom showed the dryness of the season. Wisps of rushes stuck up in enormous clumps, and the little meadow pond lay in a wash of bright gold from thousands of bladderworts. Lillian smiled at the lovely sight and, in a secret daydream, contemplated her adventurous first swim.

Kari and Julia joined Lillian on the limestone ridge, Kari proudly displaying her bouquet of flowers.

"Aren't the Indian paintbrushes beautiful this year? And we found asphodel and lobelia!" shouted Kari as she held up a clump of colorful flowers.

"And smell these," called Julia as she waved sweet-smelling wild savory through the air and under the noses of the other two.

"Where did you find those?" Kari called out as she watched Lillian add purple gerardia to her basket with one hand and pick up a folded piece of paper lying on the ground with the other hand.

Lillian glanced momentarily at the note but then stuffed it into her apron pocket to examine later. *It might mean something*, she thought.

"Behind the icehouse," Lillian added in distraction because she had other thoughts on her mind, "I found the purple ones back over there." Without turning around, she motioned behind herself.

Kari sensed Lillian's aloofness. Lillian seemed different since her time away, but Kari dismissed any fear over a dissolving friendship as a ridiculous thought. As Kari set her flower basket on the ground, she thought of their many best-friend talks, deep-felt sharing that would surely never end. Unwilling to spoil the magical moment, a long-anticipated afternoon reunited with her best friend, Kari bent forward, her tawny braids dangling down and brushing against the ground. She pulled the Bates sisters toward her, linking arms as companions do. The three breathed deeply of the summer air in Lakeshore County on beautiful Lake Michigan.

The shore meadow was their special place. It changed with the seasons, and they mutually proclaimed late spring as their favorite, at least until autumn came, making that season their top choice. For a moment, the girls stood together, enjoying friendship and solitude and love.

"Hey! Julia! Larry! When are we going to eat?" Luke's sudden appearance startled the three.

Lillian turned around and laughed scornfully. "Never, unless Mother packed us a lunch."

"Of course, she did," Garrett countered. "When doesn't your mother pack us something to eat? She wouldn't want us to die of starvation over here!"

"C'mon back by the dock," suggested Luke. "Mother packed plenty for all of us, Larry. Let's eat now and watch the men finish up the load-ing." Luke liked to call his athletic twin sister "Larry." It was his way of protecting her, even keeping her humble as her blossoming femi-nine beauty was becoming more and more obvious.

"Good idea!" shouted Gabriel who immediately turned and ran back to the *Sadie Thompson*.

The early afternoon weather held no flaws. The breeze that had kicked up cooled the advancing heat of high noon, an unusually hot day for early June in Lakeshore County. The children found a spot to observe the action and anticipated a good show, watching the sailors finish their cobblestone shoveling job.

Abruptly, a cry pierced the air. This time, it was not a harm-less yelp from Charley but something sounding serious. The deep masculine voice, colored with an uncharacteristic shrillness, was a tone quite unlike anything the six had heard before. The commotion made them stare at the scene ahead.

A fifth man on the ship made a sudden appearance. Unlike Charley or Ross or the other two silent-working sailors, this one had the look of importance. He lifted his arm and, with a tight fist, made a pounding gesture upon Charley who crumpled to his knees on the deck of the schooner *Sadie Thompson*.

"I'm sorry, sir, Captain, sir. I'll get the last of them limestone pieces on board right away," cowered Charley. "I didn't mean to dally none. I was about to—"

"Mind your tongue, you miserable morsel of a man!" shouted this fifth figure on board, obviously the man in charge. "Get to work!" His voice pierced the air, and Gabriel felt sure that his father heard the din miles away at Cobblestone Island Lighthouse.

By now Gabriel decided he liked the scraggly Charley and felt bad at his present mistreatment. Charley surely meant well, and somehow he seemed to hold hope for an adventure. Gabriel was always ready for that.

He decided right then and there that he did not like the mean captain of the *Sadie Thompson*. He wasn't sure about Ross or the other two, but he swore undying loyalty to old Charley.

Charley staggered to his feet and began loading the last cobbles into the ship's hold. His biceps bulged majestically as he scraped up stones with the shovel. The cantankerous captain stood afar off and watched, arms akimbo, looking ready to burst out in anger at any further delays.

From another boat came a distant though distinct cry, "Sam Steele! Sam Steele!"

And just as meadow flowers wither and die upon the first frost to await new life in spring, Captain Sam Steele's demeanor transformed. His arms relaxed, and he stood statue perfect, a godlike image washed in warmth and conviviality before he thrust one foot forward and waved confidently toward the call from the lake. Totally unlike his actions before, Captain Steele blazed back an uncharacteristic smile that suggested he was everyone's uncle or at least best of friends with the man who had called his name from the distant boat out a distance in the water.

Lillian's keen observation caught Captain Steele's physical signal to the caller off shore. She saw Steele make a hand gesture, a pact that seemed to indicate both boatmen were to meet out on the lake.

Lillian's thoughts were suddenly disrupted when she heard her name called out accompanied by a friendly wave. She looked up to see in the distance Dr. Federmann giving her a thumbs-up. "Glad to see you finally up and about!" he shouted out to her.

Lillian thanked the kind gentleman with a wave back. Behind the doctor, she observed a definite scowl from the crewman they called Ross as he bent down on the dock to retrieve his shovel. Ross

then jumped aboard his ship and quickly disappeared below the deck. Momentarily, however, he popped up his head one last time to throw out another angry snarl toward the watching children.

Before long, the sails of the *Sadie Thompson* plumped out as she headed out of the harbor, south toward Milwaukee. Captain Sam Steele, his two mates Ross and Charley, as well as two other sailors seemed to have the beautiful schooner under control, cobblestones safely stowed in its hull ready for delivery.

As she had predicted, Lillian saw in the distance the two ships briefly meeting on the windswept lake. She noticed a flurry of activity and an exchange of some sort before the two boats parted ways. Storing the occurrence in her memory but not particularly caring that it meant anything, Lillian returned her focus to Julia and Kari who were chattering about flowers and picnics and meadows. The boys, however, tugged at the girls and pointed toward the approaching yawl, its single headsail jib billowing in the breeze. Finding their adventure on Washburn Island over, they were eager to catch their transportation back to Cobblestone Island. The boys had no time and certainly no desire to bask in the sun to admire the day or to fawn over a bunch of flowers; more important things called for them back home.

By stark contrast, as Lillian waved good-bye to Kari Hansen on the pier, her thoughts bloomed with wildflowers and friendship and of Miss Garnet standing on the cobblestones.

Thankfully, she had dismissed all thoughts of her annoying nine-year-old brother Thomas from whom she was glad to have escaped. The first one to step onto the boat that would sail the group home, she smiled in a renewed determination and desire to swim. Her cravings grew stronger as she felt soft waves rock beneath the sailing yawl.

Nearing Cobblestone Island, Lillian felt she had contemplated her own adventure long enough and decided to finally act upon it. *Splash*. Without warning, just before the sailing yawl close hauled its final tack toward Cobblestone Island, Lillian jumped overboard, plunging herself into the cool shallow waters of the bay.

Chapter 4

A Visit to Cottage Parakaleó

Sunday evening at Cottage Parakaleó on Cobblestone Island

The boys hadn't seen the action coming. They had been digging around in the pail of worms that Captain Jonas Driver had dug and brought along for his coming fishing expedition. Julia as well had been distracted by leaning over starboard to watch the pattern created by the wake as Lillian, in a streak of grayish blue, simply dove overboard portside.

"What are you doing, Lillie?" shouted Gabriel, rubbing his eyes in disbelief. "Do you want to drown?"

"Lillian!" Luke called in alarm to his twin.

"Did you fall overboard?" chimed in a frightened Julia now at the left side of the sailboat where the commotion had begun.

Garrett simply laughed quite uncontrollably once he realized his cousin was in no danger. Wasn't it just like a girl?

Lillian broke into an automatic breast stroke, pushing back the clear water with rhythmic force as she dunked her head upon each push forward, spitting out water as she brought

her head up for air. Imitating the swimmers she had watched in Galena, she moved toward shore with the gracefulness of a seasoned swimmer. She felt cool and refreshed and exhilarated. And as she climbed out of the water onto the cobbled embankment, she met the smiling gaze of the ever-watchful Miss Garnet.

Clumsily, the barefooted Miss Garnet clambered down to meet Lillian and offered her a hand. "Well, I see you took the plunge, my dear. And if I didn't know better, I'd say you've been practicing a long time. Such grace you show."

"Oh, Miss Garnet! Miss Garnet! It was wonderful, wonderful! Swimming is ever so much better than I even imagined. I saw you standing on the hill, and I thought I heard you say, 'Do it, Lillie. Do it. Do it.' So without a moment's thought, I was over and in."

"And I see the swimming costume fits nicely."

"Yes, I, I," she proceeded cautiously, "slipped into the icehouse when the others were busy. I saw the door latch ajar and went in. I quickly changed into what you gave me and put my clothes over it. It was the perfect chance to change!"

"And change you did, my dear. Considering your experience with icehouses, I am shocked that you went *inside* the icehouse!" Lillie caught Miss Garnet's coy expression that betrayed greater meaning. Lillian had indeed had a most unpleasant experience with an icehouse upon her recent stay in New Jersey visiting her uncle, aunt, and cousin. But perhaps she was trying her best to forget that unfortunate incidence had ever happened. Miss Garnet interrupted her thoughts. "You loved it, didn't you?"

"I did." Lillian smiled back feebly. "Well, not exactly the ice-house, but it was the only place to change." And then dismissing thoughts of dreary icehouses and instead remembering her mother's directive to think about love, she added, "I did love the swim though." Somehow her spat with Thomas seemed trivial. He was only nine. She could forgive him for being nine. Except that he acted thirteen. She had trouble loving him for that.

By that time the yawl had docked and the four other children were stumbling up the steep embankment of cobbles, Captain Jonas, standing at the stern with one hand on the wheel, pursed his lips and

shook his head but with ever so playful a smile suggesting he understood Lillie's impulsive urge. In his right hand, he held up a pile of familiar-look-ing garments.

"Oh, Julia, please run back and get my things, would you?" pleaded Lillian.

"Lillian Elisabeth! Where did you get that?" Julia demanded, indicating the unusual blue woolen outfit with which her sister had adorned herself.

"Never mind just now. Please get my clothes so Captain Driver can get on with his fishing," countered Lillian.

Julia thrust a large bouquet of wildflowers towards Lillian, the blossoms she had so carefully shielded against the wind during the sail back to Cobblestone Island. "Hold these while I go please," she urged as she turned away, then back again with a look that suggested Lillian looked ridiculous. Soon, Julia was off and back in no time with Lillian's clothes folded in a neat pile. The boys dismissed the whole jumping overboard and spontaneous swimming experience as something only a silly girl would do. Luke, Garrett, and Gabriel sped off on the trail through the woods of Cobblestone Island on the mile-long path that led to the lighthouse.

"Girls, do you want to come up to the cottage?" Miss Garnet began. "I have freshly baked cookies, and Lillie, you need to dry off. C'mon up for a bit, will you?"

Lillian needed no further prod-ding, and Julia was just as eager to visit their three new friends at their hillside cottage. The sisters each took hold of Miss Garnet's arm, and with her in the middle, they plod-ded upward on the north road until they came to the stone steps leading

up the hill to Cottage Parakaleó, their new favorite home away from home.

Lillian was practically dry by the time they had finished the climb to the little stone cottage on the grassy wooded hill. Miss Garnet offered to place the colorful assortment of spring flowers in a vase and promised to bring back fresh cookies.

The sisters waited outside on the stone porch, each one leaning on two of the four tall cloud-white pillars that held up the roof loft. They tried to slowly breathe in the gorgeous lake view, but the scene took their breath completely away.

Julia felt happy to be back on Cobblestone Island after the long winter months at their farm on Washburn Island. Throughout this time, the lighthouse had lain idle.

From the first of December through the first of April, ships did not travel the ice-covered lakes throughout the cold months, and a lighthouse keeper was not needed. Lillian though had been on the island recovering from an illness, but not at Cobblestone Lighthouse. She turned around to glance inside the cottage she had learned to love. She had introduced her siblings to her newfound friends, the women who lived here—three special ladies who had nursed her back to good health. Lillian and Julia visited as often as they could to enjoy the white miniature southern plantation-style building and especially "the Three" who lived inside. All three were friendly, friendlier than most adults they knew. *They care so much for us. They guard us as their own children. It seems as if they've known us for years!*

Lillian closed her eyes to picture in her imagination the inside of the cottage. She had not visited in a while. *Living space on the left and kitchen on the right. Will Miss Garnet invite us in?* She smiled as she viewed in her mind the sleeping loft where she had been quarantined and where she and her sister occasionally stayed when invited overnight. Opening her eyes, Lillian approached the door on the stone porch and held her face close to the screen to peek inside. She delighted to see the far wall of the living room, a sturdy oak ladder running straight up its center, the entrance to Miss Tourmalina's loft. *Is Miss Tourmalina up there, creating a poem or song? I wonder how she climbs up that ladder at her age. She seems too old, but she's up there all the time, and that's the only way in. I've seen her head poke through the entrance at the top of the ladder. I wonder if she'll ever invite me up. I'd like that! I wonder if her loft has the same low sloping ceilings as my loft . . .*

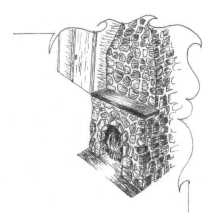

Lillian referred to the loft she and later Julia and the other girls had claimed as their own. This loft was accessible from a ladder running at an angle in one corner of the kitchen that lay south of the living area. It was divided by a floor-to-ceiling stone wall that was the back of a fireplace exposed in the living room. This upper room had been Lillian's sleeping quarters for weeks, and now she and Julia slept there when they stayed at the cottage. Lillian thought about this loft, *I wonder if the trap door is open so I can scuttle up there and read.*

Meanwhile, Julia had wandered over to the porch loft, accessible only by a ladder attached to the outside wall of the stone cottage. Similar in size and structure to the kitchen loft, this was the room claimed by Luke, Garrett, and Gabriel when they once had stayed for the night. Its two gabled windows, providing a breathtaking view of the water, gave the boys a rustic outdoors' feeling inside. The trap door leading to this more rustic loft was wide open, secured by a varnished piece of latch wood designed to hold up the trap door for entrance. The very sight seemed to beckon the boys inside, but they were not there that day to accept the invitation. They had already gone home. Julia sighed. It would have been fun for the five of them to play *The Mansion of Happiness* in the lake-view loft to see if Lillian could beat Luke to heaven. He had won the last round and was rubbing it in. The floor, which was actually the ceiling of the porch itself, lay covered with braided rugs, a splendid play area.

Quietly, Lillian moved away from Julia and opened the screen door of the cottage. As familiar with the building as she was, she still felt cautious about entering without an invitation. Still, she didn't think the women would mind if she stepped inside. Turning toward her left, she saw Miss Garnet's room. With longing, Lillian glanced away from Miss Garnet's bedroom door and looked at the many books lining the living room wall. Book shelves covered the wall, separated only by the loft ladder that stretched straight up between them. Lillian would have tiptoed inside to grab a story, if these books were indeed stories and not just research material for Miss Ruby, but noticed Miss Ruby herself seated in the far right corner absorbed in work at her trusty writing desk. Miss Ruby's desk faced the wall perpendicular to the book-lined wall. Her bedroom door, next to the expanse of bookshelves, stood shut. *I wonder how long Miss Ruby will be studying and thinking at her desk?*

Lillian had seen both Miss Garnet's and Miss Ruby's rooms. She enjoyed Miss Garnet's the best. Her room lay at the opposite side, to the left of the great ladder and the left shelves of books. Miss Garnet's room afforded a magnificent view of the lake. The stones from the old Cobblestone Lighthouse, restored to this site, showed through a side window. The feeling was cheerful and inviting. Miss Ruby's room, on the other hand, felt dark and secluded. Miss Ruby had told Lillian she liked her woodsy window view because "the seclusion affords no chance to witness bright coruscations of light from the lake to distract my ponderous thoughts." Although Lillian had no idea what that meant, she was sure that Miss Ruby's focus on life was quite different from Miss Garnet's.

Miss Ruby dressed formally, and this appearance matched her personality. She liked to remain indoors and enjoy her quiet, studious writing desk environment. By contrast, Miss Garnet dressed casually and liked the outdoors, preferring to walk barefoot on the many island cobblestones that lined the shoreline. Lillian enjoyed Miss Garnet best because she liked to talk and listen. That suited Lillian's tastes completely. Lillian needed someone to listen to her tumbling, jumbling thoughts. After all, she was a young lady of twelve, practically grown up and with many ideas and dreams of her life to come.

Lillian decided not to disturb Miss Ruby, so she quietly stepped back outside to rejoin Julia on the porch. As she tried to catch the door so it would not slam, she looked up at the majestic living room ceiling that rose to a cathedral height. Dark wooden beams ran horizontally across the ceiling. Artistic open diamond shapes carved out of wood at the center of each beam created an airy effect of rustic medieval majesty. The deep rich oak invited an atmosphere of cozy warmth.

Lillian paused a moment before she stepped onto the stone porch outside. Her eyes ran up the living room ladder running straight up the wall between the array of books. She glanced toward the top at the diamond-shaped entrance to Miss Tourmalina's loft, the same shape continued from the beams crossing the ceiling. Her head churned with thoughts: *Is she up there working on a new poem to recite to us? Will it be a song for us to sing together? How I love this tall graceful woman. How enchanting is her smile! But I know her the least of the three. I've never been inside her loft. She isn't around as much as the other two. I wish I knew her better.*

A sudden flurry of activity from the right distracted Lillian. Miss Ruby had suddenly risen from her desk chair to step into her bedroom, the door closing with a slam.

This is my chance, thought Lillian. *Why, I could quickly slip into the little storybook library and grab an adventure. I could be back outside before anyone notices.* Deciding to act on her sudden impulse, Lillian quickly stepped back into the cottage. She tiptoed lightly across the room past the great stone fireplace wall that separated it from the kitchen. Large island limestone cobbles of various shapes and colors fashioned the fireplace and defined itself as the room's most picturesque feature.

Directly across from Miss Ruby's door, on the far side of the living room next to the stone fireplace, Lillian stood before another door. This entrance opened into a tiny library dominated by floor-to-ceiling bookshelves. The room was just large enough for one or, at most, two small people. A ladder on wheels enabled anyone interested to climb up to pull a book from a top shelf. Unlike the deep topics of the living room books, this library was a treasure trove of storybooks for young and old, an absolute delight to any reader. And unlike the traveling book case that the lighthouse tender brought to

Cobblestone Lighthouse, these books stayed here for good. *What a thought!*

Before entering, Lillian stood transfixed as she stared at the familiar plaque above the door. Painted in gold on wood against a deep-sea background of dark blue, she read and whispered the familiar words. The phrase never failed to engulf and hold her in a grip of mystery. She could not easily disregard the glinting gold reflected in the elegant lettering. Today light flooding through the cottage windows to her left especially illuminated the words so its message sang out like an angelic choir: "Walk as Children of the Light."

The sentiment stopped her in her tracks. *But I must hurry*, Lillian reasoned. Somehow, the words held her a moment longer, halting her harried pace. The plaque begged time stop as she pondered what those words could possibly mean. Lillian believed she and her siblings and their two visiting cousins were Children of the Light. She believed the three women at Cottage Parakaleó, whom she had known only a short time (but for what seemed a lifetime) somehow contributed to their being so. She had felt this especially when Miss Ruby had read to her, to all of them now, from the Book.

Lillian rushed inside and gazed momentarily at the many shelves adorning the little library. The sight was eye candy. More colorful and filled with more pictures than the books the lighthouse tender *Trillium* brought to the lighthouse, she preferred reading these; she had read quite a few during her recent stay. Lillian was thrilled at the open invitation to choose a new book whenever she liked. She selected an interesting title printed in forest green against a log brown cover. As she turned to leave the library, she believed she had made a wise choice not to select a book from one of the living room bookshelves. Many were written in Latin and Greek or German or French—or another unknown language to her. They were thick and difficult, books whose content was way above her understanding; yet she was somehow drawn to one day try one. She would have to ask the women for help to understand their messages. *The women are learned*, Lillian pondered. *Their books prove that. They are gifted and intelligent, different from one another yet one in spirit.* As Lillian stepped onto the porch with the new book clutched close to her chest, her thoughts turned to wondering whether the women were sisters. *They haven't told me they are. But I seem to think so! Or had someone mentioned that they are? Why, I'll have to ask Miss Garnet about that.* She smiled proudly. *I can talk to her about anything.*

Moments later, Miss Garnet backed into the screen door holding a heaping platter of soft ginger snap cookies; she had broken Julia's silent contemplation and Lillian's admiring reverie of recent Cottage Parakaleó memories. "Oh, ho! Here we go! Now where are those strapping boys who love my ginger treats? Why did they rush off so fast?"

"They wanted to get back home," answered Julia. "They said they had had enough of girls and flowers and swimming." She reached for a ginger snap and sat on the edge of the porch, her feet on the flagstone step leading to the walkway.

"Luke made it to heaven first. And Garret the time before. I think he wants to keep it that way. To make sure the girls don't beat the boys to heaven."

Miss Garnet smiled. "You've been playing games in the loft . . . *The Mansion of Happiness.*"

"Yes, but it's too lovely to play board games inside today. Too bad the boys are missing the best part of the day on this end of the island," sighed Lillian. She had put her book down to stack three cookies on top of one another until she created a tall brown sandwich. She was ravenous from her cool lake plunge. "I love it here, Miss Garnet. And I loved my swim. Thanks for the swimming costume. I guess watching the others at Galena Beach must have taught me how to swim." She beamed, thinking of her accomplishment.

"The Galenans may teach you many things, my dear. Swimming is one thing to pick up from the villagers, but it is best not to imitate some of their other habits."

Lillian pondered the words but decided not to ask for a lengthy explanation. "May I change?"

"You have already." Miss Garnet winked.

I've already dried off, if that's what you mean, Lillian thought as she opened the screen door, turned right into the kitchen, and scurried straight up the kitchen ladder before climbing into the loft to change clothes. In no time, she scampered back down the wooden rungs. She held a damp silly-looking woolen suit that she hung outside to dry on a clothesline strung between trees.

"There's a storm brewing toward the west," Miss Ruby called from the screened doorway. She had retired from her writing desk. "Look. The clouds are gathering fast. We certainly need the rain." The command in her voice was as crisp as the starch in her immaculately pressed white blouse. But the look on her face was as stark as her trim black skirt and as stern as her tight waist jacket. No need to look out the window to check the weather. Miss Ruby's predictions were never off. Julia stood up to look toward the west where she saw a low curtain of dark clouds hovering over the horizon.

"We'll never make it the mile home, Lillie."

"Then we'll have to stay," reasoned Lillian with a delighted smile. "The boys will make it back. They're fast on the trail, and they left a good while ago. But we'd never make it. Luke will tell Mother where we are. She won't worry. She knows we like to come here."

So the girls stayed the night in their cozy home away from home. They huddled under patchwork quilts, pulling them close toward their noses as thunder crashed and raindrops pelted the low slanted roof in the kitchen loft. It was a place where they always felt safe, always felt secure. Somehow, the ladies of the house made them feel as if they were the only creatures on earth and that no disaster could ever befall them. It was a rare feeling of security unmatched even by the loving closeness of their family at Cobblestone Lighthouse. Love at home and love at this cottage felt strong but were different kinds of love. The sisters never stopped to analyze why this was so, but they basked in delight at their overnight stay at Cottage Parakaleó, which gave them a protective, heavenly feeling.

The rhythm of steady rain on the roof soon lulled the girls to sleep. A storm followed, but Julia and Lillian were far too exhausted from the day's activities to be aware of pounding rain and wailing winds. They slept soundly. The last thing they heard was the lovely musical sounds of Miss Ruby's recorder, Miss Garnet's guitar, and the soft jangle of Miss Tourmalina's tambourine. Neither had heard voices below engulfed in a lively debate over the pros and cons of impulsively jumping overboard and swimming toward a cobblestone shore.

Miss Tourmalina had hailed Lillian as a brave soul and had that night composed a poem celebrating her confidence. Miss Ruby, on the other hand, had seen no sense whatsoever in such activity, noting little wisdom behind Lillian's wild and foolish impulse. To jump overboard when her siblings thought she couldn't swim was reckless abandon. Sternly, Miss Ruby urged Miss Tourmalina not to share the poem as it might encourage Lillian to indulge in further carelessness.

Eyebrows arching now and then at various comments made, Miss Garnet had merely listened to the comments of the other two. She knew that Lillian needed to grow, to learn, to make mistakes. To be forgiven. Miss Garnet also knew how important it was for Lillian to understand the real reason she had followed her strong urge to swim.

♋♋

Monday at Cottage Parakaleó on Cobblestone Island

In the morning, Lillian finished her pancakes at the large kitchen table and joined Miss Garnet who was outside tending her flowers. Miss Garnet was unusually inquisitive about Lillie's recent swimming incident.

"I just wanted to swim and feel the cool water," explained Lillian slowly. "I wanted to be like the others, like everyone else my age, in Galena."

"In Galena! Was it more for refreshment or more to be like them?" Miss Garnet emphasized *them.*

"Does it matter?"

"It matters entirely. Your reason for doing something means everything."

"I was hot and sticky, and I wanted to cool off."

"And that was all?"

"Well, no, I . . ."

Lillian's admission was cut short by an approaching commotion and the sudden appearance of Luke who was out of breath and

51

anxious. "C'mon, Lillian. Mother needs you girls now!" called Luke. "Where's Julia?"

Wildflowers in her hand, the tiny blossoms looking uncharacteristically as fresh as when they had been picked the day before, Julia bounded out the screen door when she heard her brother's voice. Her tongue licked off an upper lip, the last lingering taste of home-tapped Cobblestone Island maple syrup. She had used a plentiful supply on her generous pile of breakfast pancakes.

"Good-bye, Miss Garnet," Lillian gladly switched the tide their conversation had taken, a topic far too heavy to deal with that morning. She felt relieved at the new tone but was mostly spurred on by the urgency in her brother's voice. "I'm sorry we can't continue talking because we're needed at home. Thanks for the stay. C'mon, Julia."

No sooner were all three children off the cottage porch and onto the wooded trail than Luke blurted, "It's Dellie. She's sick. Very sick. Julia, Mother needs you. Run home with me now! Lillian, Mother wants *you* to go to the General Store for medicine." Luke handed his twin a folded piece of paper describing Dellie's illness. "Mother says Mr. Scarsley will know what to give you. Go quickly!"

A pang of recent memory swept over Lillian as she grabbed the paper and ran down the stone walkway and disappeared onto the pathway that led to the General Store.

Chapter 5

Trip Back to Galena

Tuesday on Cobblestone Island

The Wrede family referred to Florence Delight, Garrett's younger and only sister, as "Dellie." Garrett and Dellie were staying at Cobblestone Lighthouse during the summer to be with their seven Bates cousins. This suited Dellie because she loved being with her cousin Paulina who shared her interest in drawing and artistically creating.

Dellie and Garrett lived on Berrie's Island with their parents, Frederick and Violet Wrede. Like his brother-in-law Curtis Bates, "Uncle Fred" enjoyed life as a keeper. He kept Berrie's Island Lighthouse burning for the important and frequent lake traffic on the western side of the Lakeshore County peninsula. Berrie's lay some ways away but, by sailboat when the wind was right, not too far in the distance south of Cobblestone Island in beautiful Emerald Bay.

The two mothers of the nine children could not have been more opposite. Garrett and Dellie's mother, Violet Wrede, could barely manage two. Iona Bates, on the other hand, handled seven siblings with competence and ease. For Iona, adding two more for the summer, especially the fact that they were her brother's children, meant a challenge she willingly embraced. She had agreed to take on Garrett and Dellie for several months so Violet could enjoy a respite from a mysterious, unnamed, seldom mentioned or talked about illness, a condition the children heard discussed only in whispers. All Garrett and Dellie knew was that their mother's childfree summer would help her cope with domestic duties the rest of the year and afford her cherished time to paint. Painting was Violet's passion, and Garrett and Dellie proudly acknowledged their accomplished mother's talents. Growing up as the daughter of a professor from Oxford, England, she had once trained under master artists in Europe. The summer months away from home staying with their Bates cousins afforded Garrett and Dellie an unexpected treat. They weren't that far away, a day's sail to Berrie's Island and back; and what's more, they could always count on an adventure or two at Cobblestone Lighthouse. Garrett had visited the Three at Cottage Parakaleó; and within a year, he, Dellie, and their seven cousins would come to realize their standings as Children of the Light.

Dellie had inherited her mother's artistic talents and brought out the best in Paulina who, although not as gifted, also loved to draw and design and create. The cousins looked alike and acted alike and delighted in anything creative.

Now Dellie was sick. She had contracted some illness, as children do, and Iona Bates had sent Luke to Cottage Parakaleó to enlist the help of her two eldest daughters. Dellie's disruptive catarrh had taken a turn toward bronchitis, possibly pneumonia. Keeper Curtis Bates, his wife, and the older boys had tended the light during the worst parts of the storm that had overtaken the island Sunday night. Paulina and the younger twins had tended to Dellie. Lillian and Julia's absence was felt, their help sorely needed.

Paulina feared for her bosom pal's recovery. She fretted and sniffled with worry, which only aroused fear as to what was happening to Dellie. What's more, Thomas Silas Charles's heady lectures telling Paulina what to do and what not do had done no good whatsoever. Little Maddie was left to do her best as Dellie's sole productive nurse. Patient Maddie, beautiful Maddie, with the striking golden hair matched against striking chocolate-brown eyes which often made strangers stare, had held Dellie's hand in quiet kindness all night. Maddie dutifully obeyed her mother's instructions to administer two-grain doses of quinine throughout the night to her older cousin while parents and older siblings tended the light throughout Sunday's storm.

Thankfully, the medicine that Lillian had brought back on Monday from the General Store in Galena, a well-supplied apothecary that served all the islands in upper Lakeshore County, had helped Dellie turn the corner on her illness. This medicine, given three times a day, effected Dellie's cure. Lillian thanked her lucky stars that rather than enduring scowls from her family for jumping off a sailing vessel the day of the storm, she had received congratulations for hastily bringing home the miraculous prescription. For the moment, her siblings lauded her praises—she had saved Dellie. Her jumping overboard venture hadn't even been mentioned. Hoping to continue her fame as heroine, when the scant amount of medicine ran out, Lillian quickly volunteered to walk to Galena on Tuesday to renew the prescription. And naturally, Julia agreed to go along.

Upon reaching the General Store, the girls were surprised to see Garrett and Dellie's father, their uncle Frederick Wrede, inside the store. Lillian and Julia walked in at the tail end of a conversation between Uncle Fred and Mr. Scarsley, the apothecary, who stood behind the counter.

"On board the *Sadie Thompson* docked over on Berrie's Island."

"Hope it's enough medicine for the sick sailor."

"I trust it will be. Good-bye, Mr. Scarsley."

"Good day, Mr. Wrede."

Lillian and Julia exchanged glances. Something sounded familiar to Lillian. *Sadie Thompson? Wasn't that the boat at Morrison Harbor the boys were captivated by? Hadn't her brothers and cousin watched four sailors load stone onto a ship called Sadie Thompson? Wasn't that the ship led by a bellowing captain who had distracted Kari, Julia, and me as we picked flowers Sunday afternoon?*

"Wasn't the *Sadie Thompson* bound for Milwaukee?" whispered Lillian to her sister. "What's it doing over at Berrie's Island?"

"Yes, I'm certain it was bound for Milwaukee," answered Julia, also curious about the conversation.

Lillian broke away, feeling the need to tell Uncle Fred about his daughter's medical condition. After informing him of Dellie's illness and near full recovery, she began to question him about his talk with the storekeeper. "Uncle Fred, did you mention the *Sadie Thompson*?"

"Yes, she's lodged at Raspberry Harbor over on Berrie's Island. Must have sailed into Emerald Bay coming in from Milwaukee. The captain had to deal with a sick sailor and was concerned about managing the ship down to a skeleton crew, considering Sunday night's storm brewing and all. Don't know how they will manage to set sail with only four men able to work the schooner, the fifth no good and needing medicine—" Stopping abruptly, thinking he had given out more information than he ought, he continued, "Why? What do you know of the ship?"

"Well, nothing actually. But we watched it being loaded with stone on Washburn Island on Sunday."

"Why, come to think of it, it was still loaded with stone. I wonder why they hadn't taken it straight to Milwaukee. Berrie's is the opposite direction. Well, that's none of my concern anyway. I best be leaving to run some other errands before I deliver this medicine, Lillie." He held up a package from the storekeeper. "You say Dellie's all right?" he asked with a wink, knowing he needed no affirmation from his trustworthy nieces. "Keep her healthy now." Dellie was an engine of faith in their family, and he had no fear that the young girl's prayers for recovery had been numerous and quick.

"How is Aunt Violet doing?" Julia managed to squeeze in as Uncle Frederick turned to leave.

"Pretty well these days, Julia. Pretty well. Come see us soon. Would you?"

"We'd like that. When Dellie is completely cured though. Mother is giving her the best of care."

"As I am giving your aunt Violet the best of care," Fred added, stopping to turn and smile briefly before leaving the store.

Remembering again the reason for her visit, Lillian approached the man behind the counter to request Dellie's medicine refill.

"This is the last dose of iodide of potassium for you, Missy," the apothecary barked his response to Lillian's request. "Why, you just filled an order yesterday. It's not to be taken like candy, you know!" Lillian was stunned by the loudness and the tone.

Nearly his height, she looked the short scowling man straight in the eyes and countered in a calm level voice that made her seem older than twelve, "You may recall, Mr. Scarsley, that you only gave a day's dosage yesterday. Mother sent me for more, just in case. This refill should take care of our needs." She snatched the bag from his outstretched hand, walked toward Julia, took her by the arm, and pushed her toward the exit. Pausing briefly before turning around to face the apothecary, Lillian offered a curt, polite direction, "Put it on Keeper Bate's bill please."

Mr. Scarsley growled something unintelligible back, to which Lillian could not help but respond, "And my name isn't Missy. It's Lillian."

Once outside, Julia joined in, "I don't understand that man, Lillie. He is always so mean. So angry."

"He can't get over that his wife died, and he takes his pain out on everyone else."

"But it was his overdose of medicine that killed her. It was his fault. Shouldn't he feel bad about what he did instead of being angry at everyone else?"

"Shhh, Julia, not so loud. He'll hear you and come out and say something mean again." Pulling her sister away from the store entrance, she continued in a quiet voice, "He won't own up to what he did and takes his anger out on everyone else instead."

"I just don't get it," Julia murmured.

"It is as it is, Julia. C'mon. Let's go home."

But instead of turning homeward, the girls decided to take a detour in the opposite direction toward the beach, just for a peek. They scurried down the grassy path behind the store toward the  southern edge of the island. Passing the beach house, they climbed the hill to glance upon the doings on the sandy shoreline below. The girls looked downward upon a sizable crowd of children their age splashing and making a great deal of noise in the water. It didn't take long for the swimmers to notice the two girls standing high on the hill. Like a chain reaction, one by one, hands pointed upward, accompanied by shrieks of laughter and spiteful stares. Frightfully embarrassed but with head held high with pride, Lillian turned Julia around and shoved her forward. She steered her back down the hill, past the beach house, onto the grassy path, and away from the Galena Beach.

"They're just no good!" Julia fumed. "Everyone else in Galena is just as mean as Elliott Scarsley at the store. I don't understand."

"Neither do I, Julia. But sometimes I wish I had what they have. And I suppose I shouldn't. I almost feel bad for swimming because that's what they do."

"They fill their time swimming because they don't do what we do, Lillie. We can't take time to swim with all the living going on at the lighthouse. And when we have time we spend it at Cottage Parakaleó, I wouldn't trade the time we spend there for anything."

"I don't understand why the people in Galena never visit Parakaleó. They don't seem to know it's there . . . even though they do speak of the Three."

"Yes, but I've heard some call them the Corwin girls. Are they the Corwin triplets? I guess they're about the right age to be them."

"They're Miss Garnet, Miss Ruby, and Miss Tourmalina to us! As far as I'm concerned, they don't need any other names!" Lillian stopped suddenly. "Oh look, Julia. Here are the stone steps. Let's stop at Parakaleó to say hello. We don't have to stay long."

"But, Lillie, the medicine. We should get home! We already took time to walk to the beach—"

"Just a quick visit," Lillian pleaded and won.

Julia, however, wasn't at all sure about her sister's reckless idea. She felt a strange foreboding and wished they had gone straight home.

Chapter 6

Another Visit to Cottage Parakaleó

A visit to the Three on top of the hill helped Lillian and Julia counteract the bad feelings they had just received from not only Mr. Scarsley but their encounter with the nasty children at Galena Beach. They determined to make their visit a quick one. It seemed like ages ago rather than the night before last since they had stayed there. Taking two steps at a time, they raced to see who would first reach the top of the steep hill. Lillian won without effort.

"Oh, look at how the sun shines on the old Cobblestone Lighthouse! Isn't it beautiful?" Julia gasped as she pointed to the conical structure standing near the little cottage. The door at the base of the lighthouse stood open. The open entrance to this navigational aid now turned watchtower seemed to invite the girls to come in and climb its spiral staircase. They raced up the winding iron stairs to find Miss Garnet in the

59

outdoor parapet outside the lantern room. She held a small telescope and was glancing toward Morrison Harbor on Washburn Island.

"Just watching the ships, girls. How have you been?"

"We are well, Miss Garnet," Julia answered for both of them using the perfect grammar her teacher-mother had taught her.

"It's Dellie who's been sick. We have to take her the parcel from the store."

"From Mr. Scarsley."

"I know," Miss Garnet replied.

Lillian narrowed her eyes in concentration to figure out what Miss Garnet meant. *What does she know? That we have medicine? That it's from Mr. Scarsley? Or that Dellie is sick?*

"Miss Garnet," Julia began, "why is Mr. Scarsley so mean to everyone? It's been awhile since Mrs. Scarsley was buried. Isn't he over it yet?"

Lowering the instrument in her hands after taking some time scanning the expanse of the bay, Miss Garnet slowly collapsed the handheld scope as she spoke, "Mr. Scarsley needs your love and understanding, girls. His wife is gone." She looked at Julia with exact focus. "Gone! Unlike the two of you, he has nobody to go home to now."

Julia's heart aimed toward compassion. As if trying to let Miss Garnet's words sink in, she nodded in agreement and understanding.

Lillian, on the other hand, horrified at the thought of loving such a terrible person as Mr. Scarsley, contorted her face into a particularly ugly expression. "He would be the last person I could love!" Lillian decided out loud. "Or would want to!" Then she smiled in amusement as a heartfelt thought crossed her mind. *We could give him Thomas. They'd make a good pair!*

Miss Garnet caught Lillian's wickedness and sought to understand. "Was Mr. Scarsley gruff toward you again?"

"Yes!" the girls answered in chorus.

"That is his cry for help. He needs your love."

Lillian had no desire whatsoever to pursue the direction the conversation was taking. Just the other day, she had been lectured by her mother about love. *What is going on? A reminder to love is bad enough coming from Mother, but I don't expect one from Miss Garnet. I am trying to love Thomas. But love Mr. Scarsley? Never!* The thought turned her stomach.

"Is Dellie over her cough?" Miss Garnet also knew how to change the conversation.

"Oh, she's getting over it. This medicine is just in case she needs it again. The worst of her illness has passed. Maddie helped her when we were gone because Priscilla isn't back from visiting her family on Washburn Island yet, or she would have helped Mother." *How does Miss Garnet know about Dellie's sickness?*

Julia, who had been circling the watchtower, bent down to her knees and reached between the iron slats to touch the cold white stones of the tower. She did so with the awe and reverence of a light-keeper's daughter. "Miss Garnet"—she straightened up again—"how could anyone move a lighthouse from one end of the island to another? And why really? Why not just leave the Old Cobblestone Light by us up on the bluff next to the new one that we live inside now? I mean, the old tower wasn't hurting anybody by just being there. Why not just leave it next to the new one?"

"To answer all three questions, my dear, very carefully because it would undoubtedly have crumbled to ruins if it had been left standing there without the repair it received here and because you have no need for two lights in one location." Miss Garnet smiled. "Why so many questions about the old lighthouse?"

"It could still be ours if it hadn't been transported! I mean, I know it wasn't useful on the bluff anymore. There is no beacon, no lens in the lantern room, and I suppose the Lighthouse Board could have asked for another one from the depot or wherever they come from if they wanted it to still shine as a light but . . ." Julia wasn't sure if she should continue. "But . . . it was the perfect hideout for us kids. I wish it were still by us at the north end of the island. When exactly was it moved? Who moved it? Why?"

"This winter. It was a mild one, you know. By the men commissioned by those who bought it. To preserve it."

But if it could be fixed up in this spot, why couldn't the government fix it up at the north end where it belongs?"

"That was not the government's decision, Julia. They built the present lighthouse when this one started falling apart and simply left this one stay put or fall apart, which was likely to happen soon, until someone bought it and decided to move it here. The conditions were simple. Anyone who wanted to fix it, pay for its removal, and place it elsewhere was welcome to do so, and that is what came to be. As you say, it is no longer a lighthouse." Miss Garnet's words sounded final.

Julia dared to press on, "And private owners had the tower moved, right?"

The jeweled necklace resting upon Miss Garnet's top caught the noon sun and sparked a flash, but as she suspected, Miss Garnet said nothing. Julia wanted to hear how the old stone lighthouse, now sturdy and majestic, had been moved and replastered and set up as a lookout tower rather than lighthouse, but her mother had given them strict orders not to bring up that subject in town. Most people in Galena did not approve of how it had been dismantled and rebuilt. Since Cottage Parakaleó was technically in Galena, out of respect for her mother's wishes, she decided not to press the issue. Plus, Miss Garnet seemed reluctant to answer any more questions.

Julia watched the reflected light from Miss Garnet's necklace dance in the sunlight, showing off its many facets, creating assorted shades and hues. The reds played together and artfully darted up, down, and around the garnet gems embedded in the heart-shaped piece of jewelry dangling against her shirtwaist blouse. Lillian too stared at its splendor.

She had been listening to her sister's conversation and wondered whether the rumors the people in Galena had spread were true. *Were these three women the Corwin triplets? The daughters of Felix Corwin, the first lighthouse keeper at Cobblestone Light decades ago? Was Miss Garnet's stunning jewel a treasure from the shipwreck that had taken the life of their mother Deborrah Corwin in the awful storm of 1849 when the Corwin triplets had been eighteen? If so, why did Miss Garnet speak in terms of "private owners this and that"? Was she one of the private owners that had the lighthouse relocated? Then why wouldn't she admit it?* Lillian had been too sick weeks ago to ponder such questions when the three ladies had taken such good care of her and nursed her back to health. But now that she had fully recovered, questions about these three nurse ladies flooded her brain. Somehow, she couldn't come right out and ask, and the ladies were not freely offering any information to help answer her many questions.

Lillian also had questions but dared not entertain inquiries about the red jewels worn by each of the Three at Cottage Parakaleó. Someday she would ask about them. At the right time, she would find out whether what she had heard in town held any truth. Not only was she indebted to the Three for her life but she also *liked* these new friends. She made a conscious effort to refrain from spoiling any chances of staying with them, talking to them, learning from them— or eating the delicious treats from their hospitable kitchen.

If these ladies *were* the Corwin triplets, returned to the island after many years away, then it was the three of *them* who had paid for the removal and rebuilding of the old Cobblestone Lighthouse at this spot—before leaving California to come back home to Wisconsin. For some reason, they did not want to talk about the origins of the lighthouse at its present location even though they freely answered other questions about the lighthouse.

They are Miss Garnet, Miss Ruby, and Miss Tourmalina, Lillian decided. She smiled at these nicknames. She had invented the names because of the varied red jewels each of them wore. The nicknames seemed to stick and find acceptance with each of the Three. *I don't care who they are really, except that they are our friends.* She tried to reason that sometimes knowing too much is knowing too much. Yet Lillian's questions persisted, even pounded within her brain.

If they truly are the Corwin girls, then this lighthouse is the one they grew up with. It does make sense that they would want to preserve it and have it brought near this lovely cottage with the fancy Southern-style porch. They aren't keepers, so they don't need the tower to function as an aid to

navigation. It makes perfect sense to make it a watchtower to enjoy the surrounding beauty from up high.

Lillian's thoughts shot into a new direction. *I've never thought of them as triplets. They are too different to be triplets. They have opposite personalities, yet there is a sameness about them. Oh, but they can't be the same age. At least, I don't think so. Let me see, Miss Garnet is the oldest. She is wise and lovable and good. So very good. Miss Ruby is surely the middle child. She is wise too in a different way. In a scary way. She is always right.* Lillian shuddered at the thought of Miss Ruby's uncanny nature to be right so often.

And then there is Miss Tourmalina. She is surely the youngest. Such fun, yet she always has a faraway look. Like the others, she is wise but so talented and creative. But hard to get close to. So mysterious, and she likes to stay at the cottage more than the other two. Completely lost in her musings, completely forgetting she was not alone, Lillian struck a pose, an imitation of one of Miss Tourmalina's postures although totally lacking the woman's graceful poise. She cocked her head in an elegant stance and lifted her left eyebrow the way Miss Tourmalina did when she felt inspired. She reached out with her right hand stretched forward, her fingers positioned as would a ballet dancer in position. Lillian smiled with longing to become close to Miss Tourmalina.

But they could be triplets! They're old. Just different kinds of old. All grown-ups look old. All three could be the exact same old.

Lillian's thoughts switched to the gossip she had heard in town. Lillian was sharp, observant, and enjoyed figuring out puzzles. What she could not immediately grasp, she would think about and solve later. The people in town talked. Their curious minds burned with questions they blurted out rather than reasoned through later: *Had the Corwin girls fled to California in 1850 with their father, Felix David Corwin, after their mother had drowned in that terrible storm? Had the Corwin girls taken off with their father and the three southern sailors who had survived the shipwreck . . . to seek gold in the California hills? Had the three Corwin girls actually married the three brothers and made their fortunes in the gold rush? Had the three brothers really gone off and fought for the South a decade later? And died in the war leaving their triplet wives and families rich? Did the Corwin triplets return to the island to relocate old Cobblestone Lighthouse? Did they build a little cottage of stone on the hill to look like a miniature southern plantation in memory of their husbands?*

Lillian's thoughts were mazes of tangled vines, of branches intermixed with tall tree ideas in a forest of possibilities. Lillian's real quest was to determine whether her newfound friends were indeed the Corwin girls and whether the jewels they wore were bought from California gold or were relics from the shipwreck they had encountered as eighteen-year-old daughters of Cobblestone Lighthouse's first keeper.

Lillian's ponderings continued, unfettered by any hand of distraction waved in front of her. Her father had told her about Felix and Deborrah Corwin and their triplet daughters. *The three women at Cottage Parakaleó seem to be the right ages.* Lillian wanted to scream out an answer, but she had none. *Why can't I come right out and ask? Why hadn't I asked when they had taken care of me this winter? I was too sick to know what to say, that's why.*

Like the boats she loved to watch sail from island to island, Lillian's thoughts raced, each thought in tow with the other. Her wandering contemplations pushed forth, her many questions fighting to be answered.

Who were the men who had built Cottage Parakaleó and dismantled the old lighthouse to stand next to it? Friends of the deceased husbands? Rebel soldiers from the South whom the Galena Yankees resented? Is that why no Yankee islander visits Parakaleó? Why had the Corwin girls returned to Cobblestone Island? Why had they agreed to nurse her back to health upon her return from out East where she had contracted scarlet fever?

Until recently, Lillian had never paid much attention to the old lighthouse when it stood crumbling at the bluff next to Cobblestone Lighthouse where she and her family lived. Now that it was gone, she missed having it on the bluff. It was her nature to want what she couldn't have. Julia and the boys had been inside more than she had, but their mother had told them to stay away. It was crumbling and therefore dangerous. Lillian stayed away from the old structure more out of disinterest than from her mother's directive. As the oldest of seven children in the family of a lighthouse keeper (only Luke's elder by eleven minutes), she had too many duties to attend to, which afforded her little time to explore. Then again, she had better things to do when she did find extra time for herself. When she and Julia and "the boys" needed to plan something, they met outside the old lighthouse and stepped inside only when the weather was bad. That was the extent of Lillian's interest in Old Cobblestone Light. Now, however, her interest was strong.

The old lighthouse seemed to fit in this wooded hillside setting. Its glittering cobblestones, sturdy now with new mortar since its relocation, matched the cobblestones of the cottage nearby. The two were a perfect duo. Lillian wondered why she hadn't noticed the tall structure on the sail from Washburn Island. The little stone cottage, nestled among trees on the hill, would not be easily seen from the lake, but surely, the lighthouse lookout tower would be. Next time she crossed over, she would look for it.

Lillian was a thinker, and her mind was filled with thoughts not only about the two cobblestone buildings but about the ladies who lived inside. Bits and pieces of speculations played about in town. Enough talk let Lillian know abundant unanswered questions flew about as gossip throughout Village Galena. Although aware it was wrong to eavesdrop, Lillian did so anyway, especially when she visited the General Store not too far down the hill from the cottage. Her excuse was to find out what people were saying so she could defend the three ladies at Cottage Parakaleó and stop any negative things she heard said about them. She wanted to find out the truth about them, yet doing so proved to her an impossible and most mysterious endeavor.

Whether the women were the former Corwin triplets or not did not matter to Lillian. But what people said about them did. *I like the nicknames I gave them. And so do they. So until I find out about their background—*

Miss Garnet's voice, which had risen to an uncharacteristic loud pitch, interrupted Lillian's jumbled reverie. "I said they certainly did a fine job repairing the tower, wouldn't you say? Shall I say it a fourth time?"

Lillian suddenly realized that for who knows how long, Miss Garnet had been pressing her with a question. She had completely lost focus. Red-faced with embarrassment, Lillian snapped to attention. "Yes," she sputtered, not fully knowing what she was responding to. Guessing and trying to appear more confident than she felt, she continued, "Yes, the tower is, ah, sturdy—much more so than when it stood at the point before they"—*Whoever they were*—"dismantled it, I suppose. Mother told us to stay away from it because it was crumbling to . . . to ruins before it was, um, before it was moved . . ."

"And the government would have left it to crumble apart if someone hadn't requested to move and fix it," Julia came to Lillian's rescue, hoping Miss Garnet would flesh out further details. But she didn't. "Even though our lighthouse serves us well, it's not nearly as beautiful as this one. And it doesn't have an underground passageway!"

"There is no need for a tunnel where we live, Julia! The light is part of our house," she reminded her sister and continued with confidence that her wandering thoughts were at last anchored in renewed reality. Before Lillian had the chance to ponder another daydream over whether this old reconstructed light tower had underground connections to Cottage Parakaleó like the old Cobblestone Lighthouse had to Felix Corwin's original keeper's house, she was cut off by shouts of familiar voices.

"Lillie! Julia!"

"Julia! Larry!"

Looking down from the tower, Lillian saw that Garrett and Luke had entered the scene, with Gabriel tagging behind. "C'mon down. We have some news!" shouted Luke.

Fearing that Dellie had experienced a relapse, Lillian raced down the winding steps of the conical stone tower, her feet making a racket as her shoes banged against the wrought iron. Hoping for the best, Julia rushed down after her sister but lagged several steps behind.

"I should have listened to you, Julia, and gone straight home with the medicine!" shouted Lillian as she continued her downward climb.

Miss Garnet stayed on the parapet of the tower. Collapsing the telescope and putting it in her pocket, she rested her arms on the railings as she watched the children below. Like talking ants, they bustled around one another, their antennaelike arms a flurry of exchanges.

"Dellie is all right. She's out of danger now," assured Garrett.

"Mother doesn't desperately need more medicine. She just wants it on hand just in case," Luke added.

"And she says the five of us can stay in Galena for a swim at the beach!" Gabriel could hardly wait to add.

"Mother suggested *what?*" Lillian blurted out in total disbelief. "I can't believe *that!*"

Two days ago, Lillian had failed to tell Miss Garnet that another reason she had never learned to swim was that her mother sensed the danger involved. Her mother was afraid. She didn't even like their wading in the shoreline beneath the lighthouse cliff. The north portion of Cobblestone Island was different from the south. Cobblestone Lighthouse stood on a steep limestone cliff, dangerous rocky shoals scattered in the waters at its base. By contrast, although there were some rocky cliffs that included Village Galena, the southern part of the island included an expansive sandy beach. But the Galena Beach was a mile away from the lighthouse. On warm days, the Bates children, who lived at the northern end, liked to take off their shoes and stockings to wade in the shallow water amid slippery jagged rocks. These rocks scored the shoreline beneath the bluff upon which their house and attached light tower stood. Their mother discouraged such activity, often warning them about a sudden drop off where the rocks stopped and the lake deepened. One slip could bring disaster.

Lillian's mind drifted to a recent drowning incident that had stricken their mother with grief. *No, Mother has good reason to caution us against swimming.*

"Mother found out about your first swim, Lillie, and she told us it's about time we all learn to swim." Luke held out his arms to display several articles of clothing. "She gave us these and told us to have fun in Galena for the afternoon," he explained.

Gabriel grabbed one of the bathing costumes from his brother, ran down the stone steps and hillside, and waited for the others to join him by the beach house. By the time the others had chosen from the pile of assorted swimwear Mrs. Bates had sent along, Gabriel was a distant speck.

Mother found out about my first swim. From whom? Lillian scowled at the thought. *Must have been Thomas although he wasn't even there. But he seems to know everything.* Dismissing aside all gloomy thoughts, Lillian relished another chance to swim. She quickly joined the other four as they raced to the beach house. They changed into the silly-looking outfits, likely handmade by their housekeeper Priscilla, and scanned the area for a sunny spot to swim. They did their best to ignore the comments and whistles, tauntings actually, as they walked along Galena's beach.

"Look at the Bates bums!" shouted one.

"They're so high and mighty," said another.

"And so fashionable," ridiculed a third. The laughing roar that followed was as piercing as the blast from a foghorn.

The children made up their minds not to be disturbed. Except for Lillian, this was their first swim. And they didn't care that sarcasm might destroy their fun, no matter how silly they looked in their awkwardly styled swimming outfits.

"Well, I guess you don't have to look good to enjoy the water!" shouted one.

"I wouldn't be caught dead looking like that!" said another.

"I'd drown myself in the lake wearing those," teased the third, clearly the voice of Lucinda Lynda DePere whom Lillian despised the most.

Far enough away from the small crowd of swimmers, the Children of the Light entered the water with cries of excitement that drowned out further criticisms. Not knowing how to swim, they stayed close to shore at waist depth. Only Lillian ventured out farther but came back closer to shore when Garrett cleverly coaxed her back for what he called "an important announcement."

"Aunt Iona . . . I mean, your mother . . . said we could all stay over at Cottage Parakaleó for the night."

"What about Dellie's medicine? Shouldn't I run that home?" asked Lillian.

"Dellie will be all right. She's out of danger, remember?"

I can't believe I've been given all these privileges lately. But I'm certainly glad to be away from Thomas Silas Charles! Lillian's real delight fell upon the realization that she was as far away as possible from her high and mighty little brother whose continual comments, truthful as they unfortunately often were, made her conscience squirm and her enviousness rage.

What a night they had at Cottage Parakaleó, the Three on the hill served a sumptuous meal around the rectangular oak kitchen table, one side of the table adjoining the stone wall that made the back of the living room fireplace. The two long sides held long benches, able to house a crowd with another smaller bench at the end parallel to the stone wall. Following later were entertaining stories in front of the great cobblestone fireplace. As always, the evening ended with music and readings from the Book. Miss Garnet strummed her guitar as Miss Ruby blew into her melancholy recorder. Keeping rhythm, Miss Tourmalina shook her tambourine. The lilting soprano of Miss Tourmalina matched Miss Garnet's rich alto to produce their usual harmonious blend. The children sang along on tunes they had heard played before. Miss Ruby did not sing; she read. Masterfully, majestically. After Miss Ruby's renditions, the children felt an indescribable glow deep within their souls and were quite sure it had something to do with their being Children of the Light.

The day had been full, and they slumbered peacefully in their respective lofts, the girls' one above the kitchen, the boys' over the porch. Frequent claps of thunder and bolts of lightning surrounded the little cottage in the dark hours following midnight. Miss Ruby's warnings of another coming storm had become another right-on-target prediction. But in such cozy surroundings, the last thoughts from the children's minds were devastations caused by the storm for those on the north end of the island near their lighthouse home.

By dawn, all traces of storm had vanished. A rush of early Wednesday morning sunlight flushed through the living room windows of the cottage. The night's terror had faded into a new day full of light and promise, even though the daytime weather continued hot and dry. After steaming oatmeal with island syrup for breakfast, the five children waved good-bye to their guardian hostesses and made their way through the woods on the path home. Midway through their homeward course, Paulina and Dellie came crashing down the walkway, barely able to contain themselves.

"Luke! Luke!" Paulina called from a distance. "Lillie! Julia! Gabe! There's a shipwreck at home!"

"A shipwreck, Garrett! A shipwreck!" piped in Dellie, too excited to let Paulina tell all.

"A shipwreck below our lighthouse," continued Paulina. "And Mother took the captain and crew in for the night."

"All five of the crew are still there. Their ship is smashed," chimed in Dellie, looking cheerfully bright from newfound health.

With a dramatic flair, Paulina added, "It's my very first shipwreck. I'll remember the crash my whole life. The wreck of the *Sadie Thompson* lies right below us under our very own cliff. C'mon, c'mon, c'mon. You have to see it!"

Paulina and Dellie's audience exchanged glances of unbelief at the mention of a ship all too familiar to them.

Chapter 7

Shipwrecked

That same Tuesday on Berrie's Island, southwest of Cobblestone Island

While Uncle Fred had ventured his way back southwest from the General Store in Galena to his lighthouse on Berrie's Island, the crew of the *Sadie Thompson*, who had moored their ship there since Sunday evening, were planning their own sailing venture.

After leaving Morrison Harbor on Washburn Island where they had on Sunday loaded their ship with cobblestones, Captain Steele and his crew launched *Sadie Thompson* on a course bound southward. For those watching him sail away, the ship appeared to head toward Milwaukee. However, Steele made his destination only *appear* to be Milwaukee. He and his crew had sailed southward only as far as Whitefish Harbor where he cut his ship through the canal that marked the southern border of Lakeshore County. He then sailed north on a new course set for Michigan. Noticing the gathering storm clouds that Sunday evening and at all costs wanting to avoid a shipwreck that would delay the delivery of their important cargo, Steele found safe harbor. He chose the north bay of Raspberry Harbor on Berrie's Island and anchored there for the night.

Unfortunately putting a glitch in Steele's plans, on Monday morning, Berrie's Island Lighthouse Keeper Frederick Wrede, whose lighthouse lay just to the west of Raspberry Harbor, had discovered Steele and his crew and had asked too many questions about where the *Sadie Thompson* had been and where it was heading. To get Wrede off his back, Captain Steele told him a false story about mooring on Berrie's Island for the night because of a dangerously sick crewman below decks. Steele's trick to hoodwink Fred into getting the needed medicine worked, and Captain Steele managed to get Fred Wrede off the island and off his back for the day. As soon as Wrede was well out of sight, Steele planned to leave Berrie's Island and follow a course north and then turn south toward Traverse City, Michigan. However, foiling Steele's plans, the bumbling crewman Charley Skruggs managed to get himself lost that afternoon. When Steele sent First Mate Ross Clow to find Skruggs, neither of the two returned to the *Sadie Thompson* for hours. This made Captain Steele furious. His hopes to leave became as entangled as seaweed in a fisherman's net. And Steele always took his anger out on the crew, focusing on Ross and Charley because he had banished the rest of the crew to the cabins below. After all, supposedly sick and in need of medicine, at least one of the two other sailors was strictly warned to stay out of sight. In his anger, Steele forced them both below decks.

Charley Skruggs had as few brains in his head as teeth in his mouth, which weren't many, and poor Ross Clow, a brighter although more self-centered glow in his brain than Skruggs, suffered because of Scruggs's inability to think before acting. Ironically, Steele could have set sail immediately had he not chosen to waste time by berating the sailors before storming off when the two finally returned from visiting Violet Wrede at Sandy Point west and a little south of the island's lighthouse.

"We already have Frederick Wrede knowing our whereabouts. Now you have to get the wife in on it too!" bellowed Captain Steele. "When I think of the crew I left behind in Chicago, I could spit. You two promised you could handle this! Does anything good come out of Milwaukee? If it does, it sure ain't the two of you!" Then to manifest his disgust at his crewmen's insubordination, he stomped away in a huff and didn't return until nightfall.

The captain's absence gave Charley time to think as he swabbed the deck to hopefully appease Steele's anger. Besides, Charley had nothing better to do as he waited for the captain's return. Earlier in the day, Charley had simply decided to take a walk.

While ambling along, old Charley had taken a friendly interest in the lovely Violet, wife of Uncle Fred. He had spied her painting on the far end of a spit although within view of her husband's lighthouse standing majestically upon a distant sprawling hill. He blamed his delay on an overwhelming fascination watching her paint the lake. For a while, he had studied her long straw-colored hair blowing casually across her face on the breezy afternoon. He had watched her continuously sweep her shiny locks aside with one hand and skillfully paint with the other. In all his years, Charley had never seen such beauty and grace. To Charley, Violet Wrede's casual elegance was pure and simple. Not attracted to anything remotely urban, he found her manner as opposite to rich city style as a three-masted schooner is to a row boat. This woman appeared completely at ease, even though, as he found out later, she lived far from her native country home in England. He felt a pull to speak with her, if for no other reason than to make sure she was real flesh and blood and not some apparition made from his imagination.

As Charley mopped the floorboards, he decided that talking with Violet had been worth the tongue lashing from Captain Steele. So what if Ross Clow had yanked him by the ear to pull him away from the lovely painter? Charley would never forget Violet's melodious English voice. He smiled, recalling her refined accent, the flow of it smooth like churning butter. Her soft words had charmed him as she explained the blending of colors on her palette, of how she marked on canvas three different water depths with three different colors. "They are emeralds and sapphires laced with teal as they dance upon the waves and shimmer in the sun," she had said. "Nature's gems worth more than pirate's treasure." He remembered the distant look in her eyes, a gaze that told him she loved her island and her painting. But even dimwitted hair-

brained Charley Skruggs in sensitivity felt she longed to be on a far distant island an ocean away.

Later, she actually admitted that while she lived in America, her spirit was rooted back home in her native England.

Charley smiled broadly because a beautiful woman had paid attention to him. Violet Wrede, a heavenly being sent to Lakeshore County for a moment in his measly existence, had touched his heart. Charley believed in angels and determined she was one. Yes, indeed, the verbal assaults from Ross Clow and Sam Steele had not been easy to endure, but the visit with Violet had made up for it. Talking with her was life handing him a gift.

Skruggs slapped the mop on the aft deck and rested his arm on the wheel. He was ecstatic that any beautiful woman cared enough to speak with him much less explain to him a topic as important and beyond his comprehension as oil painting. He mostly enjoyed the attention, and his feelings went no further than that. After all, she was a married woman. He was clear about that. And he was a simple sailor in need of a friend. Because Captain Steele's harsh manner and clipped tongue continually dampened his spirits, he often felt the longing for a kind heart that cared for him as a human being. Violet Wrede had filled this order.

Charley set his mop down. He breathed deeply and felt a south wind kick up. They should set sail immediately. He wondered where Steele had gone. They should have shipped off hours ago. He hadn't planned to pause and chat with Violet, and he certainly hadn't designed the disturbing ruckus that resulted afterward from his late return to the *Sadie Thompson*. He had only wanted to stretch his sea legs before their long haul to Traverse City. How did he know he'd run into someone like Violet Wrede? How did he know she would be painting on the same spit he had chosen for a walk? How did he know she would befriend him as few people ever dared befriend the lowly Charley Skruggs? Charley knew he was ugly, and he knew others knew his ugliness too.

But the lovely painter whose hair matched the blowing reeds on Sandy Point and whose gray-green eyes matched the distant hue of the water lapping against the sandy shore had seen him in a different light. Skruggs only knew that for a moment in his life, he felt handsome and strong and alive. He liked the feeling and wanted, if only for a moment, to make the comfort last. Blast Captain Steele for berating him. Blast him for taking off now when they should set sail immediately. Charley knew Steele had done these things out of spite, to leave without saying where he was going or give no hint as to when he would return. Charley felt anxious because he understood the signs of the weather, and the weather was urging him to set sail.

A noise rumbled below in the aft cabin. Ross was attempting to straighten things below decks so everything would be in order to sail. Poor Ross. Charley had made a mess for this sailing buddy. Not far from Raspberry Harbor, from atop the hill at the lighthouse, Ross had spotted Charley and another figure in the distance at the sandy point that cradled the bay. Ross had raced down to snatch his sailing buddy from the scene, pulling him by the ear, barely noticing Violet and certainly taking no time to speak with her. Ross knew Steele would boil because of the delay. And boil he did.

"Wrede's woman knows where we're going now!" Steele had bellowed at Ross when they returned to the ship, yet it was Charley's stupidity, not Ross's ineptness for talking with Violet that caused the great disturbance within their captain.

"What kind of lines did you feed her about our plans?" Steele accused.

Poor Ross had to endure Steele's injustice and sharp disciplinary tongue. It was a cruel world. Cruel for Charley who had found and lost a friend in Violet. Cruel for Ross who had to suffer for simply doing his duty by retrieving the dim-witted Charley. As for telling Violet what the crew was up to, Charley had not said a word.

"Pull anchor!" Sam Steele's roar blasted through Charley's thoughts. Appearing out of nowhere, the captain's abrupt reappearance startled the sailor. Charley picked up his mop to resume swabbing the deck. Instinctively, he quickened his pace, his ample muscular strength making up for his lack of gray brain matter. "We have no time to waste getting our special cargo to Traverse City," bellowed Steele. "Put that scrub mop away! If we miss our chance, we miss a mighty big bundle of booty to go with it! They're going to miss us in Milwaukee, but Conrad Warren said we had to head straight to Traverse City or we'd miss our connection. So let's get the job done there and then head back to Milwaukee and deliver the cargo of stone."

"Ain't they gonna miss us, C'ptain . . . if we take the time ta go over ta Traverse City first?" Charley asked in complete innocence.

"We'll make up a good story why we're late, old guy. Just leave those details to me," ordered Steele. "Now move it, boys!"

"Aye-aye, sir. Right away, sir!" obeyed Charley who was stunned at the captain's appearance out of nowhere and his apparently cooled anger. Ross had come up from below and now stood at the ship's wheel, awaiting the call to set sail. The other crewmen stood nearby, awaiting their directions.

Once upon the water, with the south wind behind their backs, Captain Steele took over and easily steered his ship northward on a steady course.

Then, late that night, disaster struck when a sudden burst of a northeasterly gave no warning, and gale force winds broke loose upon the water. Steele had little luck maintaining a straight path ahead. He desperately tried to spill excess wind from his sails by holding an even course.

Steele ordered Ross to ease the sheets without tightly cleating them down. By loosening these ropes, Ross could constantly adjust the billowing sails. Raising his voice above the fierce whistling wind, Steele roared at Ross to be ready at his command to let the ship fly. Ross, in turn, shouted for Charley to tighten the smaller jib sail.

Ironically, Charley's immediate obedience proved disastrous. As Charley tightened the jib, Ross was unable to slack the main sail. As a result, the boat picked up speed alarmingly fast, heeling dangerously, the entire ship tipping over like a pouring teapot.

The ship's drive came from both wind-filled sails as the schooner flew downwind in an unplanned race across the water, its tilt more hazardous than ever as it pounded hard against the waves.

As this was taking place, Captain Steele ordered his crew to reduce the sail area to match the wind. Like four swarming bees, they bustled about, trying to control the puffing sails. However, they were helpless against the wind's mighty force.

Rain pounding in his face, Steele beckoned for Ross to switch positions with him to steer at the helm so Steele could try his hand at the sails. Fighting the pelting rain, Ross clambered from the back of the boat and proceeded from stern to aft so he could position himself as captain. At the wheel, Ross desperately attempted anything he thought might work. Unfortunately, he made a bad decision by changing the ship's direction.

As Ross headed the ship through an unbroken stretch of water, Steele pulled in the sails to keep the ship close to the wind. Making ready to "come about," Ross screamed out the command, hoping Steele would hear. But the boat lost momentum, and they suddenly found themselves caught "in irons." The boat shuttered, then stopped. The *Sadie Thompson* struggled as her sails began to luff, clouds of white flapping madly and shaking wildly. The boat was stuck in the storm and could not move.

Now it was Steele's turn to clamor back over the deck to once again steer the ship to some kind, any kind, of safety. The captain tried to maneuver the schooner back onto a course that he felt could find refuge downwind on a nearby shore. He knew the area and sensed an island lay dead ahead. He scanned the gray scene for a promised lighthouse, both clearly marked on his well-worn lake chart as well as etched upon his memory. He saw no sign of a light. Visibility had turned to zero. But he knew land was near.

At last, unable to find clarity through the heavy rain and fog, Steele dropped his fourteen-hundred-pound anchor to avoid an inevitable crash. But as the ship pulled away from its long chain, it drove toward the island's rocky coast.

In vain, Steele searched for the comforting beam of a lighthouse, but the thick atmosphere prevented any success. A new and uncomfortable sensation for him, Steele felt hopelessly disoriented. The ship buffeted in the wind and tossed about on the waves until finally, with a loud crash, it ran aground on the jagged rocks at the craggy cliff base of Cobblestone Island.

No glint from the lighthouse had saved *Sadie Thomson* as it coursed through the rocky waves. Without a foghorn to blare off a stern warning, its crash that night was inevitable. Even the mighty Cobblestone Light had not protected *Sadie Thompson* from near ruin.

The ship dashed ashore, her starboard side slanting slightly toward the rocks. Like a child rocking in the comfort of its mother's arms, she teetered from side to side in the less comforting grip of cold, wet limestone. Its tattered jib boom extended over the rocky shore.

Lighthouse Keeper Curtis Bates, who had witnessed the crash, lost no time in securing the help of his wife to begin a rescue attempt at what he determined was a shipwreck. They raced from the lighthouse to the lakefront. Bates screamed over the din of the storm as he instructed whomever was on board to jump from the starboard deck, even though what lay ahead on the right side of the ship were dangerous rocks. The gale was wild and furious, and only courage and a sense of futility in doing anything but follow orders urged Charley and Ross as well as the other two to jump blindly and quickly.

All went well until Captain Steele took his turn to leap over-board. Once he landed, he slipped on the slimy rocks, immersing himself up to his neck in the turbulent water. It was Iona Bates who had acted quickly that night to save him. And for this act of courage, he became indebted to her.

Chapter 8

The Delirious Captain

Wednesday late morning at Cobblestone Lighthouse on Cobblestone Island

"But the *Sadie Thompson* is supposed to be at Berrie's Island!" Lillian argued as the children entered the wooded trail that led from Cottage Parakaleó to Cobblestone Lighthouse.

"Berrie's Island?" questioned Luke. "Don't you mean Milwaukee? We saw them loading up the stone bound for Milwaukee."

"No, no! We saw Uncle Fred at the General Store in Galena. He told us the *Sadie Thompson* was on his island," piped in Julia.

"At Raspberry Harbor," continued Lillian.

Paulina and Dellie jumped up and down with enthusiasm over their first shipwreck. They didn't care if the others acted confused. Their thoughts centered on the excitement of the previous night, and they couldn't wait to tell their brothers and sisters all about it. They had so many details to deliver that their words tumbled out.

"Paulina and I had to sleep on the floor in your mummy and dad's room," Dellie began.

"Since you three weren't home, the men were put up in our bedroom," Paulina added with matched excitement. "*Our* bedroom, Lillian! Can you imagine *that*?"

"They are frightful-looking men," continued Dellie. "I was glad to be on the first floor, as far away from them as possible."

"How many are there?" asked Luke.

"Five!" Paulina and Dellie answered together.

"And the captain is very mean," said Paulina.

"Like the very devil," added Dellie.

"Dellie!" reprimanded Julia, but Dellie simply stared wide-eyed back at Julia, wondering what she had said wrong in such an honest declaration.

Luke looked at Garrett who nodded knowingly. They knew about Charley and Ross and the two other crewmen. They knew of the angry Captain Steele. They knew about the *Sadie Thompson*. To think that it lay shipwrecked at their very home.

"So where will they be tonight?" questioned Lillian. "Will they still be there?"

"Their ship is a wreck. They're not leaving anytime soon," filled in Paulina. She made a face that mixed disgust with adventuresome anticipation. "And the captain is very sick. He has a hot fever."

"And he talks funny," added Dellie.

Paulina and Dellie chattered the whole mile home to the light-house, delighting themselves for once in their young lives over the chance to dish out details unknown to their older siblings. They answered questions as best they could, every now and then making an attempt to embellish the story ever so slightly through what they believed was simply good storytelling to a captive audience. For a moment at least, they stood at the center of their world. And it felt good.

Because of the heavily wooded trail from Galena to the light-house, the winding upward climb cooled the children as they walked and talked. Now and then, they glimpsed Lake Michigan sparkling through openings in the trees, the shoreline a long drop below the limestone cliff. Excited chattering made the walk seem effortless, and at last, the children found the trail's end, a clearing atop the north-ernmost point of the island where their all-in-one lighthouse and home stood proud and majestic.

They ran up the last bit of incline and broke through a clearing in the woods. No longer held in by a narrow path, the seven children spread out helter-skelter across the extensive yard in the back of the house, an area clear of woods and underbrush. They breezed between their barn and vegetable garden to the right and a small orchard to the left. Paulina and Dellie, parched from exhaustive explaining, stopped momentarily for a cool drink at the water pump that stood within steps from the summer kitchen, a recent add-on to the back end of the lighthouse. To satisfy their needs, the boys scattered off toward the outhouse, strategically tucked among a cluster of sweet-smelling lilac bushes just beyond the apple trees.

Lillian felt relieved to be home but hesitated to enter the lighthouse. She had outrun Julia and felt reluctant to plunge ahead. *Were Paulina and Dellie's amazing stories really true?* She decided when Julia came, Julia should go in first and make the discovery. Lillian "decided" things quite often, and her decisions usually won.

As she waited for Julia to catch up, Lillian glanced upward at what everybody called the "new" lighthouse. Built in 1858 and already twenty-six years old, over twice her age, the building hardly seemed new. Lillian surveyed the magnificent lantern room jutting up from the rooftop and saw the prisms of the Fresnel lamp glisten in the sunlight. *Why hadn't the light warned the sailors last night?* she wondered. *Why was the Sadie Thompson shipwrecked? Had it really been that foggy?*

Julia had now caught up to Lillian, and the sisters stood on the steps leading into the summer kitchen. Hesitant to meet the uninvited shipwrecked guests who might be sitting inside that very moment, Lillian spontaneously grabbed Julia's arm and pulled her down the steps around the house to the side entrance.

"Let's go in through the front hall door," panted Lillian as she paused to ponder her next move. "Or should we enter from the cliffside?" Lillian's mind was crammed full of images conjured up by Paulina and Dellie's tale of last night's terror. She imagined her mother fast asleep, suddenly awakened by her father's urgent command to help. Lillian could picture her mother throwing on her robe and running barefoot out their bedroom door, an entrance facing the cliff that allowed for quick access to any emergency on the lake. In her mind, Lillian clearly followed her mother racing down the long flight of steps to the water in an attempt to lend aid in the rescue.

Her eyes widened with fear as she pictured her parents helping to save those aboard the *Sadie Thompson*.

"Enter through Mother and Father's door?" Julia was stunned. "Why on earth would we do that?"

You're right, Julia, Lillian thought. *We mustn't go through Mother and Father's bedroom door. We're not supposed to do that.*

"Lillie, c'mon!" shouted Paulina from the pump as she wiped her sleeve across her wet chin. "Where are you going? Let's go in the kitchen!"

Feeling a bit confused over how to proceed, Lillian yanked at Julia's arm again and surprisingly obeyed her little sister's command. *After all*, Lillian pondered, *Paulina had been there last night. She ought to know what best to do.*

Suddenly, Luke and Garrett broke through the apple orchard and ran up the hill facing the side entrance to the lighthouse. They took the stairs two at a time and disappeared quickly inside. Without hesitation, Paulina and Dellie followed. Lillian then switched directions for a third time, going in first and pulling Julia with her. The group soon found themselves in the small foyer of the lighthouse, wondering what to do next.

The immaculate parlor, empty of people, lay to their right. They heard no voices down the hallway in the main kitchen, and they sensed no activity behind the staircase in the direction of their parents' bedroom. Perhaps everyone was upstairs.

Led by Luke, the boys ascended first and were soon lost from sight as they climbed two flights of stairs and then the steep steps leading to the lantern room. Luke hoped his father, from a man's point of view, would fill them in on the details of the shipwreck.

As Lillian led the girls cautiously upstairs, she met the ever cheerful, ever smiling Bates's housekeeper, Priscilla Rhoades. "Priscilla!" Lillian shouted. "You're back already from Washburn Island? Do you know what has happened here?"

"I just returned this morning, Missy. But it's a mighty good thing I has come back early. Looks like I'm needed real bad here. We has unexpected guests, and you and Julia come back just in time to help me change things around. I just moved myself into the visitor's room, so you girls can sleep in my quarters."

Priscilla helped Mrs. Bates with housework and cooking but came and went as she pleased to visit her sizable family on the southwest side of Washburn Island where five other African American families lived. As an African American somewhat unique to Lakeshore County, Priscilla as well as her entire extended family upon visiting Cobblestone Lighthouse, found themselves loved and respected within the Bates household. Their acceptance in Village Galena was not as welcome. As opposed to some opinions from residents in Village Galena, skin color made no difference to the Bates family. To them, people were people.

"Priscilla, you're forced out of your space!" Lillian gasped. "You must be cramped in the visitor's room! And what if the inspector arrives unexpectedly?" Lillian referred to the sporadic but certain visits by the official US government–appointed lighthouse inspector who came to check on conditions at this and other area lighthouses.

"Not as cramped as the five of you missies will be in my room." Priscilla laughed back. "I sure do have the better end of this bargain! But the switch mayn't be for long."

"I don't know about that. The men will have to repair their ship before they sail out, won't they?" countered a worried Julia. She thought of *Sadie Thompson*'s size. "And to fix it quickly will take a crew of twenty!"

Lillian smiled upon being called "Missy." She liked Priscilla's use of the term but recoiled remembering how the apothecary in Galena had used the term in a negative tone. His manner suggested she was a juvenile offender not worthy of a Christian name.

Priscilla saw that the three younger girls had joined them. "Julia and Lillian, quickly gather your things and bring them in here, will you now? Do it before them men return from the lake. You young ones better gather up the rest of your things too."

"They're at the lake?" questioned Lillian. "Good! I don't want to go into our room when they are in there. Paulina says that's where they slept last night. Those sailors gave me the creeps at Morrison

Harbor, and they will surely give me the creeps here, especially since they are staying in our room, in our beds!"

"The captain's in your bed right now, Missy. You'll need to get your things out for sleeping now that you're moving into my room. And be mighty quick and still about it. You be quiet as a mouse and don't go waking up that captain man sleeping in your bed. He's sick and ornery, he is."

"Right now?" Lillian gasped and looked at Julia for support. "Must we go in our room this minute?"

"*Our* room, Lillie? You mean, it *was* our room," sighed Julia. "C'mon, Paulina."

With Priscilla's sizable bed as a sleeping space for two children, their mother had set up two additional cots and also provided a sleeping mat on the floor for the fifth girl. Although not as spacious as their own room with the wood-burning stove, the girls found Priscilla's room workable for the time being. What they liked best was the magnificent view of Lake Michigan through Priscilla's window. This was a scene they could not see from their own bedroom, which had windows overlooking the backyard apple trees and, at one time, the old Cobblestone Lighthouse, now a mere remnant foundation.

Having decided who would sleep where, the five girls proceeded to get their things.

"What's that horrible sound?" asked Julia as she tiptoed into their actual bedroom.

"There's someone in our bed!" exclaimed Lillian who stood frozen in horror. Yes, she knew that a stranger had invaded her room, yet the grim reality took her by surprise.

"Shhh! That must be the captain," whispered Paulina. "He was hurt pretty bad last night. Mother spent a lot of time bandaging him up."

"He seems to be sleeping," murmured Dellie. "Listen to that awful snore!"

"It's more like a rumble and roar," observed Lillian at barely a whisper. "Let's just hurry and get our things. And do it quietly so we don't wake him up. I don't want to explain what we're doing in here."

The girls tiptoed about the room, finding what was precious to them. Although they had few "things," Lillian directed her energies toward finding the book her mother suggested she read. *Now where did I put that? Oh, under my bed!* Ever so gently, she knelt down beside the bed where the sleeping captain lay snoring. She tried to pull the book free. Suddenly, a giant arm came down upon Lillian. She screamed in frenzied panic, which startled the man and woke him up. He shouted, "Blast you, Charley! Keep that crate safe, I say. We have to get it to Traverse City."

Lillian was as frightened as a child facing a bear in the woods. The other girls scampered out of the room and stood safely in the hall, peering inside. Lillian's arm lay in a death clamp under the strong arm of Captain Samuel Steele. He continued to mutter, "Ross Clow, I'll have you for this. Where did you put it? Did you save it from the wreck? Did you save it?" Apparently suffering from some kind of delirium or nightmare, he kept repeating, "Did you save it? Did you save it? Did you save it?" His arm, tattoos dancing as his muscles flexed involuntarily, tossed this way and that, each time beating down upon Lillian. With a quick jerk, his left arm released Lillian from its grip.

Clasping the book she held in her hand, Lillian crawled quickly on her hands and knees across the floor, fleeing from the bed. Then she stood up. Too suddenly. And in so doing, she lost her balance. Her hand opened up to brace the fall, sending the book flying across the room and landing with great force right on Captain Steele's face. Lillian flew out of the room, and the four girls who had witnessed everything raced with her down the steps, out the front door, down the small hill, and into the apple orchard. They lay panting and gasping for breath but soon broke into peals of nervous laughter and embarrassment.

Meanwhile, upstairs, Captain Steele hurled the offensive book from his chest where it had bounced off his face. It went flying across the room, hitting the wall with a thud, falling open-faced onto the floor, wrinkling its pages. In exhaustion and with a great cry of anguish, Captain Steele flopped back onto his pillow. Mrs. Bates, who had heard the commotion from the kitchen, first from the girls tramping down the stairs, then from the thud against an upstairs wall, walked briskly upstairs to check on her patient.

Captain Steele lay moaning.

"Are you all right, sir?" Mrs. Bates inquired.

"No!" he thundered. "I've been attacked. Hit in the face by the enemy."

"Whatever are you talking about?" challenged Mrs. Bates. "My girls were up here gathering their things. Surely, they haven't attacked you." Then as an afterthought, she muttered to herself, "You are still quite delirious."

"I've been attacked! Attacked, I say!" thundered the captain as he swept the embroidered quilt to one side in an attempt to get out of bed. "Ohhhh," he moaned as he flopped back down again. "I must get out of here."

"You're going nowhere," Mrs. Bates ordered. "No one has attacked you, and no one is about to. You need to stay calm. You need to sleep. You were badly hurt last night."

"Ross! Charley!" the captain shrieked. "Where are you? Where are you? Where did you put . . ." His loud mutterings continued as he tossed his head this way and that until he was finally quiet and resumed his annoying snore.

Mrs. Bates covered the patient with the quilt and fluffed the pillow beneath his head. She felt the captain's forehead for fever and was relieved that his temperature seemed to have lessened. Bending over, she picked up the book whose crinkled pages lay facedown on the floor. She smoothed out the pages as she delivered it to Priscilla's room. *Susan Warner*, she thought as she read the author's name, *you don't deserve such treatment.* She smiled at the title, an often-reread favorite taken from the bookcase supplied by the lighthouse supply ship. She set it on the nightstand beside the bed.

Outside on the lawn, the girls discussed what had happened. "I thought he would kill me," sighed Lillian who was now more relieved than scared. "When his hand fell onto my arm and held me tight, I saw my funeral procession streaming before me. I saw the very hole in the graveyard where they would drop me in."

"We were scared for you too, Lillie," comforted Julia as she put her arm around her sister.

"I'm just glad we got out of there. Who cares about that old book anyhow? I should have left it under the bed—"

"But it is Mother's favorite, Lillie!" Unlike Julia, Lillian clearly valued her safety over her education.

Paulina and Dellie had wandered over to the cliff in front of the lighthouse, and Madeline had taken off looking for Gabriel.

Lillian and Julia, by themselves now, sat on the grass under an apple tree. "Did you hear what he was talking about, Julia? He wasn't making much sense."

"Yes, I heard him," agreed Julia. "I wonder what he was so worried about. Is something on the ship? Something he wants to keep safe?"

"I don't know, but I don't trust that man. Out of his head or not, he's up to something. And it's probably no good. Fever or not, he sure was jittery about something he had left on that boat. Let's find the boys and see what they say about it." Whenever Lillian spoke of "the boys," she referred to Luke and Garrett and Gabriel. Never Thomas. Thomas was different. He wasn't really one of "the boys." *All he was, was . . . annoying.*

"They're probably down at the dock, looking over the shipwreck. C'mon."

The two girls raced around the back of the lighthouse in the hope of leaving Paulina and Dellie behind. No use making things more complicated by inviting the ten-year-olds. They clambered down the wooden stairway, lifting their skirts so they wouldn't trip on any of the one hundred fifty-four steps leading to the lake.

A cool blast of lake air brushed against their cheeks as they stepped onto the rocky shore. They slowed their pace as they walked on the jagged white stones, keeping close to the tree-lined cliff wall.

Looking ahead, they found a perfect hiding spot, an area of layered limestone jutting out toward the lake from one section of the cliff.

Behind this rocky projection, the girls found a cavelike hiding space just big enough for them to slip into. They stepped into the opening and sat upon their ankles, their long skirts dusting the rocks beneath their feet. They hid ever so quietly to make their presence unknown. Barely breathing, they kept as motionless as the rocky ledge above them. They silently strained to see what was going on up ahead. On the stretch of shore in front of them, they saw Luke, Garrett, Gabriel, and Maddie picking through the scattered ruins of a ship run aground. A fearsome sight, the *Sadie Thompson* lay tipped slightly on its side. A large portion of its main, top, and jib sails billowed in the wind, parts of them flattened by the ship's two lacerated although unbroken masts. The scene suggested a gathering of ghosts grounded upon a rocky grave.

Chapter 9

Annoying Thomas

Immediately following at Cobblestone Island lakefront on Cobblestone Island

"The magnet's bin ruined, Ross," sputtered Charley. "Look-ey here. It's a mess. All broken apart. She'll never pick up ag'in."

"The magnet's the least of my worries," barked Ross. "I don't even care about it. Keep looking." Ross descended out of sight to join the two sailors in the lower portion of the ship's forecastle, slanted slightly on its side.

"I looked, I looked real hard," answered Charley. He glanced up and noticed the boys and Madelaine. "Hey, what's this I see over there?" With a friendly wave, Charley jumped off the bow of the wrecked ship onto the large jagged white rocks that, along with assorted water-covered smooth cobblestones, lined the shoreline.

"I've seen you before," he called out in surprise. "Them's the kids we seen a few days ago over to Morrison!" he shouted more or less to himself since Ross was not within hearing.

Startled by this discovery, Luke jumped up, urging Garrett and Gabriel to follow suit. Wide-eyed with interest,

Lillian and Julia kept watch at a distance tucked within the shelter of the rocky outcropping. They were careful not to lose their balance as they crouched low upon the rocks underneath their limestone safe haven. They were hidden but could clearly watch the action ahead.

"Hey, don't run away," Charley called. "Wutcha doin' here?"

Gabriel liked Charley, so he was inclined to stay. He turned around to address the sailor who in his heart he determined was a friend. He didn't want Luke or Garrett holding him back. "C'mon, boy. It's old Charley. You remember, don'tcha?"

"Hi, Charley. Yes, I remember you. You told me about the magnet on board. I guess it's wrecked now, huh?"

"Oh, she be wrecked, sonny. She be mighty wrecked." Gabriel cautiously turned toward Luke and Garrett to seek their approval, but the two boys were nowhere in sight. Luke and Garrett had run away with lightning speed. Startled, they had taken cover in the very hiding spot of their sisters within the limestone outcropping enclosure.

Madelaine, who had not run away but had seated herself on a large chunk of flattened limestone, stood up slowly, engrossed in the strange conversation between the old guy and her twin. She trusted Gabriel, so she decided it was safe to join in.

"This is my sister, Maddie. She's my twin," invited Gabriel.

"You ain't no look-alikes." Charley smiled, noticing her striking eyes. "She's a might more handsomer than you, boy."

Madelaine smiled. "Are you going to try to fix her?" Madelaine asked, pointing toward the ship.

"That be the plan, girlie, ifin it's possible."

"Charley, Charley! I think I found it. And it ain't even crushed! Man o' War, are we lucky! Get down here!" yelled a booming Ross from below the ship's bow. "And I want to show you something else I found."

Fearing Ross and the others would suddenly appear, Gabriel grabbed Madelaine's hand. "We have to go, Charley," he said. Mouth gaping, Maddie stared closely at this unusual sailor whom Gabriel seemed to know. Gabriel yanked her from her daydream, pulling her along swiftly as he climbed over the rocks, making Madelaine scurry behind. "We'll see you later!" Gabriel's voice trailed as the two rushed off.

Ross's head popped up from the forecastle hatch. "Are you waiting for the leaves to fall or are you getting your big frame down here?" he called. "What on earth is keeping you? I said I found something." He noticed Charley on all fours climbing over the rocks. "What are you doing? Collecting specimens for your rock collection . . . to add to the ones already filling your head?"

But Charley hadn't heard Ross's insults. Charley had bent down to pick up a handkerchief Madelaine had left behind when her brother had forced her abrupt retreat. The sailor promised himself he would return to the charming young lady her missing hanky with the lacy tatted edges. "Comin,' Ross," he answered and stuffed the hanky into his pants pocket.

By this time, Paulina and Dellie had made their way from the lighthouse on the cliff down the wooden stairway to join the others.

Thomas Silas Charles was with them. He was full of questions, and although envious that he had not been at Morrison Harbor with the others to see the *Sadie Thompson* get loaded on Sunday, he boasted that none of them had seen the *Sadie* get shipwrecked that Tuesday.

Why does Thomas annoy me so much? Lillian tried to ignore her brother's superior tones. *Is it because of his red mop of hair that's so different from the rest of us? Or is it the green of his eyes, which are gleaming right now. He's up to something!*

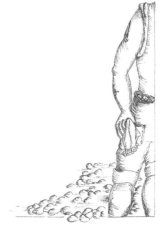

When Thomas was up to something, his eyes indeed gleamed like morning sunlight hitting the crystal green waves of Emerald Bay. They were stunning and clear, intelligent eyes that accented his quick mind. Although Thomas Silas Charles was nine, he seemed older. He was his own little man and fiercely independent.

You are so awfully annoying. And persistent. And bothersome. Lillian's annoyance grew as she heard Thomas prattle on about the shipwreck.

"It was quite the rescue attempt," chattered Thomas with the air and confidence of a sea captain.

As if you had been there! Lillian knew he had been fast asleep in the lighthouse during the entire rescue. Their mother and father had braved the storm alone with no help from the sleeping children.

It must be his "red attitude," thought Lillian. *Red, red, fire, fire. This isn't right. That isn't right. I'm right; you're wrong. Red, red, fire, fire.*

"You didn't rescue the crewmen," Lillian snapped at last. "Mother and Father did. You were asleep, and you know it. I'm going up to help Mother make lunch," Lillian spat out the words and attempted to leave.

"I was here the night of the shipwreck, and you weren't," he spewed back with utter authority before running ahead to be the first to climb the stairs back to the lighthouse.

Lillian's scowl was meant to sink his spirit. She stuck out her tongue and kicked at the rocks with her boot, which had little effect upon Thomas. Like a tugboat chugging through a foggy blur, Thomas had propelled himself out of sight. Lillian fumed in anger as she was suddenly caught off guard. An unexpected breaker had broken loose upon the shore. Dismayed and disgusted, she looked down at her feet doused with cool lake water, the depth of which was not quite sufficient to cool her fiery temper.

Chapter 10

Stolen Goods

That Wednesday noon at Cobblestone Island Lighthouse on Cobblestone Island

In the lighthouse, with Captain Steele finally settled in bed, their mother had begun preparing a noontime meal for the family and the crew of the *Sadie Thompson*. Two floors above in the lantern room, Curtis Bates polished soot off the lamps. Unexpectedly, Uncle Fred appeared in the summer kitchen, bearing mail brought up from the mainland.

"Hello, brother," greeted Iona Wrede Bates.

"Hello, sister," greeted Frederick Wrede in his usual exchange.

"How's my little Dellie?"

"Oh, Fred, she'll be fine. Her sniffles and coughing had turned into something alarming for a while, but nothing like what Lillian suffered. No quarantine necessary, we managed to doctor her up quite well."

"That's what the children said, but Violet was pretty concerned, so I thought I'd check. Always thought you'd make a fine nurse, sis."

"They're all down at the lake watching—" Iona stopped herself, thinking she best not admit even to Fred about the five newcomers to her house. She smiled as she recalled how she frequently reminded her outspoken children not to tell everything they knew. "Watching ships go by," she finished. "Did you dock way back at Galena?"

"Yes, I did. The climb uphill is good exercise. I don't mind. Say, did the girls mention anything about the *Sadie Thompson* being over at my place?"

"*Sadie Thompson*?" Iona stalled.

"That's a ship, sister, not a woman."

"Oh?"

"Yes, well, she was moored over at Berrie's. At Raspberry Harbor. And then she disappeared. Kind of strange actually. I talked with her crew for a bit and even went over to Galena to get provisions for them. The captain said they needed supplies real bad. The guy was a bit rough around the edges but mighty polite, mighty polite. So I took down a list and picked up some necessary items. Medicine even. The captain must have changed his mind, I guess. The crew wasn't there when I returned. Their schooner was gone. Then again, I did get back quite late. Perhaps they were in a hurry to leave. Still, it seems odd that they left before I gave them the medicine. They had paid for it too. Kind of strange actually."

Something told Iona Bates not to mention she knew of the *Sadie Thompson* or that she housed her captain upstairs in Lillian's bed. She couldn't say why, but she determined to say nothing. Instead, she glanced at the newspaper her brother was holding and changed the subject. "Anything of interest in the paper?"

"Well, this and that for local interest. But nationally, something interesting, yes. A bit unusual. You know that talk about internal gas combustion engines that everyone's so fired up about and that Curtis keeps dreaming about for lake navigation? Well, someone over in France built a single-cylinder four-stroke engine that runs on stove gas. Seems to be quite advanced. The last issue talked about it some, but there's a whole lot more information in this issue and something surprising too."

Iona wasn't sure she was interested in this particular subject but listened politely. What could be interesting about a gas engine?

"I know Curtis will want to read more about this invention in the *Lakeshore County Advocate*." Fred held up the latest issue of the county newspaper before he continued, "Bound to get him a bit excited." Sensing the subject at hand was of little interest to his sister, Fred walked into the main kitchen and placed the *Advocate* prominently on the table for his brother-in-law Curtis to read before dinner. Fred made sure the paper lay open to the featured article. "I can't stay, Iona. I promised Violet I'd pick up some things for her in Galena. Mostly came to drop off the mail and ask about Dellie. You're sure she's doing all right?"

"Perfectly, Fred. What about Violet? How is she faring?"

"She's been good, Iona. Thank God, she's been real good lately. Painting always seems to calm her down."

"Good. I'm glad to hear that. We'll come visit soon."

"She'd like that." Fred walked toward the summer kitchen door. "Give Dellie and Garrett our love and remember to show Curtis that article." Then he disappeared out the door on his way through the woods down to Galena.

Iona stirred her family's favorite bean and ham dish flavored with Cobblestone Island apples and maple syrup. She bent over and opened a cupboard door as she reached for a brown bottle. *The sailors ought to like this*, she mused as she poured a half cup of dark rum into the mixture. She checked the pot of hot oil into which she would soon drop by spoonfuls another family favorite, a recipe from a keeper in Camden, Maine. She stirred the batter that would soon create hot crispy cornmeal hush puppies. Captain Steele was in no shape to join the family for dinner, but more than a dozen others

crowded around the large kitchen table. Momentarily caught in wonder by the magnificent wildflower bouquet, Mrs. Bates stopped to stare at the vase full of colorful buds that graced the table as a centerpiece. It never ceased to amaze her that the wildflowers brought by Lillian and Julia after visiting Cottage Parakaleó always stayed fresh for days. Wildflowers normally wilted soon after picking. But then again, Mrs. Bates believed in miracles.

Rather than seating herself among her family and guests at the table, Mrs. Bates opted to serve them first and eat from the leftovers later.

"Your father was here, Dellie," their mother began.

"Mother too?" Dellie asked.

"No, but she is doing well, he says."

"And Uncle Fred brought interesting news," their father decided to take a new tack and not get into a discussion about illnesses. "Mighty interesting news I read in the last *Advocate* that he dropped by. Seems as if an Edouard Debouteville from France invented a new internal combustion gas engine." Curtis Bates believed gas combustion engines were the wave of the future in powering all lake crafts. He spoke of the subject often. "Seems as if the prototype has been stolen though," he continued. Keeper Bates had indeed found and read the more recent article that Uncle Fred had left out for him.

Crewman Charley's eyes widened with interest, and his mouth hung open in surprise.

Upon this apparently extraordinary news, observant Lillian noticed the distinct threatening glance that Ross Clow shot across the table at his buddy, Charley Skruggs. Luke, who had also caught the expression, saw how Charley lowered his head like a wounded puppy. Lillian and Luke exchanged knowing glances. *What were those looks supposed to mean?*

"Yes, the *Advocate* says the engine prototype was out and out stolen," their father repeated. "Right here in the States. Somewhere down south when the inventor was showing his patent at a convention. Paper calls it 'an advanced design, the best conceived engine of its type to date.' Sure don't like to hear about this theft. I've been waiting for that invention to be perfected. If it's stolen, none of us will be the wiser for its use here on the Great Lakes." Their father said nothing further as he concentrated on eating his wife's delicious dinner.

Lillian looked closely for more signs of interest from either Ross or Charley, but their lowered heads suggested they were too intent upon consuming beans and cornbread. The other two sailors followed suit, downing their food like they hadn't eaten in a month.

After dinner, Gabriel, Thomas, Madelaine, Paulina, and Dellie delighted in clearing the table and washing dishes because the sailors offered to help. To be treated to a wild sea story from Ross, with humorous interjections by Charley, made up for having to wash dishes, which was hard work. Despite the recent storms, the cistern was dry. Because of this lack of water supply, the two skinny but light-on-their-feet sailors offered to haul buckets of water up the long flight of steps from the lake. They said they would do anything as a thank-you for the delightful home-cooked meal they had just devoured.

Sunday and Tuesday nights' sudden storms did little to change the heat and dryness of the daytime hours. The cistern outside the summer kitchen begged for a period of steady rain. But with no such luck, the children had recently been duty bound to fetch water for washing from the lake far below the tall cliff upon which the lighthouse stood. Looking like a pair of matching stickpins, the two quiet sailormen surprised the five young children by hauling water easily and quickly and thus proving their muscle.

After the dishwashing and storytelling, Ross, Charley, and the other two sailors continued their work at the lakefront, trying to salvage their ailing ship. They seemed content to have their captain upstairs and out of range. Without his bellowing remarks and cantankerous orders, they seemed to know what to do to get the work done while he convalesced in bed.

Meanwhile, the other four children, using their usual spot, the apple orchard, had convened in a conference. The talk around the dinner table and what they had observed down at the lake held signs of a mystery they felt sure they were destined to unravel.

Chapter 11

A Mysterious Note

Immediately following on Wednesday at Cobblestone Lighthouse on Cobblestone Island

"I'm telling you, they're hiding something on that ship," observed Luke. "We watched them a long time, and they weren't just trying to repair things."

"They were obviously searching," added Garrett.

"And they found something too," added Lillian. "I heard Ross say so to Charley. He was yelling at him to come below deck to see it." She paused, considering what this might mean. "Did you see how Charley looked when Father said how the gas engine was stolen?"

"Yes," Luke broke in. "And then Ross gave Charley a look that could kill. What do you suppose it meant?"

"This may not have anything to do with anything," continued Lillian, "but I'm putting two and two together."

Julia raised her eyebrows in anticipation of what her sister would say next. She admired how Lillian, older than she by a year, could figure things out. Julia held more admiration for her sister than enviousness.

"Do you remember that piece of paper I showed you? The one I found Sunday at Morrison Harbor?"

Julia narrowed her eyes in thought. Yes, Julia had remembered the note. But that memory did not help her figure out how the note fit into the conversation. She edged in closely to hear more.

"Something strange is going on concerning the *Sadie Thompson*, right?" Lillian took on an intelligent air. "We figure they're looking for something important too, right?"

"Something more important than getting that ship fixed and getting out of here," added Garrett.

"Correct," agreed Lillian. "Well, this idea may be crazy, but look at this." As Lillian spoke, she reached into her apron pocket and carefully unfolded a soiled piece of wrinkled paper. She pressed it out flat against her skirt.

Luke strained to see what mystery the paper would yield. "So what?" he scoffed. "There's a couple of initials and words and numbers scribbled this way and that. The writing is so faint I can barely read what it says. It doesn't make much sense."

"Maybe yes and maybe no," put in Lillian with sly wisdom that made Julia certain her big sister was on to something. "It says 'E.D.' and it says 'gas.'" Lillian opened the copy of the *Lakeshore County Advocate* she had snatched from the kitchen. She searched for the article that her father had mentioned at dinner. "The Frenchman inventor that Father spoke about is . . . is . . ."—her eyes scanned the paper for the article—"is Edouard Debouteville. That's the 'E.D.' And the 'gas' could refer to his invention, his gas engine!"

"Do you have any idea what 'cotton dealers' and 'New Orleans' mean?" questioned Luke who was gaining enthusiasm as he made clear the faint words on the note.

"I don't know," Lillian answered carefully, "but do you suppose the work that cotton dealers do in New Orleans is associated with gasoline engines? I mean, like it could make their work easier and faster so they can make more money?"

Julia and Garrett listened closely to the interesting reasoning, trying to figure out how the sailors figured in.

"You mean the crew of *Sadie* stole the engine and are trying to find it in the wreck so they can sell the patent themselves?" Garrett speculated.

"Something like that. Remember when we were on Washburn Island watching them load stones? Do you remember that fellow in the boat out on the lake at Morrison Harbor that yelled to Captain Steele?"

A memory flashed through Luke's mind. "The one whom Captain Steele was all smiley about? Right after he had been yelling at Charley?"

"Yes, that one. Well, did you see that his ship was called *Cotton Belle*? I'll bet that ship has connections with the South, maybe even New Orleans, and has something to do with this note."

"Maybe when the *Sadie Thompson* met with the *Cotton Belle*, that man on *Belle* passed over the stolen gas engine to Captain Steele!" Luke was excited over his own revelation.

"What else does the paper say?" asked Garrett. "There's more writing."

Julia, who had the text memorized, volunteered the information. "Sketch."

"What do you mean 'sketch'?" asked Luke.

"That's what else the paper says," said Julia. "'Sketch.' Who knows what that is supposed to mean. And 'S. S.'"

"Sam Steele!" Garrett announced, pleased he could continue his contributions. "But I wonder what 'sketch' is. Sketch, gas, cotton dealers, New Orleans, and E.D. That's all?" questioned Garrett, now on a roll.

"There's a name and some numbers too," continued Lillian. "Perry Hannah."

"Maybe he's the guy who sold the patent to the inventor Debouteville for his gas engine!" Garrett remarked.

"And twenty-four by twenty and fourteen three-eighths by twenty-two."

"Are the dimensions of the engine or its parts or something!" Garrett beamed with satisfaction over his hunch.

"Oh, and there's one more word that I can barely make out."

"Let me see," said Luke as he reached for the paper. "Paced. Raced . . ."

"Races!" Garrett decided as he looked over Luke's shoulder.

"Steamboat races?" suggested Luke, turning his head around and snapping his fingers. "The gas engine powers steamboats for river races."

"Well," began Lillian, "I found the note by the *Sadie Thompson*, so it must have come from the pocket of either Ross or Charley or Captain Steele or one of the crewmen. We just figured what it might mean, so all we have to do is find out whether we're right."

"I think we have a perfectly splendid mystery at our lighthouse," Julia beamed, "and I think we are the ones who will eventually figure it out." A glint sparkled in Julia's eyes, perhaps not as bright as her sister's but certainly as sincere because of the obvious adventure she and the others hoped to embrace.

"Maybe Captain Steele is a betting man," volunteered Julia who had no idea what she was suggesting, but it sounded good. "And the sketch could be a sketch of the racecourse on the lake where people bet." She smiled at this thought, but soon, her grin faded. "But that's pretty far-fetched, isn't it? I wonder if *any* of our hunches could be true."

Chapter 12

A Discovery

Immediately following on Wednesday at Cobblestone Lighthouse on Cobblestone Island

Thomas Silas Charles is up to no good. Lillian knew it and felt it. *Why had he been in my room talking with Captain Steele? He had no business in there. If anyone should talk to the captain, it should be me. What does Thomas know about the mystery anyway? What could he hope to find out when he isn't even a part of our plans to uncover the mystery?*

"What were you doing in my room, Thomas Silas Charles?" Lillian frowned.

"It isn't *your* room anymore," countered the wise little brother.

He is truly up to no good.

"I think the captain is a very nice man." Thomas smiled.

To Lillian, the smile seemed a bit too sly. Exasperation washed over her. "Have you heard the way he yells at his crewmen, Thomas?"

"No, I wasn't with you on Washburn Island, remember?"

Lillian savored the memory. *No, Thomas, you weren't!* "He isn't kind at all," insisted Lillian. "He is mean and wicked to Ross and Charley."

"He speaks of the two continually."

So you discussed Ross and Charley with him, did you? Lillian's frown deepened.

"Captain Steele is intent upon their finding something on the shipwreck, getting the schooner fixed in a hurry, and then leaving the island. I offered my help," said Thomas.

Offered your help! Stay out of this, Thomas! "I don't think Ross and Charley need help from a nine-year-old," Lillian fumed.

Thomas looked hurt, but Lillian didn't notice. "All right then," he murmured as he walked away. Stopping abruptly as if he had forgotten something, he turned around to add, "But I may just be helpful to you in solving the mystery."

What do you know about the mystery! How could you know anything? You weren't in on any of our discussions. What has Captain Steele told you?

Lillian decided to drop the matter for the time being, but she did wonder what Thomas Silas Charles knew and how on earth he thought he could be helpful in solving the mystery. She felt a sudden longing to visit Miss Garnet at Parakaleó. The idea captured her thoughts, but her mother reminded her to go outside to weed the garden.

How she hated that chore. Especially when it was hot. Sometimes she resented being the oldest girl who always had "to be the most responsible." Finding Julia who was always willing to help, she went outside to attack the little green enemies popping up all over in their vegetable plot.

"What do you think the captain has been telling Thomas?" inquired Julia in complete seriousness. Julia's utmost concern over the matter that bubbled hot in her sister's brain was obvious.

"I don't know, but knowing Thomas, he has found out something. And that something is probably just what we need to know."

Julia yanked at a particularly stubborn intruder as it popped out, root and all. She shook off the dirt and threw it on the grass where other weeds lay piled. Julia wondered why Thomas annoyed his sister so much. Truly, he could act uppity, but he was such a smart boy. And Julia knew he could be useful to them. But Lillian seemed to resist his contributions and knowledge. Lillian seemed to resist him completely.

"We don't need Thomas, Julia," Lillian pronounced as she stood to brush off her skirt. "At last! We're done! Let's take that walk to see Miss Garnet." She had convinced Julia a walk would refresh them after working in the heat for what had seemed like hours. Lillian felt certain in the coolness of the woods the sun, still quite high in the sky, would excuse itself from their presence.

When the girls arrived at the cottage, they found Miss Garnet in her own garden, a wild and wonderful assortment of flowers.

"Your flowers are gorgeous," beamed Julia who loved the scattered arrangements.

"Oh, hello, girls," called the jolly lady who looked up from the ground. She was on all fours, cultivating the dirt around a cluster of orange and yellow nasturtiums. "What brings you back so soon for a visit?"

"We just had to get away. It's always good to talk with you. You always turn dismal situations into something good," Lillian shot out, her real intention being to as quickly as possible discuss the situation concerning Thomas.

Miss Garnet flashed her famous smile and laughed heartily. She stood up somewhat stiffly. "I was thinking about going into town actually. Care to join me?"

Not exactly what Lillian had in mind, she soon found herself in the General Store around people she didn't really care to see. Not

only was Lillian reluctant to exchange words with Mr. Scarsley, she certainly had no desire to chat with Galena's busiest wagging tongue, the intimidating Mrs. Gwendolyn DePere.

Lillian didn't know who she despised more, the formidable Mrs. DePere or her cutesy thinks-she's-better-than-anyone-else twelve-year-old daughter, Lucinda Lynda Pinda Pudding and Pie Wish You'd Go Away and Die DePere. Lucinda was the ring leader of those who had ridiculed her at the beach the other day.

Lillian still felt angry over Lucinda's cruel laughter, her hurtful stares, and all those who had pointed fingers at her bathing costume. *Lucinda acts so high and mighty. She thinks she's smarter and more important and richer than we who live at the lighthouse. I hate how she boasts about her rich Aunt Miranda of Milwaukee. So what if Lucinda has an aunt who married a rich and prosperous businessman? Why should that make her a better person? My Aunt Violet is a wonderful artist. So there.*

"And my sister Miranda was mightily disappointed, mind you," chattered Mrs. DePere to Elliott Scarsley, the storekeeper as well as apothecary. "She had expected that shipment of limestone cobblestones days ago, and it never showed up. Boat never came. How can she expect to show off her rock garden if it isn't completed? Those glistening rocks will add beauty and elegance to her roses. Oh, such roses she has. From France. Fragrant ones. They'll be the talk of Milwaukee . . . if they aren't already. Perhaps the talk of Wisconsin."

She sputtered on as if sensing someone would shut her up before pouring forth her full load of prattle. "Mrs. Fred Pabst is on her guest list. And Mrs. Edward Allis, all the Uihlein wives, Mrs. Thomas Cochran, Mrs. Fred Vogel, Mrs. Emanuel Silverman, Mrs. Guido Pfister . . ." She looked up to make sure she was properly impressing Elliott Scarsley through her mention of all the important people of Milwaukee. "The party is set for mid-August. Imagine the inconvenience of canceling! Can't have a garden party when the garden isn't presentable. Don't know what she'll do without those limestone cobbles to enhance it."

"Frederick Wrede was in the other day," Elliott Scarsley managed to break in while he wrapped her purchase. "He said something about a schooner *Sadie Thompson* being docked over at Berrie's Island for the night. Said something about having limestone in her hold."

"Well, I never!" dramatized the woman, forcing her voice to a high then low pitch. "Why would Miranda's order of limestone cobbles be clear over to Berrie's Island?" Forming a hasty conclusion, she leaned in close to her captive audience of one to whisper a confidence, "It is probably the missing shipment, you know." She pursed her lips tightly and, with smug confidence, continued her bragging drone, "My sister, Mrs. Joseph Adler, is high society, you know. People cry to be put on her guest list. To think that she might have to cancel her gathering. It's a crime. Simply a crime."

Then wrapping up her thoughts, she manufactured a satisfying smile and arched her eyebrows. "I cannot wait to tell her about this wandering ship. She knows people in high places. Between the two of us, we'll make it right. You'll see. Why, Mr. Scarsley, I'll have you dispatch an immediate telegraph message to secure a United States revenue cutter in finding that missing *Sally Tompkins*, or whatever it was, that pirated away her garden stones. We'll get that limestone back to her garden where it belongs."

It's Sadie Thompson. Lillian's silent correction echoed through her brain. She hid behind Miss Garnet who, also at the counter with her purchase, decided to join in on the conversation. Up close, she was fascinated to watch Mrs. DePere's mouth aflutter. *How can anyone talk that fast?* Lillian's stare at the strong-willed woman broke only as she watched Miss Garnet's graceful handwriting sign off for her items put on charge.

What was that? Lillian suddenly took notice. *Had Mrs. DePere just scowled at Miss Garnet? And had Mr. Scarsley nodded in agreement? How can this be? How dare they treat her so? Miss Garnet is an angel if I ever knew one.*

On their way back home, Lillian conversed only briefly with Miss Garnet. Because Miss Garnet gave no indication for a long chat, Lillian decided to leave her alone and dropped back to discuss a matter with Julia. "Did you hear what Mrs. DePere said in the store? Her sister was supposed to get limestone cobbles. And that's just what the *Sadie Thompson* had on board."

"Yes, rocks for her sister's garden in Milwaukee or something like that."

"So she can show off her fancy flowers from France, I'll bet. I'm sure Miss Garnet's flower garden is much prettier anyway, with or without limestone cobbles."

"Do you think she'll send a government boat, a revenue cutter, out looking for *Sadie Thompson*?"

"Probably, knowing Mrs. DePere. She goes after everything she wants. Whatever it takes. At all costs. We'd better tell the boys." Then Lillian's face grew red with anger. "You know, Julia, I came to Parakaleó to talk with Miss Garnet about Thomas. I can't take him anymore. I need her advice. Miss Garnet knows how to handle difficult people. But she didn't seem to be in the mood to talk at all."

Then her expression softened as she sensed something important about their visit. "Actually, Julia, I feel better for just having been with Miss Garnet. I can't believe how nice she treated Mrs. DePere. Did you notice?"

Julia had.

"And did you notice how Mrs. DePere scowled less after talking with Miss Garnet?"

Julia did.

"I don't even want to talk to Mrs. DePere. Or her daughter Lucinda Belinda Melinda! But Miss Garnet was so pleasant toward her. Even when Mrs. DePere acted fierce. How can Miss Garnet be so nice to someone so awful?"

"I know what you mean."

At this time, Lillian had no idea that her mere observation of Miss Garnet had taught her exactly what she had come to find out at Cottage Parakaleó.

Chapter 13

Sadie's Comeback

Thursday morning at Cobblestone Lighthouse on Cobblestone Island

Throughout Wednesday, Captain Steele had burned with fever, but by late afternoon, he began to show some improvement. In his weakened condition, his thankfulness to Iona Bates showed in his eyes as he watched her care for him. If it hadn't been for her total devotion to his medical needs, he knew he would have perished. She had checked him continuously. She had coaxed him to a restful sleep.

Although Mrs. Bates had made a hearty supper meal Wednesday evening, Captain Steele had not dined with the family. She had brought up his meal later, after he slept peacefully for several hours that afternoon. He then managed to muster enough strength to swear to Ross and Charley that he'd be out and about the next day.

He kept his vow. Late Thursday morning, Lillian peeked into her old room to find it curiously empty. Empty, that is except for Thomas who stood by the window, looking out at the apple trees. He turned when he heard Lillian in the hallway. "Conrad Warren," he said with annoying authority.

"What are you talking about, Thomas?" Lillian stepped into the room. "And what are you doing in my . . ." she corrected herself before he could, "*the guest room* for Captain Steele and his crew?"

"I'm thinking of what the captain said about Conrad Warren."

"Who's Conrad Warren?" Lillian was irritated that Thomas knew something she did not. *Who on earth is Conrad Warren?*

"He transferred a large package to Captain Steele out on the lake the day he left Morrison Harbor. The day you and the others were there."

So they had been right about the meeting between ships and transfer of goods from the Cotton Belle to Sadie Thompson.

"Captain Steele said something about Ross finding a package that Conrad Warren had given him in Morrison Harbor."

"Conrad Warren is captain of the *Cotton Belle*," Lillian deduced. "*Cotton Belle?*"

Oh, I shouldn't have mentioned that detail. Thomas doesn't have to know everything. "Oh, never mind." *Why did the captain have to tell Thomas about that meeting?* Lillian was incredulous that if Steele was trying to hide something, he certainly would refrain from handing out information to a nine-year-old boy. *And hadn't Captain Steele been sick with a terrible fever? How had Thomas managed to get information out of someone as sick as the captain? How does he do it?*

"He was talking kinda crazy, and I just listened," Thomas ventured, studying her upraised eyebrows, seeming to know Lillian's thoughts.

Lillian pondered the captain's delirium. *He hadn't offered information of this sort to me.* Lillian didn't believe for one second that he had actually *told* Thomas anything. Thomas had just overheard the captain's feverish gibberish. *Yet the words could mean something.*

Like a breaker's explosive crash upon rocks, Lillian recalled Miss Garnet's calm demeanor toward annoying Mrs. DePere. She remembered how Miss Garnet's graciousness washed away Mrs. DePere's anger. *Maybe a little grace toward Thomas might dissolve his know-it-all attitude.*

Then she added a devious afterthought, *After all, Thomas could be valuable. Then again, he is terribly annoying.* Lillian decided to dismiss Thomas's contributions. He couldn't possibly be useful in solving the mystery at hand. *Thomas is perhaps even more annoying than Mrs. DePere. How unfortunate that he is my brother.*

Moments later at breakfast, their father shared exciting information. At last, the government tender *Trillium* was coming to bring workers and bricks to build the oil house that had been promised to

Cobblestone Light. The failure to begin this project grieved Keeper Bates, who resented the Lighthouse Board for continually failing to deliver on its promises. The Board knew of the fire hazard that existed by storing kerosene in the lighthouse even though the basement could be considered secure. But surely, the authorities knew that Iona taught school there.

For four years, the lighthouse board had recommended that a separate flameproof oil house be built to store the mineral oil or kerosene. Since 1880, Curtis and Iona Bates had burned kerosene at Cobblestone Lighthouse. The older children remembered the days before when their mother and father melted lard on the stove and, in winter before it cooled, rushed it up two flights of stairs to fuel the lamp. Four years ago, this had all changed when a new fourth-order Fresnel one-wick lamp was installed that burned kerosene instead. For three long years, they had waited for the safety of an oil outhouse to store the flammable liquid.

The *Trillium* supply ship arrived that very morning. The tender came from the district depot commandeered under Captain Jonathan Joseph, two officers, and a large crew. Like all lighthouse tenders, she was named after a native flower, in this case the lovely Cobblestone Island white trillium characteristically speckled with pink on the outer edges of its three white petals, turning pink to lavender to a deeper purple as it aged. The tender's formal orders included moving out the old lard-oil lamp fixtures stored in the cellar of Cobblestone Lighthouse. These artifacts were ordered back to the lighthouse depot. The crew was also commissioned to at last build a fireproof brick oil house separate from the lighthouse itself. A third Lighthouse Board order was to fell local trees to build a wooden fence for safety's sake in front of the lighthouse on the northern cliff overlooking the lake. The open bluff was an accident waiting to happen, but luckily, no child had yet fallen over the cliff wall. With seven of his own children on the premises and two more added for the summer, Curtis Bates would be thankful for the completion of this job as well. And besides, the lighthouse tender's arrival was always exciting for the entire family because with the necessary supplies came a new case full of books and magazines.

Captain Steele, seemingly as good as new and intent upon leaving Cobblestone Island to get on with his work, lost no time in enlisting the help of *Trillium*'s crew to quickly finish repairs on the *Sadie Thompson* so that he could be on his way with what he mysteriously called "important and necessary business."

The able-bodied crew of *Trillium* launched themselves immediately into helping Ross Clow, Charley Skruggs, Captain Sam Steele, and also Steele's pair of skin-and-bones crewmen repair *Sadie Thompson*. Captain Steele could be charming when it worked to his advantage. He somehow hoodwinked even the two officers to pitch in and help with the repairs. The able crew fixed the torn rigging, chopped away the tangled stays, set the mast, shrouds, sails, and rigging, and repaired the damaged rudder so the ship could once again sail upon the lake.

Much to Charley Scruggs's dismay, the first pile of junk hauled away were pieces of the broken-up magnet he so loved. The limestone cobble cargo loaded onto the ship at Morrison Harbor would be left behind for now. Bit by bit, the storm-torn ship took shape again as a sailing vessel. The large crew worked steadily and made the repairs quickly. Time left over afforded the able crew of *Trillium* to at last get to the work it had been sent to perform for Keeper Curtis Bates. Without having the plans to assemble the promised brick oil house, Captain Steele instead ordered the crew into the eastern forest to cut wood for the fence building project.

Luke, Garrett, Thomas, and Gabriel volunteered to help paint the *Sadie Thompson* late that afternoon. They hoped to overhear something of importance as they worked close to Ross, Charley, the two sailor crewmen, and Captain Steele as some of the government-sent *Trillium* crew worked on their commissioned lighthouse projects.

"Is *this* the color we're painting the ship?" Luke blurted.

"Shhhh! Captain Steele says it's the only thing *Trillium* has on board. He's putting up with it, so let's not make him feel bad."

"But, Garrett, I can't see Captain Steele commanding a boat of this color! It's not a schooner color, do you think?"

"It'll do, boys. It'll do!" shouted Captain Steele. "It isn't my first pick to dress up my damaged schooner, but it'll do, boys. It'll do. I don't turn down free goods. Why, it'll do just fine as a memory of my little stay here, boys, and the ship that supplied it. It'll do just fine." With a bellowing command, Captain Steele ordered the painting job to commence.

Embarrassed at being overheard, Luke and Garrett helped paint the ship with not so much as another word about the odd color. They did, however, remark about the only one on board *Trillium* who had not pitched in to help.

"Where did Captain Joseph go?"

"I don't know, Garrett. He seems to have disappeared."

"I saw him take off his wool jacket. It's hanging on the water pump with his lighthouse cap."

"Well, it's hot outside," defended Luke. "I don't blame him for shedding that thick coat of his. It's so dry and hot again. I'm just glad we don't have to wear all those official government clothes."

"But the captain of a tender should help with duties, shouldn't he? How can he just take off and leave?"

"I can tell you one thing, Garrett. If Captain Joseph had stuck around, Captain Steele wouldn't have taken over and gotten Joseph's

whole crew to help repair *his* ship first. Man, was he barking out orders at everybody!"

"What was it he said to some of the crew of *Trillium*?" Garrett asked as he comically imitated Captain Steele's demeanor and voice. "If Captain Joseph wanted to get his jobs done first, he would have stuck around to get it done. So get to work fixing my ship here that needs repairin' and paintin'. And if there's time left over, my crewmen will help you get at what you're supposed to be doing. *I'm* your captain now, so jump to it!" Luke laughed at Garrett's accurate interpretation.

Captain Steele was indeed back to normal again, throwing around his authority by bossing everyone in sight—that is, everyone except Iona Bates to whom he was eternally grateful for saving his life. After hours of labor in the hot sun, the repair work and repainting completed, Captain Steele gratefully acknowledged the unexpected help that had blown his way.

"This here ship's done some wanderin' lately, and we're going to give her a new name," he bellowed. "Ross, you swing that paintbrush of yours and christen this here rig *Wanderer.* Make the letters big and black so they stand out in contrast to the new color," Captain Samuel Steele ordered, his eyes sparkling with newfound health.

As Ross began to paint the new name he had sketched in charcoal onto the boat, Mrs. Bates called from the lighthouse, "Girls, come quickly. I have some exciting news!"

Chapter 14

Caught

That Thursday evening at Cobblestone Lighthouse on Cobblestone Island

Mrs. Bates was taken aback because the girls were less than excited about the strawberry-picking excursion she had suggested for the following morning. It was exciting news that Iona Bates planned to take the family knockabout sailing craft to Berrie's Island for a short visit with Dellie and Garrett's mother, Aunt Violet. Normally, a trip would have thrilled the girls because they enjoyed any chance to sail, but Lillian especially felt dismay over the prospect of leaving. The timing couldn't have been worse. She and "the boys" had plans to figure out what Captain Steele was hiding below deck on his newly restored schooner. Leaving at this time would complicate matters. Their mother insisted, however, that the berry-picking trip take place the next day.

Lillian knew something had to happen that night if she were to help solve any kind of mystery tied to *Sadie Thompson*, now named *Wanderer*. Putting herself in charge and also having no intention of being left out, Lillian called an immediate meeting in the apple orchard with Julia and the boys. "I think Aunt Violet wants to make sure Dellie is well, so Mother is sailing with us girls, weather permitting, to Berrie's Island tomorrow to see her."

"Father says this hot, dry weather is to continue," added Julia.

"Then if there is any wind at all, we're bound to make the trip. Mother says the trip is for strawberry picking. She knows we love doing that. Garrett, I think the real reason is to reassure your mother that Dellie is all right."

"We can't leave now," interrupted Julia. "We have investigating to do."

"I know. The timing is not good," agreed Lillian. "How long do you think *Sadie*, I mean *Wanderer*, is going to be here?" she asked the boys.

"Now that it's repaired and painted, the crew is going to leave soon. Like tomorrow. We can't let that happen without finding out about what they're hiding in the ship's hold," ventured Luke.

"While we were painting, we heard them talk about keeping a package safe and secure down below," added Garrett. "We're sure they're hiding something."

"And they want to leave as quickly as possible to take the box somewhere?" Julia asked.

"Right," answered Garrett.

"Don't even think of investigating without us!" commanded Lillian. "We'll have to do it tonight while Julia and I are still here. We must find out whether they really have the stolen gasoline engine. According to the note, we're on the right track." She paused to think how she should offer the next information. "And Thomas tells me that Captain Steele did have a meeting with that man—he called him Conrad Warren—in the other boat, the *Cotton Belle*." She paused again. "We might want to bring Thomas in on our plans since he knows about a possible mystery anyway." Lillian bit her lip, regretting the words as soon as they had tumbled from her mouth.

Julia, however, was thrilled to include her little brother. "Thomas is small and quick and fast. Let's get him to go down to *Sadie* with us tonight and find out," encouraged Julia. "He'd be perfect for nosing around in small places."

But the boys thought too many involved would complicate the success of a late-night snooping investigation. Lillian quickly confirmed the idea of "four is enough," so Lillian was thankful when everyone agreed that Thomas was not to be included in their plans.

Later, nearing nightfall, Captain Joseph of the *Trillium* seemed to appear out of nowhere. His crew immediately recognized his unmistakably loud voice. He staggered out of the wooded path from Galena into the clearing of the lighthouse lawn. Apparently, he had spent the day getting his fill of liquid refreshment at a Galena establishment, coming back just in time to fulfill his orders from the Lighthouse Board. "Haul them logs outta the woods and over, over to that there cliff," he barked as he staggered toward his assembled crew. "Watch whatcha doing there, over there. Don't lay 'em down so hard."

He hadn't noticed that the tree cutting had already been completed. He had no idea logs were set to go for the fence building in the morning. "You wanna hafta start all over again, again? I ain't choppin' any more trees if them ones don't do no good, no good." Then he laughed so hard that his staggering made him sprawl onto the grass near the apple trees. "Don't think I'm gonna do it again if it ain't done right." He spit as he rose, fell onto one knee, and rose again to say, "Done right!" Then he started to sing some miserable sea shanty tune, out of tune.

Still bellowing, he stumbled over to the pump and put on his official woolen jacket and fumbled with his hat before he managed to put it on straight. Since he had done no work at all, his threat, "I ain't gonna do it again" made no sense. In fact, his whole demeanor made no sense. He pulled himself to a standing position only long enough to fall down again, too dizzy to be of any use except for barking more orders.

Iona Bates came to the rescue and wittingly convinced Captain Joseph that it was silly to "continue the fence building project" so late in the day. Since it was already evening, she firmly pointed out that tomorrow was another working day. For the besotted captain, she fashioned a makeshift bed in the cool fruit cellar under the kitchen next to the basement area she used as a school classroom. Having taken care of him, she then fed her own sizable family and her five sailor guests, excluding the crew of *Trillium* who used their own facilities for eating and sleeping. Big-hearted Iona graciously persuaded Captain Steele and his crew to spend one last night in the comfortable accommodations of the lighthouse before taking off the next morning in their newly repaired ship. Even stubborn, gruff Captain

Steele who felt it was too great an imposition could not argue with Iona Bates who promised that her maid, Priscilla, would be of great help. After all, he was indebted to Iona for his very life.

That evening, along with marking down dry weather conditions, Curtis Bates entered into his official Lighthouse Board. "Wood cut by *Trillium* crew today but waiting for a sober captain to commence building the north fence."

An hour before midnight, taking a secret pathway down to the lake, well out of range of the great light and their father's detection, the four oldest children met on the deck of the newly repainted *Sadie Thompson*, now *Wanderer*. On this moonlit night, their dark clothing made them partners with the shadows.

"Everything's open below," announced Luke, holding up his lantern as he ascended the steps coming up from below deck in the aft cabin. "They didn't lock a thing. We can go right down and start looking for the crate. Just be quiet. We don't want Father up in the lantern room, or anyone else for that matter, to know we're down at the lake."

Lillian wrapped a woolen shawl tightly around her shoulders. The summer night was cool. She looked out at the vast inky lake and shivered.

The gibbous moon on this twelfth night of June had given them the necessary light to climb down to the lake although she and Luke

now held oil lamps to guide their detective work on board the ship. Although the darkness did not frighten her, a feeling of foreboding for what they were about to do did.

"This has to be the place," whispered Lillian after a seemingly endless time searching without luck around the dark cabin for some kind of storage closet or cabinet. She passed her lantern to Julia who lifted it high in the air. Ghostly shadows threw themselves against the walls and ceiling. In one corner, the Charlie Noble exhaust pipe extended upward from the wood-burning stove. Suspended in mid-air, it resembled a hovering demon. Its skinny arm seemed to reach toward the ceiling as if trying to nab an intruder. Lillian shook off her fright as she felt her way around the stove. "Those are the bunks, four of them. I found them before, but I also found a cabinet. Let's look in the other direction."

Julia brought the lantern closer and exposed a large cabinet on the other side of the stove. Lillian felt for the latch she had detected earlier despite the blackness of the cabin. It wouldn't budge. Luke and Garrett tugged with mighty force and finally opened the door, which exposed shelves holding several crates and barrels. It was too dark to see exactly what lay inside them.

"Let's drag this barrel out," Luke ordered Garrett. "Careful, it's wet and dirty, and whew, it smells!" They had rolled it inches away when Lillian clearly spotted a clean square crate behind it.

"That must be it," she called. "Hurry up, boys. It's cold and damp in here. Let's open it up and see what's inside."

As the boys pulled the barrel forward and lifted it down onto the floor in the area of the galley kitchen, Julia held the lantern lower to aid Lillian as she dragged the crate over the floorboards.

"Oh no!" shouted Lillian. "Look at all this twine." She tugged on the ropes covering the crate. "We'll never get this box open tonight. And this was our only chance."

"Unless you use this knife" came a voice from behind the four. They spun around quickly to see a figure in the shadowy darkness. The voice and sly grin looked unmistakably familiar.

Chapter 15

Something Found

Immediately following that same Wednesday night on Cobblestone Island

"Thomas!" Luke and Garrett shouted.

Julia spun around, nearly dropping the lantern on the wooden plank floor.

Lillian gasped as she turned around, her hands clutching the ropes on top of the package that had fallen over with a loud thud. "Shhhhhh, someone's going to hear us if we aren't careful!" whispered Lillian.

"Thomas," Julia whisper shouted. "You brought a knife. That was brilliant of you. Give it to Lillian."

In her excitement, Lillian no longer cared that her annoying brother was in on the proceedings. She reached for the knife to begin sawing through what seemed to be iron-laced twine.

"Not so fast," Thomas began, "you're about to search the wrong crate."

"How would you know?" ventured Luke, a little too loudly. "Thanks for the knife, but no thanks for the advice. Give me the knife."

Lillian frowned at the suggestion since she had hoped to cut the ropes and make the discovery herself.

"That crate is too small." Thomas stayed fixed in his position as he placed the knife carefully into a pocket. He produced a measuring stick from behind his back.

"The boat is repaired, Thomas," Luke offered sarcastically. "We're done with measuring."

Lillian rolled her eyes. *Thomas has to be so precise about everything. What is he up to? Just hand over the knife.*

But Julia knew instantly. She sensed Thomas had a plan by bringing a measuring stick.

Thomas, who had stood in the background shadows long enough, now made his grand entrance into the light. His confident commanding steps took Lillian by surprise, and she instinctively moved aside to let him through. "Definitely too small." He squinted as he measured the crate. "Julia, I need more light. Over here please. No, this can't be the engine. This box is far too small."

"We're opening it up anyway," commanded Lillian. "Hand over the knife." Now it was Thomas's turn to raise his eyebrows as he dutifully obeyed his older sister. But when Lillian opened the box, all she saw was hard tack biscuits. With a sigh, she took a new approach and suggested they search a different storage cabinet on the wall.

Julia exchanged places with her sister and held the lantern so that Thomas could see into that cabinet. It was completely empty. *Now what?*

"I don't think it's here in the main cabin. Let's check the fo'c'sle," decided Thomas, a bit too self-assured for Lillian. But they all agreed to his search plan.

Silently, they climbed out of the main cabin, crossed the hold, and came to a small square opening leading deep down into the ship's forecastle. One by one, they climbed down the narrow hole and sandwiched themselves within a tiny storage area. The foremast took up much of the room, its massive diameter and height making it look entirely out of place for such a small room. A large anchor lay wedged in an upper shelf. Dirty ropes and riggings surrounded it.

"The gas engine box has to be hidden in here. Nobody would look in here for anything but gear," announced Thomas proudly. "You look while I hold the lantern."

Lillian and Julia slipped behind the mast to allow room for the two older boys to search the open storage areas. Thomas sat on the hatch with his feet firmly planted on the ladder as he held the lantern low so that his brother and cousin could search. The closed-in room was dark and damp and smelled of fish. Thomas was glad to be in the fresh air above. The girls knew they were moral support for the boys and, although they felt faint from the stench, determined to stay put.

Several crates all bound in twine were wedged in a large compartment where the boat widened toward the hold. Luke searched for one larger than the one they had opened in the main cabin. He found a new box jutting out from between two smaller ones on either side. Appearing larger, it offered some hope. Luke pulled on it and saw that it too was wrapped in twine. He yanked on the cord, dragged it forward, and carefully let it drop to the floor. In his excitement, Thomas had jumped down from the ladder, handed Garrett the lantern, and helped his brother scrape the box along the floorboards until it rested in front of the mast.

Not to be outdone by his nine-year-old cousin, Garrett took center stage by shoving the lantern back at Thomas and helping Luke turn the crate at a better angle to search. Not wishing to miss one moment of this exciting midnight quest, the girls clutched the mast and peeked around, one on either side. Julia sensed that Thomas wanted to be included and exchanged positions with him. She took the lamp and stood on the ladder half in and half out of the tiny forecastle. She was glad to breathe fresh air.

"Twenty-four by twenty," Thomas measured with his stick. "Yes, this could be the one." The boys looked at Lillian who rolled her eyes again. Julia smiled with understanding. "The note said fourteen and three-eighths inches by twenty-two inches. The other carton was far too small. This one is the right size for the dimensions written on the note, with room to spare. I knew it would be in the forecastle. Nobody would think of looking here."

"Except us," whispered Julia, proud of her little brother's calculations.

Then in her excitement to solve a mystery and to perhaps catch a thieving sailor who had dared to sleep in her very bed, Lillian spontaneously dismissed her mounting anger toward Thomas. At least for the time being, she no longer cared that he had somehow found out about the note. In her thrill to catch the sailor's dirty work, she no

longer cared. She raised her eyebrows and tossed her head in resolve. Thomas had let his brilliance shine through once again—however he managed to do it—and had saved the day.

The knife was a smart idea; she would agree to that. He had also saved them time by knowing where in the ship to look and for what kind of crate to search. He had saved them the bother of opening the wrong box and having to start over and over again looking for a new one. So far, the search had only taken them off guard once. They wouldn't have to bind back too many crates. *Wait. Bind up crates. We don't have any more twine to do that. I destroyed the old twine when I opened that first crate in such a hurry.*

But then she saw a ropey snake trailing from Thomas's back pocket. *He thought of that too. He found extra twine to repack the boxes and stuffed it into his pocket. Oh, Thomas thinks of everything.* She also noticed that he had worn dark clothing to hide himself during the night. *Thomas really could be useful*, she considered.

Thomas stepped back and leaned against the ship where, outside, the repaired bowsprit was reattached in regal majesty. From this cozy spot, he watched as the two older boys cut the cords from the large crate. Garrett held the string taut as Luke sliced through. Snippets of twine fell and scattered over the dark floorboards.

Once the box was free of string, Lillian stepped out from behind the mast. She decided this was the moment she and Julia should take over the leading roles. *We should be the ones to pry open the box and make the discovery. If the gas engine of Edouard Debouteville lay hidden inside, we should be the first ones to discover it.* Lillian dismissed the eager looks on her brothers' faces. She ignored how Thomas willingly stood in the background to let his two older sisters take the credit.

Julia handed the lamp over to Garrett, which he held near Lillian. The space was awkward and crowded. The air offered a tray of sickening smells: wet wood, spoiled fish, potent whiskey. The space inside the forecastle was too close for five people, even though they were children. But none of them seemed to care about the squeezed-in quarters, the pungent odors permeating their nostrils, or that the time had ticked past midnight.

Luke crouched over to watch while Thomas remained at his post in the background. The smart little brother smiled in anticipation. He entertained thoughts of what he could buy with the reward money once they exposed the wandering pirates.

"This package is quite light in weight," Lillian whispered in surprise. "But it *is* the right size," she added hopefully. Quietly, she snapped open the top of the crate. Julia held the crate boards apart as she and Lillian peeked inside. "It's too dark I can't see," Lillian called out impatiently. "Bring the light closer."

Inside, the crate was littered with crumpled paper. Lillian dug through the padding, tossing the wads carelessly aside. Finally, she found three long rather thin packages. Each was covered in brown paper tied with more twine.

Lillian lifted out one of the long packages. "The knife, Thomas. Give me the knife!" She cut the thinner grayish twine easily and shoved the cords to one side. *This is no engine!* Luke pushed more crumpled packing to one side.

"It's, it's, a painting!" gasped Julia. "A painting of, of . . ."

"Of an old man in a top hat pressing down on white fluffy stuff," interjected Luke.

"And another man in a straw hat walking away from whatever it is," added Garrett.

Lillian was too stunned to say another word. She was hoping the next package would hold some connection to a gas engine. She quickly cut more string and slipped the second package up and out. It too was light and thin and picturelike.

"Horses in the country?" questioned Garrett when he took a look at a second painting. "I can't believe it."

"I like the dog sitting on the carriage, watching," interjected Julia, trying to make the best of a disappointing situation. She glanced at Lillian who seemed utterly befuddled, which made Julia want to cry.

Feeling a lack of motivation but knowing it was her duty to continue, Lillian cut and lifted the final package. This one revealed a black-and-white canvas of . . .

"Two girls!" Luke dismissed the drawing with a laugh. "Well, Thomas, you were wrong. These are just some old pictures wrapped up in a very large box."

"I can't believe it!" Garrett added, trying to see clearly in the dark.

"We can't leave without putting everything back," sighed Lillian. "Or they'll know we were here. Thomas, give me that twine from your back pocket, and I'll tie these all up again. Then let's clean up the mess on the floor."

The boys stuffed their pockets with twine snippets and were off to clean the mess they had left in the main cabin.

Soon, the children had everything back in order. As they climbed the steps up the cliff, one of them let out a long drawn-out yawn. The hour was late. Their attempt at discovery had failed miserably, and they were far too tired to think of what to do except trudge back up to the lighthouse and get some sleep.

Lillian, however, was wide awake. Stunned by the unexpected turn of events, she felt helpless at her failure to solve the mystery. Her disappointment at not finding the right crate overwhelmed her. As she stumbled up the steps in the darkness, she sadly realized that later that very morning, Captain Steele's repaired vessel would be leaving Cobblestone Island. She had no further opportunity to continue the exciting hunt for the stolen gas engine that surely lay hidden on board. She felt doomed to fulfill her mother's wish to instead search for baskets of boring wild strawberries that were anything but hidden all over Berrie's Island.

Chapter 16

Surprise

Friday on Berrie's Island in Lakeshore County

"I like how you capture the colors of the lake, Violet. There's something special about the upsweep of your brushstrokes and the light tints at the end that create the look of light shining on the waves."

Violet turned around with an incredulous stare. "That's more or less what Charley Skruggs told me the other day, Julianne."

Julianne Wrede had also come for a visit to Berrie's Island. She was Iona and Uncle Fred's eighteen-year-old sister who still lived at home with her parents, Rev. and Mrs. Wrede from Bexley Bay on the Lakeshore peninsula. Because of her varied interests and independent spirit, Julianne was a favored aunt to Lillian and Julia. "Who is Charley Skruggs?"

Lillian put down her book and perked up when she heard Charley's name. She raised up on an elbow to listen. Julia, also reading, lay beside her on a patchwork quilt spread across the ground at Sandy Point within view but a fair distance away from the Berrie's Island Lighthouse. Lillian nudged her sister to attention. She and Julia had been out of sorts the entire morning, lamenting the previous evening's events.

Upon awakening, their mother had proclaimed the day perfect for sailing, and she was right. With sails trimmed in flat, they close hauled the Cobblestone Lighthouse knockabout on a steady beat to

Berrie's Island. Against their will, Lillian and Julia forced themselves to go along with their mother's plan to visit Aunt Violet. Upon their arrival, they declined to join their mother, Paulina, Madelaine, and Dellie in strawberry picking. They decided instead to stay behind with Aunt Violet and Aunt Julianne. The young girls' lack of enthusiasm, even in watching Aunt Violet paint the various moods of the lake, clearly betrayed their unwillingness to be on Berrie's Island at all. And besides, they were tired.

"Charley Skruggs is just an old sailor who drifted by," answered Violet. "Was here one day and gone the next. He was a crewman from a schooner lodged on the island for a night . . . or was it two? Anyway, he and I had an interesting chat. He seemed mesmerized by this painting. I had just started it. Was developing the waves."

"It's easy to admire your work."

"It was funny, the comments he made. He didn't seem terribly bright, but he talked as if he understood art. He was sincerely friendly. And so complimentary. I rather enjoyed our conversation, and he clearly enjoyed the attention I gave back."

"What did he tell you?"

Mouths hanging open, Lillian and Julia exchanged glances. They couldn't believe their two free-spirited, artistic aunts were discussing old Charley Skruggs of the *Sadie Thompson* turned *Wanderer*.

"He said he much preferred my lake pictures to 'dumb old paintings of cotton sellers,'" Violet mimicked Charley's slow, less-than-articulate speech. "Or racehorses. He talked as if he referred to specific works of art."

"Oh?"

Violet's eyes blinked, then blinked again. The motion stopped, then started again in rapid succession. She chuckled. "Well, Julianne, he also said, 'I'd for sure take *your* painting over that black and white scratchin' of two dancing girls."

They both laughed at Aunt Violet's perfect imitation of the dull-witted sailorman.

Then Julianne became serious. "Why, Violet," she said, "cotton sellers, racehorses, ballerinas? Sounds as if this old sailor knows something of painter Edgar Degas."

"Oh yes, indeed he does. He told me so. Why, he called him . . ." Violet stopped to compose herself before launching into another imitation of Charley, "He called him 'Mr. Dee-*gas*'!" She overemphasized the "gas" so powerfully that both aunts could not control their laughter. "I had all I could do to hold myself in, Julianne. Imagine, an old sailor talking so about the French impressionist master."

Lillian's eyes widened in disbelief. *What did I just hear?*

Julianne spoke next, "Remember our trip to New Orleans? I was only eight, yet you sensed my love for art. And you knew I would love Edgar Degas." Her pronunciation of "duh-gah" was sheer elegance.

"But you were mighty disappointed not to see his ballerina paintings. Why, you were even a bit put off by that exhibit of cotton marketers."

"And racehorses. *You* liked those horses."

"Yes, I did. Reminded me of England. But you didn't stay sad very long once we met the great artist."

"And I am indebted to you for that trip, Violet. You know how much it meant to me. How it inspired me at such a young age."

"That was the plan." Violet smiled.

Lillian jabbed a finger into Julia's ribs and whispered a definite command, "Let's take a walk . . . now!" Julia understood. "Aunt Violet, Aunt Julianne," Lillian began, "Julia and I are going to see how the strawberry picking is coming. Do you mind if we take a walk to meet Mother and the little girls?" In her self-proclaimed maturity, she emphasized the word "little."

Aunt Julianne gave an offhanded consent. Eyes blinking, shoulders rising up and down, Aunt Violet smiled in a mutual consent as she dabbed her brush onto her palette. Her artistic sweeping of the paintbrush added another wet sparkle to her lake on canvas. Julianne sensed Violet's need to talk and waved off Lillian and Julia so the sisters-in-law could be alone.

"It was over a decade that we took our trip to Louisiana, Violet."

"Yes, I was a new bride to your brother, Fred. And you were only eight. But such a promising artist, Julianne. The trip was a rare opportunity to view the works of Edgar Degas."

"At that time, I had no idea who he was or what marvelous paintings he produced. To think you'd take me to New Orleans to see his work. Have I thanked you enough since?" Julianne Wrede smiled at her artistic sister-in-law. Violet was a talented painter, who had studied art not only at her native town Oxford in England but also in Scotland, France, and Italy. She had been quick to recognize Julianne Wrede's budding talent.

"Yes, you have."

Julianne understood the reason behind her dear kin's sigh and desperate need to relieve her loneliness as an isolated lighthouse keeper's wife. Her release came through painting. The unmarried Violet Harcombe had put a promising career in art on hold when she had visited America and ended up married to Julianne's brother Frederick Wrede, Jr.

"I know you would have liked to continue your studies, Violet. You hadn't planned on falling in love with my brother."

Violet fell silent, allowing Julianne to continue the conversation. Violet thrived on their kinship and trusted Julianne completely. "Some of the blame has to go to your own brother though. Daniel was the one who urged you to come to America and visit him. I think he felt you were working too hard on your art, and he wanted you to have a change of pace. Can you blame him really?"

"I had no idea what a lighthouse keeper assistant did. Naturally, being as close to Daniel as I was, I wanted to visit him, so I took him up on his offer to come to Lakeshore County. Parts of it remind me of my grandmother's place in Cornwall, you know. That always makes me feel less lonely. It seems so long ago now when I was visiting Cobblestone Light, and your brother came to visit Curtis and Daniel to discuss lighthouse things."

"But Frederick really came to see you!"

"Yes." This time, Violet sighed in genuine happiness. "Yes, that was a wonderful time for us."

"Your courtship was a quick squall." Julianne laughed. "Not that it was stormy, but it sure came about quickly. You had no problem at the time giving up your pursuits in art. No, how willingly—"

"Yes, I know. I know. But I miss Grandmother." Violet laid her paintbrush on the wooden palette and looked directly at Julianne. "You know, I should take you to visit Grandmother. She is a bit eccentric, but we would have a good time together. I do miss her. She was my greatest inspiration, and she paid for my schooling."

"I know. But don't feel guilty about that. She did that as willingly as you married Fred. And she is happy for you now."

"America seemed right to me at the time. But sometimes now I'm not so sure. My physical condition seems to have worsened again, if you haven't noticed."

Julianne had noticed but choose not to mention it.

"My condition certainly hasn't improved since Garrett and Dellie were born. But to have them and to have Fred is worth any trouble that I have physically. I don't mean to imply that I attribute my physical ailments to them." Violet picked up her brush and dabbed it in a splotch of bluish green, then capped it with white. "It's just that I feel so isolated in my permanent move to America. If I could go back to England again just for a visit." She swept her brush on the canvas to create more sparkling waves. "You could learn so much studying art in Europe, Julianne, if you came with me."

Violet saw her young self in Frederick's almost nineteen-year-old sister. She recognized in Julianne the same eye for artistic detail and wanted to spur Julianne to great artistic heights, heights that she knew she herself would never reach.

Years on Berrie's Island had been difficult for Violet. Far from her family overseas, she endured terrible bouts of homesickness. She especially missed her Cornish grandmother. Although her children, Garrett and Dellie, the joys of her heart, loved life on Berrie's Island, she herself struggled with its isolation. Put simply, her entire existence seemed a struggle. She felt the mysterious illness that plagued her was amplified by her intense homesickness. Ironically, her only salve against isolation was to paint, in isolation.

Violet seemed to forget her loneliness and seclusion by wielding a paintbrush and palette. Her growing tics and body twitches, something she had been experiencing since childhood, had not seemed to lighten upon her move to America. She knew no cause and could honestly not lay the blame for her worsening condition on the move to the States, on the rigorous duties of a keeper's wife, or on trying to live up to the standards of motherhood. In her mind, the mounting evidences of her strange illness might have been brought on by something entirely different.

Violet was indebted to Frederick's sister Iona for taking Garrett and Dellie to live with them at Cobblestone Lighthouse for the summer so she could pursue art; she dearly hoped it would lessen the effects of her undiagnosed illness. Although separating herself from her children was not a welcomed idea, she found a physical boost in moments of uninterrupted artistic endeavor. Her body tics seemed to subside somewhat when she would spend summer days creating landscapes of the lake in quiet repose at Sandy Point. For entire afternoons, she could completely relax while she painted and also kept an eye on the distant grounds of Berrie's Lighthouse.

Fortunately, Garrett and Dellie loved their summer on Cobblestone Island, so Violet was not guilt ridden over having them away from her in a stay with their cousins. Besides, every once in a while, like today, the children would pay her a visit. Violet welcomed these visits and also felt thrilled to have her young sister-in-law and confidante close at hand so she could offer her a painting lesson or two.

During Violet and Julianne's confidential chat, Lillian and Julia had scampered away from their aunts. Side by side, they traipsed across Sandy Point with no intent whatsoever to pick strawberries. Lillian fluttered with excitement. "Dee-*gas*, Julia! Did you hear Aunt Violet say, 'Dee-*gas*?'" Lillian imitated Charley Skruggs with only a slight trace of mockery.

"Yes, I did, Lillie." In great excitement, Julia ran in front of her sister and momentarily stumbled backward a few steps, Lillian nearly bowling her over with her swift sprint.

"It isn't a gas engine at all!" shrieked analytical Lillian as she stopped abruptly, grabbing her stumbling sister's shoulders in a tight hold. "Those pictures on *Wanderer* are Edgar Degas's originals, and Captain Steele probably stole them and wants to sell them for lots of money."

"Or something like that."

"Now that I think of it, that first painting with all that white and fluffy material is . . ."

"Cotton!" they shouted together.

"And that country painting of horses could have been race-horses!" Julia could barely contain her excitement.

"And remember the note said 'sketch'? That last picture *was* a sketch, Julia. A black-and-white sketch of two dancers. I remember their toe shoes."

"Ballerinas!" exclaimed Julia. "Degas is famous for his ballerina pictures. Aunt Julianne taught me that."

"And Charley obviously knew about that cargo when he described all three pictures to Aunt Violet."

"And he knows they are by . . ."

"Dee-*gas*!" they chorused in a fit of giggles, once again empha-sizing the "gas," this time in definite mockery. Joining hands, they skipped around in a circle, at last falling onto the sand and flinging piles of it into the air. They laughed in amazement over how wrong they had been about the note Lillian had found days ago near the *Sadie Thompson* on Washburn Island.

They were stunned to learn the note did not refer to Edouard Debouteville's newly invented gas engine but to three of Edgar Degas's famous works of art.

"Oh, how are we going to sleep tonight? How can we wait until tomorrow to tell 'the boys' of our wondrous discovery?"

"I guess we'll have to, Lillie. C'mon, let's find Mother and help her pick baskets and baskets of strawberries." Julia smiled.

"Paulina and Maddie and Dellie know nothing of this mystery. Let's not say a word. Let's just make like we're sorry for being so uppity about leaving Cobblestone Island for the day. Let's apologize and make up by being as good as gold from now on."

"Yes, and soon they will know why we have been so glum. And they will forgive us for our angry moods this morning." Julia hoped things would turn out well for them. "Oh, how foolish we acted, Lillie. Will they ever forgive us, do you suppose?"

"I don't know. Mother wasn't too happy when I jerked the sheet on the knockabout as we came about. I think she knows I don't want to be here." Then Lillian paused to contemplate their future. "But they'll have to forgive us." She smiled. "After all, we'll be rich when we turn in those horrible stealing sailors. When we return the masterpieces back to Mr. Degas, he will give us lots and lots of reward money and . . ." Lillian stopped. Her eyes narrowed in determined thought. "And nobody in Galena will ever laugh at us again."

Chapter 17

Running Away

Saturday morning at Cobblestone Lighthouse on Cobblestone Island

"I thought surely Thomas had gone with you, Iona," said Curtis Bates. "He is often off by himself. He lives in his own world, you know. It doesn't matter if he is surrounded by nature, his siblings, or by a group of women. He finds his own way. I thought nothing of his being gone. I thought surely he was with you womenfolk."

That was all Lillian needed to hear. From the tone in her father's voice, she sensed that something was terribly wrong, and she also sensed that her parents were not taking the matter seriously enough. *Thomas is gone. Father and the boys had not missed him because they figured he had come along with us to Berrie's Island . . . to help us sail the boat. Not that we girls need help, of course*, she added decisively. Then guilt overcame her, and terrified thoughts coaxed her to a dismal conclusion. *This is my just punishment for treating Thomas so badly. I wanted him out of my life, and that is what I've got. He's gone. I should be happy, but I'm not.*

I'll bet Wanderer has taken Thomas captive. I'll bet he has been kidnapped. Those horrible, thieving, art-stealing, child-snatching good-for-nothing sailors have taken my dear little brother and, and . . . who knows what they have done to him.

Lillian's conscience was blanketed with guilt. Yes, she disliked Thomas Silas Charles most of the time. She hated his know-it-all attitude and his being three years younger but four years smarter. Yet he knew things. He sensed things. He understood things far more clearly than she ever did. Her enviousness had always been strong. In her anger, however, she had never once dug deep into her hatred to discover an even deeper layer of love underneath. *Now it's too late. Thomas is gone. Perhaps murdered. And I never learned to appreciate him. I never even thanked him for bringing the knife and measuring stick to the Wanderer that night.*

In frustration that her family did not seem as concerned as she was about Thomas being gone, Lillian decided she had to figure out this situation by herself. In a rare wave of sorrow, she didn't even look for Julia, Julia who always soothed her troubles, always calmed her woes. Lillian wallowed in self-pity, looking for some kind of understanding. She craved a soothing balm for her deep, dark feeling of guilt and grief. *What if I had been kinder to Thomas? Would he still be here? Would even one ounce of patience have made things turn out differently? Why have I shown such a lack of love?*

Lillian raced out the front door, flew down the stairs, and breezed past the apple trees. She ran straight for the wooded pathway leading to Cottage Parakaleó. She would find solace and peace with Miss Garnet. Lillian ran, at times stopping to walk and catch her breath, and then ran again until she reached the cottage.

As she raced up the last few steps, she saw the front door standing open. Streaming sunbeams dazzled the porch stones, throwing brilliance on the white pillars holding up the green roof. The old stone lighthouse also caught the sun's rays giving it a stately brilliance. Majestic and tall, it towered before her. *This building is more beautiful than ever today. But why doesn't this lovely sight make me feel better?*

Heart racing, Lillian stood silently for a moment at the front door. She saw Miss Ruby deep in concentration at her writing desk. Lillian glanced upward. A light burned in Miss Tourmalina's loft. Lillian tiptoed inside the cottage. No one sat at the kitchen table. The gaping library door showed a room full of books, but no signs of Miss Garnet.

For goodness sakes, where are you, Miss Garnet? Lillian fled to the porch and glanced through the flower beds. Nobody there. She skirted behind the cottage to the back woods. No one in sight. She dashed again to the front, on toward the lighthouse, and searched upward toward the white stone tower. Not a soul could be seen. She sprinted halfway up the circular stairway, calling, "Miss Garnet? Miss Garnet? Are you there?"

No answer.

She stumbled down the winding staircase, stepped outside, and found herself running back again into the cottage. Miss Ruby was not at her desk. Lillian looked again toward the open library. She glanced upward at the plaque above the door.

"Walk as Children of the Light." The gold letters burned her mortified heart with a tortuous fever. Feeling forlorn and tearful, she hurried outside, fled down the cobbled steps, and headed toward Village Galena. *Maybe Miss Garnet is there.*

Lillian reached the embankment where she found Captain Driver's fishing yawl. The boat made little lapping noises as it rocked in the water. "Kari!" Lillian shouted from a distance as she beheld the comforting sight of her friend from Washburn Island. What good fortune. She wanted Miss Garnet, but here was her best friend, the friend she, up to this moment, had not realized she longed for the most. Kari shared her dreams and secrets. Kari understood her feelings, and she understood Kari's. Lillian had been with her a year ago during the Hansen tragedy. Since then, their friendship had solidified into granite, shining with a mirrored polish. Kari knew Lillian had cared with an unbroken heart. *You needed me* then. *I need you* now. Lillian choked through tears.

Kari Hansen turned her head upon hearing Lillian's call as she sat on a bench overlooking the water that connected Cobblestone and Washburn Islands. "Lillie!" she called back. "Lillie, I came over with Papa . . ."

"Oh, Kari, something awful has happened," Lillian panted as she sat beside her friend. She brushed off tears that had collected in little pools.

"I can hardly begin to tell . . ."

"Lillie, what's wrong? What happened?"

Lillian knew Kari would understand. She blinked away increasing tears and looked into Kari's clear Danish-Norwegian eyes, brushing the moisture from her cheeks. "It's just like your brother Soren. When he drowned during that storm. Only now it's, it's Thomas."

"Thomas drowned?" Kari was horrified.

"No, no," Lillian sniffed, taking quick gulps of air as tears continued to flow. "He's been kidnapped. By those men on the *Sadie Thompson*. The sailors we saw loading stone in the harbor. Only now it's the *Wanderer*, and they have stolen paintings on board, and I think they've taken Thomas with them." Lillian's labored breathing broke into sobs.

Openmouthed, Kari stared at her heartbroken friend and looked into the depth of her friend's watery eyes, into the depth of her soul, and saw her little brother Soren drowning to death all over again.

She recalled last year's images of horror. In vain, the little boy tried to rescue his dog from angry, turbulent waters. Soaking and sinking, his dog Sport panted and struggled, then reached land. Soren had not. Soren had flailed and fought and fell. Kari shook her head, trying to erase scenes of Soren bobbing up and down, up and down. Cold lake water. Shivering dog. Sinking boy. Down, up, down, up, down, down, down. One last time, down. For an instant, Kari resented Lillian for dredging up the memories, memories Kari had thought were finally buried at sea. Quickly, she forced her mind back to the one who needed her, to the pressing matter at hand.

"Start from the beginning, Lillie. I'm not following what you're saying. Thomas is kidnapped? By sailors from the ship we saw the other day? What happened? Where is your family? Are they looking for him? What is *Wanderer*? Why are you *here*?"

Chapter 18

An Understanding Friend

Immediately following on Saturday at Cobblestone Island

"Oh, Kari, I just had to run. I wanted to talk to someone. I'm glad it's you. I know you'll understand."

"I can only try."

Lillian did her best to explain how *Sadie Thompson* had been shipwrecked at the lighthouse and how her siblings had looked for a hidden gas engine on board and had found only paintings. She explained about the overheard conversations of Aunt Violet and Aunt Julianne on Berrie's Island and how it led her and Julia to believe the paintings were probably stolen Degas originals and that they were planning to turn the sailors in as thieves.

Through sobs, she explained how Thomas had appeared with the knife and measuring stick when they had discovered the paintings at midnight and how the four others had done all the searching on board the ship while Thomas stood in the background and had simply watched. Lillian admitted how unkindly she had treated Thomas, how unloving had been her thoughts. And amid a free flow of tears, like water breaking over a dam, she admitted how turning in five thieves mattered little compared to having her little brother back.

"I didn't let Thomas do anything," Lillian sobbed. "I wanted the discovery all to myself. I wanted to open the package myself. Thomas never even tried to get in on it. He just let me be selfish." She glanced upward as she shook her head in despair and then continued in broken speech.

"Then we went to Berrie's Island and found out from Aunt Violet and Aunt Julianne that Charley, the old sailor, knew about the paintings and that they are famous . . . and . . . and that he thought they weren't as good as Aunt Violet's lake picture. And when we got back to Cobblestone, Julia and I were so excited to tell them that the mystery had changed but . . ." Lillian paused for a moment to gather her breath. "But the *Wanderer*, that's *Sadie Thompson*'s new name after they fixed it and repainted it." She sniffed. "A really silly color for Captain Steele, Kari. And then . . . and then one morning, the *Wanderer* was gone, and so was Thomas." Tears flowed freely. "I heard Father tell Mother that he hadn't missed Thomas because he thought Thomas was with us on Berrie's Island. That he figured Thomas was just being Thomas and went with us at the last minute to help sail the boat, even though we don't need help. Oh, Kari." Lillian stopped to catch her breath.

She squeezed her eyes together as warmth and wetness streamed down her cheeks. "I don't care about the stolen pictures anymore. I just want to see Thomas again."

"But you don't really know he is on board the *Wanderer*," Kari reasoned. She tried to piece together the scattered bits of information.

"Where else would he be? He's missing, Kari. He's gone."

Life's bitterness poured into the open wound of Lillian's heart when she looked up to see Lucinda DePere walk by. Like a salt shaker seasoning a slab of raw meat, life shook its unfairness on Lillian's weary nerves. High-class, nose-in-the-air Lucinda Lynda and two of her like-minded girlfriends pranced by in starched white dresses, stylish hairdos, and clean new boots. Iona Bates would say they looked like they had just been "cracked out of an eggshell."

By drab contrast, Lillian's plain calico work dress and grayed apron, wrinkled and twisted, looked like a war handout. Her boots, dusty and dirty from a trudge through the woods, resembled pauper's footwear. Her long dark locks, unkempt in their tangled strands, took on the coiffure of a witch. But as she glanced toward the glamour girls from Galena, she felt a change of heart and mustered a smile. *Thomas is gone*, she reasoned. *I can never be nice to him again, so I may as well be nice to Lucinda DePere. That's what Miss Garnet would do. Oh, where are you, Miss Garnet? I need you.* A sudden inspiration gave Lillian the resolve to handle the situation on her own. She resolved to put the past behind her and treat Lucinda nicely. *If that is possible!*

"Do you plan to jump off the ferry again?" Lucinda DePere taunted while her friends tittered in the background.

"This time in your country dress instead of that silly swimming costume?"

Lucinda's adoration club could not withhold their peals of laughter. The high-society butterflies breezed by the bench, making sure their immaculate clothing brushed against Lillian, giving them further reason to tease.

"Oh, I'd better launder my pinafore immediately!" Lucinda shrieked in mock drama as she lifted her billowing skirt from its encounter with Lillian. "I've been so careful this morning not to soil my new outfit ordered from the mercantile in Whitefish Harbor."

"Such a shame, such a shame," one of Lucinda's friends clucked as she edged away from the bench where Lillian and Kari sat in the close comfort of true friendship, truer friendship than Lucinda's friends could ever know. The high-minded girls gave the two wide berth, as if avoiding a pair in quarantine. Then barely within earshot of the dismal pair, the fashion parade turned to point, stare, and cackle in the lingering distance.

Can things get any worse? Lillian struggled to believe that her kind thought had been met with scorn and ridicule. *How can I possibly take any more grief?*

"Let's go for a walk," Kari suggested, pleased with her spontaneous and helpful thought spoken out loud. "I have some time before Papa and I have to catch the yawl home. Captain Driver seems in no hurry today."

Lillian liked the idea. She longed to see Miss Garnet and felt delighted to take her friend along.

"Let's go to Parakaleó," Kari continued, sensing Lillian's desire for enriched comfort.

Maybe Miss Garnet will be there now.

Visiting Cottage Parakaleó was a treat for Kari. As the girls climbed up the cobbled walkway and stepped onto the porch, both wondered who they would meet inside: Miss Garnet, Miss Ruby, or Miss Tourmalina. Lillian desperately hoped to see Miss Garnet, but there was no sign of her.

"And now abideth faith, hope, charity, these three; but the greatest of these is charity, First Corinthians thirteen, verse thirteen," Miss Ruby enunciated carefully. She was engrossed in her studies. "Charity is love, you know," she said, turning around toward the girls and glancing up and over her round rimless glasses.

Love. A dagger pierced Lillian's heart.

Faith she knew because she was comforted by Kari's "faithful" friendship.

Hope she knew because she was strengthened with "hope" to see Miss Garnet.

But she drew a complete blank when it came to *love.* She felt the love of others but had trouble giving it away.

Then in an odd instant, she felt something, a pang of charity toward Thomas Silas Charles. *Can God ever forgive me for my lack of charity toward Thomas?*

"Traitors, heady, high-minded, lovers of pleasures more than lovers of God. Ever learning and never able to come to the knowledge of the truth—from Second Timothy," continued Miss Ruby.

"Sounds like she's describing Lucinda DePere," whispered Kari with a smirk.

Lillian looked toward the library. The gold letters above the door pierced her soul. *Walk as Children of the Light*, she read silently.

Turning to Kari, she whispered, "No, Kari, I am the high-minded traitor, not Lucinda. Miss Ruby describes me."

Kari was stunned. She had only tried to lighten the atmosphere. Suddenly feeling uncomfortable in her surroundings, Kari knew she should leave Lillian alone with Miss Ruby. So she tiptoed outside onto the porch.

Lillian approached Miss Ruby. She did not want to miss her third recitation. Miss Ruby's quotes always came in threes.

"Charity suffereth long and is kind; charity envieth not, is not puffed up, doth not behave itself unseemly, seeketh not her own . . ."

Her own? Had Miss Ruby emphasized the "her"?

"Is not easily provoked, thinketh no evil but rejoiceth in the truth." Miss Ruby closed the Book. "Love endures through everything. It cannot fail." Miss Ruby broke into a smile. She reached for the brooch that had caught itself in the folds of her white blouse. Once freed, the heart-shaped gem caught sunlight streaming through the window. The bright rays reflected from the ruby and cast crimson arcs across the room. When Miss Ruby stood up, the colors disappeared.

Scraping her chair against the hardwood floor, Miss Ruby suddenly stood up from her desk. She turned toward Lillian and recited deliberately, "Love rejoices in truth. Love cannot fail. No, it cannot fail."

Where is Miss Garnet? Lillian felt frantic. *I know I deserve a lecture but . . .*

Then Miss Ruby disappeared into her bedroom and out into the backyard garden, no doubt. Lillian clearly heard her outside door slam shut.

It seemed Miss Ruby, Miss Garnet, and Miss Tourmalina were there, or not there, at certain critical moments. This happened a lot when the Children of the Light visited Cottage Parakaleó. *But now is the moment I need you most, Miss Garnet. Where are you?*

Unlike any others the children knew, these three women were special. They knew things, sensed things. Their appearances and disappearances seemed other worldly. The three women cared for each of the nine children in uncanny ways, and for Kari too because Kari was also a friend. Lately, Lillian had sensed the Three had focused an immediate concern upon her. Upon lowly Lilian. Lillian sensed the Three wanted to direct her. She hadn't acknowledged the feeling until then.

Lillian again felt the welling of warm tears. *Where are you, Miss Garnet?* Feeling tangibly depressed, she tried to resist giving in to self-pity. *Miss Ruby said what she wanted me to hear,* Lillian reasoned. *And then left. I feel so terribly alone.*

She looked up at the loft and saw a light. *I mustn't disturb Miss Tourmalina. She's probably working on something up there.*

Where is Miss Garnet? I want her most of all. Does she want me to figure this out myself? And where did Kari go? Feeling despondent, Lillian prayed for insight. She thought back to when she had first been sent to Cottage Parakaleó and befriended the Three as they took care of her in her quarantine. She recalled how closely she had talked with them throughout those strengthening weeks.

In their many conversations, the ladies had carefully counseled her into not blaming her mother for sending her to New Jersey where she had contracted scarlatina. They had shown her the light of truth in seeing that blame is a wicked thing and that what had happened to her out East was something that had provided her an opportunity for ultimate strengthening.

How could she blame her mother for entering that New Jersey icehouse when it was she, Lillian, who had? How could she blame her mother when it was her own decision to play with Great Uncle Merritt's neighbors, the Navy children who thought it fun to sneak into the icehouse and suck on the chunks of ice? She wouldn't have had to go along with that silly idea.

I am the only one to blame. Sure, how was I to know an undertaker had used that ice to pack someone who had just died of scarlet fever? How were we to know the ice was infected? I'm sure that is why Aunt Louise told us to stay away. But I hadn't listened! I can only blame myself.

Then a thought made her correct her thinking about who had befriended whom. *I didn't befriend these three women. They have befriended me. Sure, they are nurses who were sent to help me, but they helped me way, way more than getting me healthy again. They helped me in deeper ways. They don't need me. I need them. Boy, has my thinking been wrong.*

Then as if by magic, the puzzle parts Lillian had been piecing together in her mind for weeks quickly came together to form a clear picture. Her thoughts transported themselves back to one of the conversations she had had earlier that spring with Miss Ruby and Miss Garnet about the name they had chosen for the cottage.

The time had been mid-May. By this time, Lillian had just started to clear of the wretched contagious stage of skin peeling. She was feeling stronger and knew her quarantine would soon be over. She had so many questions about where she was and why. As she stood with Miss Garnet and Miss Ruby within their abode, she asked them why they called their little stone house such a strange name.

"Parakaleó?" Lillian asked. "Why do you call it Parakaleó?"

Miss Ruby pulled a large book from the shelf near her writing desk. She quoted, "'I *exhort* therefore that, first of all, supplications, prayers, intercessions, and giving of thanks be made for all men, First Timothy two, verse one."

"Oh," responded Lillian with pretended politeness because she had no idea what Miss Ruby was talking about. For that matter, she didn't always understand what her grandpa Wrede talked about in church at Bexley Bay either. But she was curious, especially since here at Cottage Parakaleó, she didn't feel she had to understand but to simply get well.

"You see, my dear," Miss Ruby explained as she pointed to a word in her great book, "in Greek, the word for 'exhort' is *parakaleó*."

"Oh, I see," Lillian responded again although she did not see. She felt the "oh" that tumbled out of her mouth seemed appropriate even though she understood nothing. She did not know the meaning of "exhort" any more than she understood its Greek form, *parakaleó*. But she dared not ask questions for fear they would be answered with more Greek explanations. Instead, Lillian kept quiet and gave into total confusion.

As if reading her mixed-up mind, Miss Garnet explained, "Lillian, 'to exhort' means to urge strongly. It is the action of a concerned person. *Parakaleó* is a move by someone who cares deeply for another." Then as if acting out its meaning, Miss Garnet rested old gentle hands on Lillian's shoulders. Lillian felt their warmth. "*Parakaleó* is an urge to do the right thing."

Lillian opened her eyes to shake her thoughts back to the present. "Oh," she now uttered out loud, "*parakaleó*. I understand now." *They want me to do the right thing. That's the direction they've steered me toward. How unhappy I have felt lately. How I have resisted truth. And they wanted me to discover this alone. That is why they left me.*

"A building cannot care and love and want people to do the right thing. It's not the cottage that is *parakaleó*. It's the Three. They are my guardians. They have urged me to understand love. When Mother sent me away, she asked me to think about love." Her thoughts tumbled out as confident proclamations. She knew she was alone in the room and believed no one overheard her. "Why did Mother choose these three women to nurse me through my illness? Where do they come from?" Then she fell silent in wonder. *Does Mother know they named this place Parakaleó? I don't think this cottage had a name before now.* Out loud again, "Did Mother know I'd find answers here?" *Love. Love. Love!* thought Lillian. *Love finds joy in the truth, and the truth never fails. I understand the truth now. I guess I always have but*

have ignored it. I did not love Thomas. But I could have. I should have. I would have had I known he would be taken away from me.

Lillian walked over to Miss Ruby's desk. She opened the Book where a marker lay. Clearly underlined were words from First John. She read, "Let us love one another; for love is of God; and everyone that loveth is born of God and knoweth God." Still oblivious to anyone listening, she read out loud, "He that loveth not knoweth not God for God is love." Lillian slammed the Book shut. So intense was her happiness in discovering the truth that she neither heard nor saw someone listening from above.

Had Lillian glanced upward, she would have seen Miss Tourmalina, hands resting on her chin, watching from her loft. Her brilliant heart-shaped tourmaline ring caught the daylight and cast dancing red reflections upon the high living-room ceiling. Miss Tourmalina sighed and flashed a celestial smile. Then she disappeared from view, and the brilliant light that had momentarily brightened the loft softened to a glow.

I know God. I love God. Lillian thought, warm tears wetting her cheeks. Eyes glistening with a flood of tears she could not hold back, Lillian read the words etched upon the striking plaque that hung above the library door. Its sentiment drew Lillian in. She stared at the golden letters against the deep blue background that reminded her to "Walk in the Light." "For the fruit of the Spirit is in all"—Lillian squinted—"Goodness and Righteousness and Truth. Were those words always there before? Or have I not bothered to look closely enough?" *Walk in the light in all goodness, righteousness, and truth. I have not walked in light. But I will.*

"Miss Garnet? Miss Ruby? Miss Tourmalina?" she called.

"Larry!" Luke suddenly broke into her reverie as he called from the front entrance to the cottage. "You've got to come home immediately." He stepped inside the room, Kari
close beside him. "Mother knew you'd be here and sent me to bring you back." Luke had an intense look of concern as he glanced about the room. "Who were you talking to, Lillian? I heard you talking, but there's nobody here." Luke sensed Lillian's hesitation to answer. "It doesn't matter," he continued. "Get home fast!"

Without hesitation, Lillian gave a parting hug to the bewildered Kari, who had waited outside for her on the porch swing. Lillian promised to fill Kari in on every detail as soon as she could. The friends parted, and the twins found the trail home. Lillian's mind mixed thoughts of Parakaleó with why her mother wanted her home. Luke hadn't told her, and she was afraid to ask.

Even though she had not seen Miss Garnet, she was happy that Miss Ruby's audible research had seen her through her personal crisis, an ordeal she did not realize was far from over.

For an instant, Lillian wished she had spoken with Miss Tourmalina. As she left the cottage, Lillian had caught a glimpse of the light glowing in Miss Tourmalina's loft. *Why had I not at least said hello?* Lillian felt comfort in believing Miss Tourmalina had been there, probably working on some wonderful, creative project. *I'll ask her about it soon*, Lillian determined.

Lillian and Luke walked through the woods to the lighthouse in silence. Lillian's thoughts danced around two questions: *Why have I been suddenly summoned home? What has happened to Thomas?*

Chapter 19

Stowaway

Earlier on Friday at Marble Island, north of Cobblestone Island

On an island in the lake passage due north of Cobblestone stood another aid to navigation. Marble Island Lighthouse was a conical brick tower with its keeper's quarters close by to the west. The Marble Light that shone at night could be clearly seen from Cobblestone's lantern room. However, Keepers Curtis and Iona Bates shared no similarity to the unfriendly pair of keepers stationed on tiny Marble Island.

Fretting over having left Cobblestone Island in such a hurry, seaman Ross Clow shook his head as he paced the kitchen floor of the Marble Island Lighthouse. Iona Bates had given them decent meals at Cobblestone. Here, the only taste temptation to satisfy his hunger was a bowl of one kind of fruit: bananas spotted brown with age, hardly an appealing morsel for a rugged sailor.

Ross wanted a hearty meal. How he longed for Iona's bean-and-ham dish or her "thick as fog split pea soup" with its man-sized chunks of ham. His mouth watered when he thought of the warm apple pie she had served with ample cream. These enticing thoughts tortured him as his pacing picked up speed.

"Do you have to do that?" Ross bellowed at Charley Skruggs who was drumming his fingers on the massive oak kitchen table. "Wonder what's takin' the captain so long."

Captain Steele and the pair of younger sailors remained on board the *Wanderer* docked on Marble Island.

Thomas sat in the parlor, alone but composed.

"I'm not sure we should leave the youngin' here," said Charley. "He seems mighty scaredlike. I'd say we should sail him back home ourselfs."

"You heard the captain," fumed Ross quietly so Thomas would not overhear. "We're days late for Traverse City. You know we have to deliver those pictures. We probably missed our contact already. Conrad Warren said the man who plans to buy the paintings is busy and won't be sitting around waiting forever. It was difficult enough for Warren to get the decent price he did in New Orleans for those three pictures. And then he made the long trip north to get them this far. If we are to make any profit on them, we'd better get them to where they're supposed to be. We ain't got the kinda time to go back to Cobblestone and still make it to Traverse to sell those pictures."

"I don't know what's so famous about them scenes we gotta get to Traverse City." This time, it was Charley's turn to shake his head in protest. "Betcha that there contact man Warren would give a heap more money for them paintings of Berrie's Island than them racehorses and balleriner dancers we got on board." Charley nodded his head in agreement with his own statement. "That lady painter on Berrie's Island paints more better pitchers."

"And she ain't famous like Edger Dee-*gas* neither," countered Ross, consciously imitating Charley's wretched pronunciation just to rub it in, emphatically emphasizing the "gas."

On the morning before the women went to Berrie's Island, Thomas had sneaked out of bed to return to the lake to do more late-night detective work. He had gone on board the *Wanderer* just before daybreak to look for the crate he was certain contained Edouard Deboutville's stolen internal combustion gas engine. Certain they had simply not taken enough time the night before to find the right crate in which it was packed, Thomas determined to complete the search himself. He was positive the engine was on board *Sadie Thompson* or *Wanderer*.

Thomas wanted to make the discovery in time to surprise the girls before they left for Berrie's Island. *Lillian would be so proud.* He longed to make Lillian proud of him.

But Thomas did not know that Captain Steele had also planned to arise early that morning to sail away with his crew on the newly repaired ship. While Thomas was still rummaging below deck, he had heard the crew come on board. With no way to escape, Thomas did the only thing he could do, hide. He found refuge in an old fish barrel in the forecastle. But once they were launched and well on their way, the rocking of the boat through ragged waves mixed with the stench inside the barrel forced Thomas to come out sooner than he had planned.

When Captain Steele discovered the stowaway, he fumed with rage and rightly so.

"Throw him overboard!" shouted Ross.

"Over my dead body!" roared Charley.

"Good, we'll throw you over too," suggested Ross.

It was Captain Steele who finally settled his men down and decided to sail ahead and leave the boy behind. The captain had grown to like the smart little boy and meant him no harm.

He was certain someone on Marble Island would sail the boy straight home. The sixteen-mile stretch would be an easy sail south. But Sam Steele hadn't counted on trying to deal with a pair of ornery lighthouse keepers who would refuse to cooperate with his plans.

Chapter 20

A Plan

Saturday noon at Cobblestone Lighthouse

"Says here the stolen engine was found!" exclaimed Keeper Bates at the table. While waiting for the others to assemble for lunch, Iona had given Curtis a recent edition of the *Milwaukee Journal* newspaper that Uncle Fred had brought over to keep his brother-in-law informed about the gasoline-powered engine. "Says the caretaker of the museum took the engine away for safekeeping while he fixed the rickety legs on the display table. Didn't want the engine to fall over when people streamed by." Curtis seemed amused. "Thought it might break."

Lillian couldn't believe her ears. *Thomas is gone. And Father is joking about an article in the newspaper? Mother and Father are too calm. Is it possible they don't miss Thomas because they have six other children? Or maybe they don't want to stir up unnecessary worry within the family. Yet I can't believe how they seem so easygoing about the whole thing.*

Lillian tried hard to defend her parents. *Our housekeeper is having trouble keeping calm about the matter, and Mother and Father do their best to pacify her nerves. Maybe holding steady themselves is their way of calming not only housekeeper Priscilla but the rest of us as well. Oh, I don't know. Their attitude just doesn't seem right.*

"Says the New Orleans Exhibition Center sends its apology for getting everyone worked up into a dither about the missing machine."

Lillian already knew the engine wasn't stolen. *Will Father read about stolen Degas paintings next? How can Mother and Father be so controlled? Who cares about stolen items? My brother Thomas has been stolen.* "We have to find Thomas!" Lillian finally exploded.

Iona, who understood Lillian's anxiety, took her hand and stepped down into the summer kitchen for a private meeting.

"Lillian, I want to read you something," her mother said. "I think it's important you know about this." She reached for a piece of paper on a shelf. "Captain Steele left a note before he and his crew took off." She read the note that thanked the Bates family for doctoring him toward good health, for feeding all of them like kings, for showing them more love than any crew of sailors deserved, and for helping repair their ship. "Captain Steele was touched by our love and kindness," said her mother.

Love again.

The other members of the household had gradually filed in to sit at the table in the main kitchen. Before Lillian and her mother joined them, Lillian felt the urge to share how she and some of the others knew all about the stolen engine and went searching for it at night on the ship. But she was too upset about Thomas being gone and decided now was not the time to make that confession. Instead, she followed her mother as they joined the others at the kitchen table.

"You have let your lights shine for our guests," Mrs. Bates announced to her family. "I am proud of all of you for that." She looked down at the note in her hand, then directly at Lillian. "I don't believe they kidnapped your brother."

"But how can you be sure, Mother?" demanded Lillian whose anxious thoughts fought with her mother's proclamation that they had acted as Children of the Light.

"The boys found that Thomas had left his nightclothes neatly laid out on his bed. You know he does that when he's up to one of his schemes," Curtis added to back up his wife's words.

"Yes," popped up Gabriel, "he does that. You know, when he goes somewhere, so when he gets back and all tired out, everything is ready to go. It's not that he's organized. He's just lazy."

"Don't say that," defended Lillian.

"We thought he went with you girls," added Luke. "We thought he was just leaving things in place for when he'd come back with you. Like he's done before."

"But now we figure he went to the ship to do some more exploring and was planning to get back to bed before any of us woke up," added Garrett. "Except that the ship took off with Thomas on board. Something like that."

"How do you know all this?" asked Lillian.

"We don't, dear," answered her mother. "We are just supposing. We've talked the matter through plenty since we discovered he was missing. Considering the situation, I wanted you to be home. That is why I sent Luke out to find you."

"We're really concerned, Lillie," continued her father until Lillian broke in.

"So what are we going to do? Just wait 'till he returns?" Lillian was incredulous at the apathy. *Thomas could be dead by now. Where is the search party?*

"The *Tonawanda* came just before you returned from Cottage Parakaleó, Lillie. It is going out soon. They're waiting at the dock. We've asked the captain to search for Thomas."

"*Tonawanda* revenue cutter came when you were gone, Lillie," Madelaine piped in.

"Revenue cutter!" exclaimed Lillian as she glanced toward Julia. "Mrs. DePere said she'd send one out looking for her sister's missing cobble shipment!"

"Yes, while they look for Thomas, they plan to keep an eye out for the ship that was to deliver them," explained Iona.

"The *Sadie Thompson*," added Dellie.

"You mean, *Wanderer*," corrected Paulina.

Iona smiled because she knew the *Sadie Thompson* would never be found, which would be sad for Gwendolyn DePere but a private victory for herself.

"All of this happened while I was gone this morning?" gasped Lillian who was trying to understand the situation.

"I'm afraid so, dear," answered her mother. "We're all concerned for Thomas. But I really do think there is a logical explanation for everything. You know it doesn't pay to worry."

Their mother smiled thinking about the part of the note she had chosen not to share with her family. Captain Steele had written how he had overheard her "stern talk" with drunken Captain Joseph whom she had accused as "a disgrace to the United States Lighthouse Board." In writing, Steele complimented her on insisting that Jonathan Joseph himself build the fence on the cliff in front of the lighthouse. And how incredulous he was that she actually got him to do it.

Mrs. Bates had reminded Captain Joseph that the US government had ordered him to build it, and build the fence he would. She then had given him an ultimatum to have it finished in twenty-four hours, by the time she returned from Berrie's Island, or else. In the note, Captain Steele joked admiringly about her pluck but secretly wondered what the "or else" would have been had Captain Joseph not completed Mrs. Bate's stern directive to build that fence. Steele wrote, "I am not sure who I would at all cost avoid tangling with, the rigid United States government or the formidable Mrs. Iona Bates, Cobblestone Lighthouse Assistant Keeper."

In the message, Steele also noted her kindness when she lovingly brewed Captain Joseph a stiff pot of coffee in the morning and fed him a hearty breakfast. What touched Mrs. Bates the most, however, was Captain Steele's acknowledgment of solid gratitude for her taking care of him at the point of death. This gruff seafaring man was grateful to Iona Bates who had cared enough to save the life of a total stranger, to save him.

Steele ended the note, "You are a loving woman, Iona Bates. You forgive and forget." And then in a PS, he added, "If you were a single woman and I was a marrying man . . ." Then over smudged print where the continuation was clearly crossed out, Steele had scratched the following, "Curtis B. is a lucky man." Iona folded up the sentimental note and placed it in the pocket of her apron. She would keep that note, at least for a while.

Lillian noticed her mother's smile. She also saw her fold and hide the note. She knew her mother had not read the entire missive to her. Someday she would ask her about it. Lillian was certain of one thing. *Under all circumstances, Mother absolutely refused to worry.* Lillian, who wanted to be like her mother, simply could not shake off her personal woes. She forgot that her mother had at one time been twelve years old herself and had wrestled with similar misgivings.

Lillian dashed from the table. She scurried down the one hundred and fifty-four steps to the lake. There it was, the mighty *Tonawanda*, a United States revenue cutter, about to take off on a search for a missing ship and a missing boy. *If Thomas can stow away,* she thought, *so can I.* She raced down the long wooden pier and climbed aboard. Little did Lillian know that her little brother was close by on nearby Marble Island.

The Marble Island keeper and his wife were the only residents on a desolate piece of land in Lake Michigan. This couple did not like entertaining visitors, and they certainly did not like trouble. Steele and his crew were clearly uninvited guests. They figured the curly redheaded young boy with the upturned nose with them was nothing but trouble. The couple could not disguise their disdain over the predicament into which they seemed to have been forced. The keeper couple made excuses about their sailboat needing repair, which meant they had absolutely no way to get Thomas back to Cobblestone Island.

"I want to leave the boy here, ma'am. You'll think of a way when and how to get him home. It isn't all that far back to Cobblestone Island. You'll manage somehow," explained Captain Steele in the nicest tones his crew had ever heard coming from his undomesticated mouth. "It's not my fault he was on board. I'm behind schedule, and while the wind is on my back to sail southeast, I have to push on."

Quite different from Captain Steele's tone and demeanor, the keeper's wife let everyone know how she felt. "I refuse to be saddled with a boy who has no business interfering with my peaceful life on Marble Island," she proclaimed.

"He's a smart lad," encouraged Captain Steele.

"He's not my flesh and blood," objected the keeper's wife. "And not my concern!"

Charley was glad that Thomas was out of earshot. He wouldn't like for him to hear the woman's scorn.

With no children in sight, Captain Steele wondered whether this lack in her life produced the bitterness she clearly portrayed. While her voice sounded harsh, she betrayed her true feelings through sad, longing eyes.

"You take him with you. He is not staying here," the woman stated with firm resolve, not wishing to continue the discussion or be the one to figure out how to get a displaced boy home.

Captain Steele was in a dilemma. He looked at Ross Clow for encouragement, but Clow merely shrugged him off. Steele didn't even bother to seek help from his second mate. Surprisingly, however, Charley Skruggs had already figured out a plan to get Thomas home.

Chapter 21

The Search Begins

Saturday afternoon at Cobblestone Lighthouse on Cobblestone Island

"I want to go along," pleaded Lillian on board *Tonawanda*. "He's my brother, I have to find him. It's important to the family. It's important to me." Lillian tried to make *Tonawanda's* captain believe she had her parents' permission to leave the island with them. In a short time, Lillian persuaded the captain to let her stay and was granted passage on board *Tonawanda*. Soon after she climbed on deck, the ship departed, leaving the towering limestone cliffs of Cobblestone Island a distant speck.

On board, Lillian's heart felt like lead, not so much heavy with fear as loaded with love. She recognized the feeling as a pulling longing to have Thomas back. As they steamed away from the island, Lillian watched Cobblestone Lighthouse grow smaller and smaller upon the rocky cliff. A melody popped into her head. *Hadn't she recently sung the Martin Luther hymn in Bexley Bay at Grandpa Wrede's church?* The words trailed along with the music as Lillian hummed the tune inside her head.

> Shine in our hearts, O most precious Light,
> That we Jesus Christ may know aright,
> Clinging to our Savior, whose blood hath bought us,
> Who again to our homeland hath brought us.
> Lord, have mercy!

More than anything Lillian begged for mercy, for love she knew she did not deserve. She understood that she had not caused Thomas's disappearance, but she felt responsible for having treated him so poorly. Her heart ached. *God is love, Miss Ruby had read. I must cling to God's love right now. If it is his will, he will bring Thomas home again.*

> Thou sacred Love, grace on us bestow,
> Set our hearts with heavenly fire aglow
> That with hearts united we love each other,
> Of one mind, in peace with every brother.
> Lord, have mercy!

Lillian's eyes felt moist as she pondered, "In peace with every brother." *Sure, I still have Luke and Gabriel. But Thomas is also my brother. He's odd and strange and obnoxious and annoying . . . and oh, how I love him. Please, Lord, bestow your grace upon us. Keep Thomas safe. Bring him home.* As the ship plowed through deep water, Lillian subdued her thoughts with prayer.

"Portage Island leeward, sir!" shouted a sailor. "Shall we stop there to search for the young lad?"

"Prepare for landing," answered the captain.

"Wait!" Lillian shouted. "What is that in the distance over there? I see something in the water dead ahead. A tiny boat . . . with . . . with two people on board."

Chapter 22

Floating Away

Earlier that Saturday on Lake Michigan

Charley Skruggs refused to leave Thomas alone in the hands of the Marble Island's lighthouse keeper. Charley hoped to shield the boy from the viscous comments of the keeper's wife. He couldn't imagine what fate might befall Thomas if left in her care or lack of it. Charley had insisted that Captain Steele take off without him so he could return Thomas to Cobblestone Island. Charley reasoned that Iona Bates would let him stay at the lighthouse for a short while until Steele picked him up on his return trip from Traverse City. He also secretly hoped he could plan a trip back to Berrie's Island to revisit Violet Wrede.

Without Skruggs, Captain Steele was not pleased to be left with only Clow and the two younger crewmen to sail the schooner. But for the sake of Iona Bates who surely missed her son, he decided to muddle through and try Charley Scruggs's plan. He felt the skimpy crew could somehow manage to get themselves across the lake to Traverse City, Michigan. Once there, he'd pick up an experienced crewman for an easier sail back.

Ross Clow, on the other hand, saw nothing good about the plan. All he could see ahead was more work for himself. Charley wasn't much for smarts but a stronger partner Ross could never find. And Charley took directions. Not too confident the younger two sailors could or would obey his orders like Skruggs took his orders, he shook his head and walked toward the ship. A tough trip lay ahead.

Soon enough, however, Captain Steele and his remaining three crewmen managed to steer *Wanderer* away from Marble Island.

From shore, Charley watched the ship depart, its mighty sails catching the wind in perfect order. Charley noted the worry washing over Thomas who seemed desperate about their own situation of perfect *dis*order.

"We've gotta git offa these here premises, boy," Charley whispered to Thomas as they watched the *Wanderer* sail away southeastward across Lake Michigan toward Traverse City. "It ain't safe here. I'd ruther be on them open waters than stay here and be lashed by the tongue of that fearful woman inside that there lighthouse."

"We should at least be able to make it to Portage Island, Charley," Thomas calculated. "Father says the keeper there is as nice a man as you would want to know, unlike the people here who won't even flash Father a signal as an alert that something is afoot. He could do that from their light tower, you know. On a clear night, Marble Island Light is easily visible from Cobblestone, but the keeper here refuses to create a signal. He keeps talking about Father and the two of us being after the gold."

"I heard the missus keeper talk about guarding the gold, buried treasure I think she means, that she plans to find in the waters around this here place. Doesn't she know we only want to git you home and don't care none for treasure hunting?"

"No, Charley. Greedy people don't understand worthy ways. Now what is your plan for getting us out of here? Shall we try for Portage Island?"

"I seen a boat landing on the eastern shore of this here island. There was some kinda rowing craft nearby too. Let's find it and

see how far we can go. Maybe to Portage. Maybe all the way to Cobblestone."

"But Charley!" Thomas shot back. "Cobblestone is over ten miles south of here. Can we make it in a rowboat?

"We can try, sonny boy. We can try." He scanned the lake and commented, "The weather is set for a fair ride today. We can only try. If we aim for Portage Island first, maybe them lightkeepers there can sail us on to Cobblestone." Charley flashed his cavernous smile as Thomas stared in fascination. Not a pretty picture, but Charley's heart was a nugget of pure gold. And this treasure was not buried either. Thomas had no need to seek the chest of lost coins supposedly sunk near Marble Island during Civil War times. He had found more gold in Charley who planned to take him on a real adventure to get him back home. Crazy as it seemed to row that far, Thomas completely trusted his buddy's inclinations and readied himself to act upon any plan this sailor had to offer.

On the eastern shore of Marble Island, hidden among rocks, Charley and Thomas found the boat landing and an old dinghy, paint peeling, a thin layer of wood at the top of one side missing. The boat lay upside down above the rocks beside a weathered, rickety pier. When Charley kicked the boat, it stood solid, so he stepped aboard to test how it would float. He found it safe and motioned for Thomas to join him on board. The dilapidated paint made the craft look shoddy, but Charley proclaimed it a safe enough craft for the jaunt between islands.

"Full sails ahead!" he shouted, even though their trip across the waves would be man powered rather than wind pushed. Luck had it that sturdy oars, in better shape than the boat, lay tucked below the wooden seats. This dinghy would get them to where they needed to go. Charley was sure of it.

Portage Island lay miles ahead to the southeast. They would aim for Portage and see how they felt to either land there or continue on to Cobblestone. Charley hoped for a kinder keeper, and as Thomas had suggested, one who might actually sail the two of them home. Although a fair journey stretched ahead, Charley Skruggs would have no trouble manning the oars, and Thomas seemed able enough to row for a short time if he had to.

With quick easy strokes, Charley launched the craft and plunged ahead going south. Soon, they saw the white stone Marble Island Lighthouse grow tinier and tinier behind them. As he rowed carefully and steadily, Charley studied the quiet, intelligent Thomas, his strong rhythmic rowing carrying them farther and farther on their jaunt ahead. With the weather seasonably fair, the air comfortably cool, and the lake thankfully calm, Charley pulled onward for a long time with firm regular strokes. Finally, his silent thoughts, too much of a burden weighing down his caring heart, moved him to utter, "Them Dee-*gas* pitchers ain't worth it to endanger the likes of a nice boy like you."

Thomas had been looking down at the water, staring at the waves lapping against the boat, making a game of it as he measured and compared their crests and troughs.

"Dee-*gas* pictures?" he inquired. "What do you mean?"

"Them three pitchers Ross and Samuel are takin' to Traverse City. The horses and the cotton seller people," he said, then added with a chuckle, "and those balleriner ladies."

Thomas, who had not only been counting waves but had also been thinking of Debouteville's gasoline engine and wondering how he could have missed finding it, looked up with a start. His green eyes sparkled with insight. Watching Charley row, barely a half dozen oar pulls later, he had pieced things together. A light flashed through his brain like lightning brightening a darkened cliff. His eyes narrowed in thought, the slits of green glowing and piercing his ponderous thoughts: *Pictures of horses, cotton seller people, and ballerinas—Dee-gas pictures . . . Edgar "Duh-gah."*

His mind raced to countless dinner conversations he had suffered through while listening to Aunt Julianne's stories of the cotton seller and racehorse paintings she had seen with Aunt Violet in New Orleans.

"Where were the dancers?" Thomas remembered Aunt Julianne saying. *"Where were all of Edgar Degas's famous ballerina paintings? I hadn't come this far to see horses,"* he had heard her complain once too

often. From his two creative aunts, Thomas Silas Charles Bates knew the artistic works of Edgar Degas. Thomas had heard more stories about ballet dancer paintings from these aunts than he ever cared to hear again in his life. But now he was glad he had listened with half an ear to their endless chatter. Now everything made sense.

The crew of Sadie Thompson were pirates, but not of a stolen gasoline engine. They had stolen famous Edgar Degas paintings and were off to Traverse City to reap a good price.

Thomas beamed with understanding as he focused again on the graceful rhythm of Charley's rowing.

"Charley," he began slowly and deliberately, "you didn't have an internal gasoline-powered engine hidden on board *Sadie Thompson*, did you?"

Charley's openmouthed, blank stare indicated to Thomas everything he needed as an answer in the negative.

Chapter 23

Unwelcomed Visitors

Later that Saturday afternoon on Cobblestone Lighthouse

Sweaty and dizzy from physical activity they were not used to experiencing, Gwendolyn DePere and her daughter Lucinda at last emerged from the long wooded path that led from Galena to Cobblestone Lighthouse.

"Well, I never had such a climb in my life. Imagine tramping that distance twice a day." Lucinda's mother sounded incredulous as she wiped her damp forehead with a handkerchief. "Imagine those  Jensen boys doing just that to come to school at the lighthouse. And to think a real teacher, Miss Mason, had been right in town. However, Lucinda, if Mrs. Bates . . ."

Oblivious to her mother's chatter, Lucinda looked down at her clothes, wanting to cry. "Mother," she whined, "my mercantile pinafore is getting dirty."

"We'll order you a new one, dear," soothed Mrs. DePere who for all the money she was worth thought little of taking care of what she had in favor of replacing it with something new.

"But how we look, Mother! What will Mrs. Bates think?"

"Hold your head high with dignity, Lucinda. You are the daughter of the richest man on the island. That will take care of any visible tarnish."

Lucinda's weak smile acknowledged her mother's advice. She smoothed her pinafore, more grayish than white, and charged out of the clearing, head held high. Not Lucinda's choice to have made the mile-long trip, she had given in to her mother's wish to come along for an unannounced face-to-face meeting with Mrs. Curtis Bates.

Midway through the teaching season, Miss Regina Mason, who had been the Galena schoolteacher for years, decided at age twenty-nine to dismiss her professional career for a domestic one. A long-time boarder at the DePere household, she had become interested in one of the workers who regularly showed up to discuss business with Mr. DePere. Regina delighted in long conversations with this ambitious man as he waited for an audience with the boss. They had married, Regina moving out of the DePere household but continuing her job as schoolteacher. She announced her decision to retire from teaching altogether when, several months after their marriage, she was delighted to learn they were expecting a child. Mrs. DePere felt compelled to find a worthy replacement. Although Iona Bates wasn't a professional teacher like Miss Mason, she felt she might do for a while as a short-term substitute.

Mrs. Iona Bates, with a solid reputation for good discipline and high learning standards, stood at the top of Mrs. DePere's list of temporary replacement schoolteachers—but only if Mrs. Bates agreed to teach in Village Galena. Clearly as a bribe, Mrs. DePere had persuaded nine families to contribute fifty dollars each, with Mrs. DePere being the first to contribute, to create a cash incentive for Mrs. Bates to switch her teaching location from the lighthouse basement to Galena's one-room schoolhouse. Mrs. DePere figured that bringing Lucinda along when she talked with Iona couldn't hurt her plan to persuade Mrs. Bates to relocate her teaching station. Therefore, Lucinda dressed up all prim and proper, ready to recite her multiplication tables and an English sonnet or two, in hopes of coaxing the able Mrs. Bates to be not just a part-time teacher at the lighthouse but the prestigious schoolteacher for all the island children—for a short time anyway.

Lucinda, who held no desire whatsoever to share a classroom with Lillian and Julia or any of the other Bates children, had only consented to the plan if Mrs. Bates indeed agreed to come to Galena. Lucinda clearly objected to subjecting herself to lessons learned in the dark dusty basement of some old lighthouse. Secretly, she was afraid that Lillian and Julia were smarter than she was. In Galena, Lucinda was top of her class, well ahead of the children of those who worked for her father. She wanted to keep it that way.

With her head held high, ready to meet eye to eye with a modest dwelling well beneath her own mighty status in life, all Lucinda could do was gasp when she emerged from the woods. She was greeted by a spacious lawn, an immaculately weeded garden, a grove of handsome apple trees flanked by blossoming lilac bushes, a sturdy barn, and a beautiful keeper's house with attached light tower. The house looked more like a dignified schoolhouse with a lighthouse tower propped upon the roof than a ramshackle keeper's cottage that she had expected. Lucinda could not contain her shock. "Mother, such an estate this is! Such a house!" she gasped. "The Bates family could be richer than we are!"

Mrs. DePere muttered that such an idea was impossible. All the same, she wondered how the Bates family could afford such luxury. Before them stood a lighthouse two stories high with a summer kitchen besides. What she failed to comprehend was that the United States had commissioned Captain and Mrs. Bates to live and work at the lighthouse. They were government employees. But Mrs. DePere never thought too deeply about matters that did not directly concern her own affairs. Up until now, Cobblestone Lighthouse held no interest to her whatsoever.

"Iona? Iona dear?" Mrs. DePere called with false friendliness as she peeked inside the entrance to the summer kitchen. No reply. "Is there anyone home?" she called sweetly at the front entrance. Then with a lowered voice, she shot a sly grin to her daughter and added, "Let's look inside."

What she saw amazed her because everything was modestly although tastefully decorated with absolutely nothing out of place and certainly everything in shipshape order. With both the main floor and upstairs checked and found empty of life, Gwendolyn DePere decided the Bates family must be below the cliff at the lake. She shushed her daughter who moaned at the thought of more walking. "Come along, Lucinda, a few more steps won't hurt you. You're young and energetic. We have things to say. I didn't walk all this way for nothing."

"A few more steps? There must be a thousand," Lucinda gasped as she placed her once polished white high-buttoned shoes on the first wooden step of the stairway going down to the lakefront. She looked down at what she perceived was a mile-long stretch of steps lying before her. "Imagine climbing *this* every day," she muttered.

"Thirty-three, thirty-four," she counted, making her way to the lake. "My fancy shoes will be worn out by all this walking, Mother."

"Never mind about that. We'll get you new shoes as well. Come along now. Don't dillydally."

"One hundred and seventeen, one hundred and eighteen . . ."

The sun created prismatic sparkles on the glassy lake. A light breeze brought forth only the faintest of ripples. Would it have predicted something outside of weather and crops, *The Farmer's Almanac* could not have made a more dead-on prediction than Gwendolyn's guess where everyone would be gathered. Looking outward at an incoming vessel, the entire Bates household stood transfixed at the lakefront boat landing. Side by side, their eyes intent upon the lake, Iona and Curtis Bates looked like museum statues.

Luke crouched down between Garrett and Gabriel who looked straight ahead. Julia, Paulina, Dellie, and Madelaine formed a hand-holding quartet, eyes fastened in the distance. Housemaid Priscilla created the only motion in the scene as she fidgeted nearby, wringing hands inside her apron.

Three others stood at the top of the cliff, leaning upon the newly built fence in front of the lighthouse. With a dazzling glow, sunshine caught their faces and reflected brilliant shades of red from a garnet necklace, a ruby brooch, and a ruddy tourmaline ring.

Chapter 24

A Horrible Sight

Saturday afternoon on Lake Michigan

"There's a boat coming. A ship!" announced Thomas who had craned his neck to check out the noise. Charley woke up from his catnap and was stunned by what he saw dead ahead.

"By jiminy, if you ain't right about that. Looks like we're gonna get us some help out here. Give me the oars, boy."

The revenue cutter approached slowly but steadily. Trying to change rowers, Charley and Thomas stood up in the boat, trying to switch positions. Thomas lost his footing, which put the boat into a precarious rocking motion. Trying to steady the craft, Charley lunged forward, grabbing Thomas. Wrapping his huge arms around the young boy as protection from falling overboard, to outsiders, Charley surely looked like a demon executing a death grip.

On deck of *Tonawanda*, Lillian recognized her brother and perceived the scene ahead as an attack upon him. "Thomas!" she screamed. A sailor standing nearby, big and burly, jumped upon hearing the shout. Horrified at what she saw, Lillian continued her wild calls, "I'll save you, Thomas. I will, I will, I will. I can swim. I *will* save you."

With barely a thought, Lillian climbed up and over the railings of the cutter and plummeted into the water. Propelling her actions was the memory of 1 John 3, which she had read and memorized from Miss Ruby's book: *We ought to lay down our lives for the brethren.*

She added thoughts of her own, *This is my brother in need. My brother whom I love.*

The icy cold jolted Lillian's senses, but adrenaline pushed her forward. With quick feverish strokes and with urgent energy, she swam toward the dilapidated rowboat still rocking in the waves. *Will I be too late?* she thought. *Will I be able to save him? Swim faster, faster, faster.* Lillian felt tears mix with chilly water. Watery eyes blurred her vision, and she told herself to close them and push ahead without thinking. *Tonawanda's crew* stood in horror. They had just watched a young girl hurl herself overboard.

Lillian swam toward the dinghy. Her long skirt and high cloth boots slowed her down, but she had neither time nor strength to remove them. At the very least, they kept her warm in the icy waters of Lake Michigan. *Will I get there in time?* she thought. *Swim faster, faster . . .*

Her conscience, however, tormented her. Accusations pounded her mind: *It's all your fault, Lillian. This horrible situation is because of you and your loveless attitude.* Her scream thrown across the waves released panic but could not quiet her nerves. "Hold on!" she shouted although no one heard her, not even herself. "I'm coming. I'm coming."

Lillian glanced up, quickly brushing the water from her eyes so she could see clearly. In her frenzy, she perceived only a dangerous monster who had kidnapped her little brother, probably about to throw him to a watery grave. *One more stroke.* Lillian's thoughts raced faster than her arms could propel her forward. *Then one more. Then another and another. I'll get there, Thomas.* Her body felt heavy from the cold, but long steady strokes pushed her ahead. Had she not felt as strongly about the rescue attempt, her body too would have sunk to the depths below.

But love spurred her on. Love mixed with hate as she saw the rickety rowboat teeter. The monstrous figure lunged forward in a seeming attack on Thomas.

Her fright and the frigid waters tried to hold her back or, worse, compelled her to change direction, but she would not turn around. She gave no thought to her dangerous situation. Finding herself far from land in the middle of Lake Michigan, she felt destined to finish what she had begun. *I have to do this!* The vessel from which she had jumped lagged in the distance as she swam closer to the rowboat. *Go, go, go!* her mind pounded. If her rescue failed, no one could save her, but she didn't care. She felt her mission, her body numb as she struggled to fight against the cold. Then suddenly, her shivering limbs relaxed as she felt an instant thaw, the waters around her looking distinctly red.

Lillian basked in the soothing comfort as she continued mightily forward, her strong final strokes sweeping her ahead. Although water splashed across her face, giving her blurred vision, she at last reached her destination. Lifting herself from the mysterious surrounding warmth, the contrasting cool air blowing against her body, she shivered momentarily without losing a second of focus. Her knuckles clunked against the rowboat. *I made it*, she rejoiced. She threw one arm, then another over the weathered sides of the battered and worn fisherman's dinghy. Her joy then turned to rage.

"Leave him alone, you monster. Pick on someone your own size, you big brute." Her words pelted the fiend next to Thomas, now hunched forward on the wooden seat. Lillian felt herself drawn upward by strong arms and then slammed onto the floor of the bobbing boat. Momentarily, she felt secure. Charley lifted Lillian with the swiftness and grace of a seagull scooping up its noon meal. But devour her he would not. Instead, he held her in his warm arms for an instant before she began to thunder her fists upon his chest. Her eyes widened in terror as she faced her brother's abductor.

"Let my brother go. Let him go. You kidnapped my brother. Now let him go." Then from sheer exhaustion, frightened tears flowed in a flood.

"Lillie, stop. Charley hasn't harmed me." Thomas tried to pull his sister away without further rocking the boat. "He's my friend. He's taking me home."

Lillian shook off her emotional frenzy for an instant to turn around and realize her brother was in no danger. She was chilled, but a shock of warmth coursed through her as she studied the scene. Thomas Silas Charles sat calmly at the back of the boat with crossed legs and arms. Lillian looked back at toothless Charley who suddenly clamped shut his mouth to spare her the sight of his disgusting toothless openmouthed grin. As he smiled without parting his lips, Lillian relaxed. "You . . . you . . . you've not kidnapped Thomas? Wha . . . what are you doing out here then?" She shivered from the biting cold.

Careful not to rock the boat, Charley took off his jacket and wrapped it around Lillian who immediately enjoyed its soothing comfort. And forgetting himself, Charley smiled, showing the cavernous horror of his mouth. But Lillian showed no alarm. Wondering if she would die from the intense cold, somehow she knew she was safe with Thomas and with Charley.

Chapter 25

Home at Last

Immediately following on Saturday at the Cobblestone Lighthouse lake-front on Cobblestone Island

Iona Bates would never let her family know the panic that had pierced her heart nor the terror that had torn her soul when she discovered Thomas was missing. She indeed trusted the Lord in every danger. She called upon his name in every need. But aside from that, she was also human. She knew that Thomas could be in grave danger. As she stood at the great lake's edge, she tried to mask her feelings that mixed faith with fear, dark fear.

Hours earlier when she watched *Tonawanda* depart, she had seen Lillian on board and understood Lillian's need to be there. She had noted Lillian's look of longing, returning it with her own look of motherly hope that linked itself with human doubt only a mother could know when someone or something endangers her child. They both had prayed.

Pray, Lillian. Pray for Thomas and pray for me.

Pray, Mother. Pray for Thomas and pray for me.

Neither had any doubt that they would be seen through this crisis, no matter how it turned out. Yet their human fears lurked about, ready to pounce in a moment of weakness.

Now, however, the dark mask of concern no longer hid this mother's genuine happiness. Within sight on deck of the incoming ship stood Charley Skruggs with her two missing children, Lillian and Thomas. Hair wet, body shivering, Lillian stood wrapped in a blanket. Their mother breathed a sigh of relief and offered an even greater sigh of thanksgiving at the welcomed sight.

Gwendolyn DePere's gaze was not upon the incoming cutter *Tonawanda*, the very boat she had ordered to search for the missing *Sadie Thompson*. She stood, staring instead at a large mound of cobbles heaped upon the assorted jagged rocks lining Cobblestone Island's north shore. "Stones like *these* were to go to my sister in Milwaukee," she announced like a queen commanding her war fleet. She lifted her skirt to walk on the jagged boulders surrounding the pile of stones. Like a tag-along terrier, Lucinda Lynda followed close at her heels.

Mrs. DePere assessed the situation. Decorative smooth cobbles piled together stood in a heap. The mountain of stone was surrounded by contrasting jagged pieces of limestone that lined the glistening shoreline. "This pile of rocks looks like the perfect adornment for a rose garden," she declared with authority. Totally absorbed in what she felt was attending to her duty in helping kin, she neglected to see that *Tonawanda* had anchored and delivered even more precious cargo. With her back toward the Bates clan, she witnessed no joyful reunion.

Lucinda, however, had seen the ship's approach and tried to get her mother's attention. "Mother," she whimpered. "Mother, look."

"Not now, dear. I must figure out if this is really Aunt Miranda's order of stones," she muttered. "She purchased enough cobbles to be placed around the roses throughout her courtyard, several tons. Let me see, would this pile be enough? Yes, I think . . ." Strictly absorbed in her calculations, Mrs. DePere neither saw nor heard Lucinda walk away.

Lucinda strolled toward the *Tonawanda* that had now landed. Curiosity compelled her to investigate the commotion, to find out why the Bates family had gathered together with such attention at the boat landing.

"And without realizing that Charley was trying to help Thomas, I jumped off the boat and into the water to save him, my lost little brother," explained animated Lillian to her family although through chattering teeth. To Charley she admitted, "Why, I thought you were strangling him! From on board, it looked like you were attacking him, about to throw him overboard!"

"I was mighty thankful, Missy, when I seen that there cutter come along to pick us up. It saved me and Thomas a heap o' rowin'! Even I was gittin' tired out there on the great ol' lake."

At last, the children's mother turned around and made a fuss over the safety of both children. Then everyone began talking at once, offering appropriate congratulations to the rescued children, and murmuring general condolences because of the anguish the situation had caused. Thomas and Charley became the centers of attention as each unfolded his own interpretation of the story.

Meanwhile, with enormous curiosity, Lillian had noticed the presence of pompous Miss Lucinda. Shocked, however, to notice in Lucinda's demeanor a complete change of attitude, not one that dared to point, laugh, or tease, Lillian walked straight toward Lucinda while the others kept up their lively conversations. Lillian remained wrapped in a thick woolen blanket marked with an insignia from the cutter. Her hair was beginning to dry, her body slowly but surely losing its chill from the cold lake.

"Lucinda?" Lillian began cautiously, "I'm surprised you're here."

"I, I'm surprised that you were so brave and jumped off a big revenue cutter," Lucinda said with eyes opened in wonder, mouth agape.

"Sometimes you have to do what you have to do." Lillian tried to smile, attempting friendship. Lucinda seemed tolerable when she was not with her fashionable fawning fan club.

Lucinda warmed to the gesture and confessed with complete honesty, "I was in your house. When Mother and I first came, we were looking for your mother, for anyone, but nobody was around. The door was open, and I went in. I went upstairs. You, you have closets in every room." Lucinda's tone betrayed unmistakable awe.

Closets were expensive. The government taxed closets like it taxed rooms, and few houses on the island had them, if they had any at all. Lucinda certainly had no closet in her bedroom in Galena. Of course, her parents did, but Lucinda accepted that as a privilege given only to adults. Lucinda felt too incredulous over Lillian's fortune to be envious.

"Sure, we have closets in all the rooms. Lighthouses are government property, you know. We don't have to pay taxes on the extra space." Lillian assumed everyone knew this common knowledge but anticipated that Lucinda did not.

"It's a lovely house, Lillian. I like it a lot." Lucinda's less than complete humility warned her against admitting the Bates dwelling seemed grander than her own. Her father, Bertrand DePere, owned a lead mine in Galena, Illinois, and now headed the lead shot manufacturing operations in the village of Galena, Wisconsin. He knew this job well from his days working at the shot tower in Dubuque, Iowa. He was the richest man on Cobblestone Island; even so, his house did not measure up to the standards of Cobblestone Lighthouse or, at least at the moment, not to Lucinda. Lillian had closets, lots of them. She was impressed. Lucinda suddenly longed to befriend the girl she had for so long despised.

"Oh, look! We have visitors," proclaimed Lillian as she looked upward and saw the Three standing high on the bluff in front of the lighthouse.

Lucinda shielded her eyes against the sun's glare. "I don't see anyone."

"It's the Conner sisters, the ladies from the cottage on the south hill. They hardly ever visit here, especially all three at once." Lillian cautiously used the women's real names rather than the jeweled nickname titles she had bestowed upon them. She was excited to share her newfound knowledge of names with Lucinda. At the General Store on Wednesday, Lillian had watched Miss Garnet endorse her charge of purchases with "E.C." and Lillian had found the courage on the way home to ask Miss Garnet what the initials stood for.

"Endeara Conner," Miss Garnet had divulged quite briefly. "And my sisters are Serena and Alvina Conner." But that is all she said on the subject of names.

"Conner sisters?" Lucinda was confused because she had never heard the name.

"Yes, the three women who live at Cottage Parakaleó on the hill at the end of the lighthouse path. The nurses who helped me through my quarantine with scarlet fever."

Lucinda stepped back at the sound of the dreaded disease. "Conner sisters? Cottage—what did you call it?" Lucinda questioned. "I've never heard those names before. You must mean the Corwin sisters—Sarah, Elsie, and Amy Corwin, the triplet daughters of the former Cobblestone Lighthouse keeper. The ones who lost their mother in that horrible shipwreck in 1849 or whenever it was." Lucinda always enjoyed a chance to show off what she knew.

Now it was Lillian's turn to look confused.

Lucinda persisted, "Are you talking about those three strange ladies who came to the island this spring? The ones who people say wear fancy red jewelry?" Lucinda held her hand to shield her eyes as she squinted at the sunshine pouring down upon the cliff. "I don't see them. I don't see anyone. And, ah, yes, I heard that you have been sick."

Luckily, Lillian had turned away. She would not have liked to hear her friends called "strange," especially by Lucinda Lynda DePere.

"Hello!" Lillian shouted upward, and all three women waved in acknowledgment, their jewels catching the sun and casting dancing ribbons of crimson up and down the cliff wall. Turning back to Lucinda, Lillian explained, "No, Serena, Endeara, and Alvina Conner. From Canada. They were on their way to visit cousins in Illinois and ended up at the wrong Galena. Since they were here and are trained nurses, they decided to stay awhile to take care of me at Cottage Parakaleó. They love it here on the island." Miss Ruby had at last confirmed the three were indeed sisters. "Miss Garnet," Endeara Conner, the oldest. "Miss Ruby," Alvina Conner, the middle sister. "Miss Tourmalina," Serena Conner, the youngest.

"Well, I see no one, and I do not know what you are talking about," sputtered Lucinda as she swayed back and forth in the sun's glare in an attempt to catch a glimpse of the figures. She could not seem to combat the blinding sun. "All I know is that the Corwin triplets have come back to live on the island, somewhere beyond Village Galena, beyond the boat dock, and that they are very strange. Mother told me so. She says they have expensive jewels from the shipwreck of 1849, or whenever it was, and they have lots of money from their dead husbands who fought in the war against the South. And like you just said, that they are nurses or midwives or something. Obviously since they took care of you."

Lillian crinkled her nose in a frown. *What fabrication has Mrs. DePere been telling her daughter?* She looked long and hard at Lucinda who still gazed upward, trying to see the visitors. *And why is Lucinda paying attention to me today? She's so different. She usually ignores me. Or taunts me. What is she up to? And why can't she see the three women on the bluff? I can see them plain as day. Why can't she? They are positively glowing up there.*

"What do you mean that the Corwin triplets are back on Cobblestone Island?" asked Lillian. She was eager to learn from Lucinda more of the stories people from Galena told about the three ladies who lived at Cottage Parakaleó.

"Like I said, they're the triplet daughters of Felix Corwin, the previous keeper at your lighthouse. Surely, you know all about *them.*" Lucinda seemed to be slightly perturbed at Lillian's scanty knowledge. "They took care of you, didn't they? Surely, they told you what had happened to them years ago."

"I've heard of the Corwins," Lillian volunteered, sensing Lucinda's annoyance. "I know Mrs. Corwin died tragically, but that's about all I know."

"Yes, Deborrah Corwin, the triplet's mother," Lucinda proceeded in a singsong voice as if bored from telling the story many times before, "drowned in a terrible storm, trying to rescue some sailors from a shipwreck. Three of the sailors from the crash survived, lived at the lighthouse while they were recuperating, and ended up falling in love with and marrying the Corwin daughters, Sarah, Elsie, and Amy. And . . ." Realizing the captive hold she held upon Lillian, Lucinda suddenly slowed her speech, deliberately pausing to make sure Lillian would comprehend what she would say next. Lucinda was surprised and pleased that someone actually had a sincere interest in what she had to say. "And there was treasure on board that shipwreck. Treasure the triplets and their sailor husbands kept as plunder. Red rubies and other gems like that."

In her mind, Lillian pictured the women from Cottage Parakaleó wearing their stunning jewels: a garnet necklace, a ruby brooch, and a ruddy tourmaline ring, all three shaped as hearts. All three red. She reflected upon an earlier day that seemed so long ago when she was first brought to them. Not remembering much else about that day, she remembered being enthralled with their jewelry. She smiled as she remembered giving them nicknames shortly thereafter, titles that befit the names of their stunning gems, names they seemed to like: Miss Garnet, Miss Ruby, and Miss Tourmalina.

"After he buried his wife, Felix Corwin gave up his position as lighthouse keeper," Lucinda prattled on, not realizing Lillian was engrossed in her own thoughts. "He took his daughters and husbands to California to look for gold in 1850, or whenever it was, and they struck it rich, or at least we think so."

"We? What do you mean, *we*?"

"It's what my mother says and my mother's friends. Anyway, we, or I mean, Mother figures the husbands fought in the Civil War and were killed, and the triplets decided to come back here with all their money. Mother isn't sure if they are rich from finding gold or from the treasure they found on the shipwreck. It's one or the other though or both. With all their money, they had that cottage built with a fancy southern porch—on that hill behind the store outside of Galena. *I've* never seen it, but obviously, *you* have." Lucinda seemed her smug self again as she delighted in supplying Lillian with background information that she felt Lillian didn't know. "For some reason, they wanted to come back to Cobblestone Island."

Enjoying the attention from Lillian, she continued, "They had a whole slew of worker men dismantle Old Cobblestone Lighthouse and move it next to their cottage. I've never been able to see their cottage from the water coming over from Washburn Island. I suppose it is next to the old lighthouse up in the trees somewhere. Mother wouldn't let me go there, with you being deathly sick and all."

Lillian's thoughts raced with questions. *So Lucinda's mother thinks the three ladies at Cottage Parakaleó are the Corwin triplets. Although I haven't known my three friends very long, I've visited them enough to pretty well know they aren't the daughters of the previous light-house keeper. If they are, they surely would have told me. They wouldn't keep that from me. They would know that I'd be interested in their lives as long ago Children of the Light . . . house keeper.*

Lillian surprised herself when she thought of the women as Children of the Light. *Are they?* Lillian decided to ponder that question later.

It just doesn't make sense for them to be the Corwin triplets. Hadn't Mother mentioned that the Corwins still lived in California?

Miss Garnet told me she was Endeara Conner. Hmmm, Conner might be her married name. And if they married brothers, they would all be Conners. But she didn't say Elsie or what had Lucinda called the others? Amy and Sarah? No, she didn't use any of those names.

Suddenly, Lillian saw that Lucinda was staring closely at her glazed-over face. Breaking out of her daydream, Lillian stepped back and asked, "Have you met them, talked with them?"

"Gracious, no," answered Lucinda. "They aren't out and about very often. Mother has seen them at the General Store, but not me. Besides, they are very strange. I wouldn't want to talk with them."

"You're *sure* they are triplets, the Corwin triplets?"

"Well, sure. Who else would they be?"

This Lillian could not answer, but she was quite sure her three friends at Cottage Parakaleó were not who Lucinda said they were. *Miss Garnet told me their names, names that do not match up with what Lucinda called them.* As Lillian thought through the matter, she suddenly realized something rather curious.

Sarah, Elsie, and Amy Corwin have the same initials as Serena, Endeara, and Alvina Conner. Lillian had many things to ponder.

"I can't see anyone," Lucinda sighed, once again looking up toward the cliff in a desperate attempt to see the mysterious figures.

"They're gone," Lillian returned. "Perhaps they decided to walk down to the lake."

By this time, a great commotion had begun, with Lucinda's mother, Mrs. DePere, in the thick of things. She talked incessantly while those around her could do little but listen.

Iona had had enough and decided quickly that the only proper celebration for such a good ending (that had ensured the safety of her children, not to mention a good excuse to escape the wagging tongue of Mrs. DePere) was to go back to the lighthouse and prepare a proper celebratory meal for everyone. Uncharacteristically, she employed the willing help of her husband. Arm in arm, the happy couple proceeded on up the long stairs to the lighthouse to prepare a feast.

"Has the ship *Stella Townsend* been here?" Mrs. DePere continued but mostly demanded, once again forgetting the ship's correct title. "Has it unloaded this pile of cobbles? I have reason to believe that the very large stack of smooth decorative cobblestones I found obviously dumped over there was to be shipped directly to Mrs. Miranda Adler of Milwaukee."

"Look at the lake," broke in Thomas. "A new ship is coming in." In the frenzy of *Tonawanda's* arrival, delivery, and departure and the excitement brought about by it, together with Mrs. DePere's demands about rocks, no one had noticed the approach of a two-masted schooner. All eyes returned to the water. The entire crowd became mesmerized by the ship's unusual color that contrasted sharply with the large black letters bearing its name. Considering its color, this craft could only be captained by a sailor, man enough to commandeer it. As *Wanderer* approached, Captain Samuel Steele, Ross Clow, and the two skinny shipmates waved from the deck and smiled at the crowd, none of the men seemingly ashamed to be surrounded by so much—pink.

Chapter 26

A Question of Piracy

Immediately following on Saturday at the Cobblestone Lighthouse lakefront on Cobblestone Island

"Of all things," gasped Iona as she heard the commotion at the lakefront. She turned around and looked out at the lake to watch *Wanderer* approach. Clinging to her husband's arm in determination to continue the upward climb to prepare a memorable meal, she mused, "Curtis, perhaps there is more of the story to unfold. We'll surely hear all about it over dinner."

Down at the water, Lucinda moved closer to her mother, occasionally glancing back and looking for three figures that might be coming down from the cliff to join the crowd. Lillian found Julia, and together, they approached the incoming schooner. With Thomas in the lead, Luke and Garrett followed. Gabriel stayed near Charley. Paulina, Dellie, and Madelaine made their own trio with Priscilla standing behind them. The colorful audience anticipated a glorious show.

"Land ahoy!" Captain Steele shouted. "Coming ashore."

Ross and the captain and the two stick poles jumped off the ship to join the small congregation. Captain Steele looked unusually happy.

"I came to pick up my able-bodied crewman, Charley Skruggs, and head south for Milwaukee."

"Milwaukee," blurted Mrs. DePere, delighted that she may have stumbled upon some good fortune to transport a special heap of rocks to where the collection belonged.

"I thought you had to git yourselfs to Traverse City to deliver them pitchers," broke in Charley who approached the safe company of his crew.

"I had no need to get myself to Traverse City, Skruggs. Traverse City came to me," the captain announced.

Captain Steele enjoyed the attention of an admiring crowd. "I met Harry Hannibal of Traverse City on my way to Traverse City. Let me explain. We were sailing just beyond Marble Island when the captain of the propeller steamer *City of Traverse* hailed us over. He asked whether Clow over here or I had seen the *Sadie Thompson*."

Mrs. DePere perked up at the mention of *Sadie Thompson*.

"When I asked what for, he told me that a Mr. Harry Hannibal was on board, looking for a ship that was selling some Edger *Dee*-gas paintings." Unlike Charley, Steele emphasized the "Dee" in his own unique mispronunciation of the famous painter's name.

Mrs. DePere edged closer, her mind set on charming *Wanderer*'s captain.

"Well, I figured he was the very man I intended to meet. But I wanted to be sure. I fumbled through my pockets for a note where I had written down the name of the rich man from Traverse City, Michigan, who wanted those paintings. Think I could find that note?" He chuckled, knowing the outcome of his story would turn out in his favor.

"Then I says to Captain Steele," broke in Ross Clow who wanted some recognition for his contribution. "I says to him, this here man is the name I remembered was written on that notepaper he lost. I tells him straight out this here is the guy. Yes, siree, Harry Hannibal is the man we're looking for, the one we're supposed to meet in Traverse City." Ross was obviously searching for praise. "How fortunate Hannibal came looking for us! He saved us the trouble of sailing clear 'cross Lake Michigan."

Julia nudged Lillian, and the two walked over to the boys. "Did you hear that?" Julia began. "Harry Hannibal? What's he talking about?"

"Sounds like the name written on that notepaper Lillian found," Garrett beamed in recognition.

"Yes, but only *sounds* like. The paper actually says Perry Hannah, not Harry Hannibal," remembered Julia who felt good about recalling such an important detail.

"I wonder what's going on," remarked Lillian who turned back to the crowd to hear what else Captain Steele had to say.

"And so I tells the captain of *The City of Traverse* that we had had a connection with *Sadie Thompson* and that we just might be able to help this here Hannibal fellow out with securing those Dee-*gas* paintings he was so eager to lay his hands on. Then the steamer captain and a man in fancy duds, which turned out to be Hannibal himself, came on board the *Wanderer*, and we showed them the pictures that had been transferred from *Sadie* to our *Wanderer*. Only when Hannibal took a look at the paintings, he said he only wanted two of the three."

"'Course I was mighty disappointed he didn't take all of them. I was expecting one thousand two hundred dollars for all three because Captain Conrad Warren promised me that was the agreement."

Lillian's eyebrows arched at the mention of Conrad Warren.

"Now this Hannibal fellow only wanted to pay three hundred dollars apiece for the cotton seller painting and the ballerina sketch."

"Says he had no use for the racehorse picture," interjected Ross Clow.

"Let me tell it," barked the captain and motioned for Clow to step back. "I tells him six hundred dollars for the two pictures weren't enough for my trouble. Why, that was half what I expected for all three. I told him flat out, no deal. So he took another close look at all three pictures and said he'd give me eight hundred dollars for just the two he wanted, and that was his final offer. He said I could keep that there third one or sell it or do whatever I wanted with it. That it didn't make no matter to him what happened to it." Captain Steele bit his lip and shrugged his shoulders. His wonder seemed sincere.

"Can't understand why he didn't like the racehorse picture. To my mind, the horse picture was the only one worth anything in the first place. Nice country scene. Anyways, Warren and me are out four hundred dollars, but all the same, we're eight hundred dollars the richer than we were before meeting Hannibal." He smiled broadly, his straight teeth gleaming white in contrast with the broken limestone on the shore.

Lillian poked Luke with her elbow and urged him to say something.

"Ah, ah, where did you get the paintings, Captain Steele?" Luke asked, trying to sound only casually curious.

"They originally came from an art dealer in New Orleans who sold 'em to a captain friend of mine. That there was Captain Warren of the *Cotton Belle*. Said he'd take the pictures as far as Washburn Island. Warren then offered the captain of *Sadie Thompson* a percentage of the profit if he would sail them pictures the whole way to that there Hannibal fellow. The *Sadie* captain said the cut from the deal was worth it to him. Turns out though, he had no time to make the full trip 'cross the lake to Traverse City. Thought he could meet up with *Wanderer*, see, on the way over. He knew I'd be sailing in the region, which, of course, I was. We met out on the lake, and he gave me that there note I can't seem to find with the name of the man in Traverse City I was to drop the pictures off with. Had the dimensions of all three works of art written on that note too, so I was sure they were the right ones. I told him I'd sail the pictures right over if he could give me a decent cut myself."

Fascinated by the fabrication of this tale, Lillian's eyes were glued to Captain Steele, wondering what else he would make up to make the somewhat true story fit his needs.

"The New Orleans art dealer said the pictures are famous, painted by a fellow with the name of Edgur *Dee*-gas from France. Said they'd fetch one thousand two hundred dollars from Hannibal, the richest man in Traverse City who wanted special artwork to decorate his new house."

Captain Steele made another attempt to look through his pockets. "I just wonder where in tarnation I put that piece of paper with the information about them pictures. Can't understand what happened to that note. I must a dropped it or lost it in a windstorm when I met up with the *Sadie* captain."

"It don't matter none, Sam," Charley contributed. "You remembered his name and didn't hafta go all the way to Traverse City. Hannibal came looking for you."

Unable to keep quiet, Lillian decided to join in. "So what will you do with the other picture? The leftover third painting."

Mrs. DePere could hold her tongue no longer and decided to answer Lillian's question for Captain Steele. She knew her offer would impress the captain and put him in the right frame of mind to do her a favor. Plus, this was an excellent chance to make a good deal attaining a famous piece of artwork. It would impress the neighbors.

"I'll take the racehorse picture, Mr. Captain! I'll take it sight unseen. Why, my husband is a member of the Washington Park Jockey Club of Chicago. It will remind him of the Washington Park Race Track he and General Philip Sheridan started last year. It is the Midwest's preeminent racetrack, you know." Mrs. DePere relished the opportunity to brag about her husband's high-class out-of-state investments and also drop in a famous name and title.

"Bertrand DePere will adore such a picture hanging in his den in Galena. He doesn't particularly enjoy my floral paintings in every room and every hallway for that matter and will welcome something more suited toward his masculine tastes."

Mrs. DePere continued her rapid chatter, "On second thought, I'll hang it in the parlor. It will be the talk of the town!" She proceeded to pronounce the Frenchman's name with great skill and care, "An original Ed-gar Duh-gah! Oh, but first do explain your connections with the ship, ah, ah, *Susan Tomkins*?"

"I believe the name is *Sadie Thompson*, ma'am. Say, what business is that of yours?" Captain Steele flashed wondering eyes at the fast-talking woman.

"Why, it is *all* my business, sir," she continued with an air of annoyance. "I have sent the United States Revenue Cutter *Tonawanda* after her!"

Captain Steele squinted his eyes. Ross and Charley looked at each other in alarm.

"I think that ship is gadding about trying to escape from something," Gwendolyn DePere announced. "No wonder its captain tried to push off these paintings on you. Why, I have reason to believe that *Sully Timpkins* is actually—a pirate ship!" Thoroughly delighted in all the attention, Mrs. DePere reveled in the shocked looks surrounding her.

"I am determined to find that elusive ship if it's the last thing I do," she continued, "and have it hauled in for pirating goods."

How odd, Lillian mused, *for Mrs. DePere to think of a Great Lakes schooner as a wandering pirate ship.* Then Lillian broke into a knowing smile. *Mrs. DePere can search all she wants, but* Sadie Thompson *is one "pirate ship" she will never find.*

Chapter 27

Mysteries Unraveled

Immediately following on Saturday at the Cobblestone Lighthouse lakefront on Cobblestone Island

"The *Sadly Thompsons* was supposed to deliver limestone cobblestones for my sister's spacious rose garden. She needed a lot of stone to fill a courtyard designed especially for her imported French roses." Mrs. DePere scanned the crowd to make sure she was making an impression. "I told her to buy our smoothest stones from up here in Lakeshore County and assured her that schooners are always making such deliveries. She is Mrs. Miranda Adler of Milwaukee," Mrs. DePere rattled on, emphasizing her sister's name slowly and distinctly to make sure everyone was aware that this famous title was *her* kin.

Lillian raised her eyebrows at the prideful prattle.

"That boat never made the delivery," the tall lanky woman continued. "Why, I have information that *Sadie Crompton* loaded up in Morrison Harbor and then spirited herself away. Through the Postal Telegraph System, I sent the armed steam vessel *Tonawanda* from the Federal Revenue Service out looking for her."

Captain Steele felt an immediate dislike for the woman, especially since she had no intention of correctly naming his former ship.

"And I believe the captain of the *Sassy Thompson* should be brought to terms when he is found. No less than a hearty fine for that scoundrel. With a jail sentence to go along with it! My sister may have to cancel her August garden party and the Milwaukee debut of her rose collection."

Captain Steele thought he'd have some fun. "Why, ma'am, in my course of travel, I met the *Tonawanda*. The captain asked about *Sadie Thompson* too. I told him I believed she was headed for the Straits of Mackinac where there is always a lot of boat traffic."

"Well, I'm certainly glad you gave him the tip. Like I said, the captain of *Sidney Tomplin* will be sorry after he deals with me."

Now Captain Steele went in for the kill, deliberately pronouncing the former name of his ship loudly and carefully because now he truly believed she was mispronouncing the name on purpose. "You think *Sadie Thompson* is a pirate ship, do you? Stealing rock cargo, eh?" He looked past Mrs. DePere's shoulders at the huge cobblestone pile in the distance. "There's enough rock right there behind you for your sister's rose garden. Why don't Clow and Skruggs and my two shipmates here load up this big pile of smooth cobblestones onto *Wanderer*, and we'll take them on to Milwaukee for you?"

"Oh?" The beam of Mrs. DePere's smile soared beyond delight. She felt she had truly charmed Captain Steele and directed him toward her wishes. "You would do that? I have reason to believe those cobbles *are* my sister's order and that for some odd reason the schooner dumped them here." She emphasized the ship's name with care.

"You don't say!" Captain Steele made sure he looked properly shocked at the horror of such reckless abandon.

"Well, actually," blurted Charley, "actually, them rocks . . ."

But Captain Steele clamped his large hand over Charley's mouth and continued the thought for him. "Actually, my sailorman here, good ol' Charley Skruggs is trying to tell you that he and Ross Clow and the boys would love to help you out, ma'am, by shoveling those garden cobble decorations onto *Wanderer* and getting them delivered to your sister in Milwaukee as quick as can be. Isn't that what you meant to say, Charley, old buddy? Wouldn't you like to do a favor for this charming woman?"

Mrs. DePere blushed from ear to ear.

Steele released his grip, stared Charley closely in the face, and added, "Wouldn't that just be something nice for us to do for the kind lady, eh?"

Taken completely by surprise, not comprehending a word his captain had said, Charley simply stared back and nodded in silent agreement.

Lillian looked in bewilderment at Julia. Luke and Garrett glanced back at their sisters equally as stunned. *Captain Steele seemed to have Mrs. DePere completely fooled, yet who was really the biggest fool of all? Seems as if Harry Hannibal, whoever he is, is the real pirate. Won't Perry Hannah who wants those three famous pieces of artwork be surprised when those paintings never show up to decorate his Traverse City mansion?*

Lillian curled her arm around Thomas who surprisingly did not try to escape her loving grasp. He understood that something in his sister had changed, which made him pleased beyond words.

"Thomas," Lillian began cautiously, "I've been wondering about something, something I'm really curious about." Thomas brightened. He liked curiosities. "How did you know we were looking for a gas engine on the ship that night? How did you know all the facts, all the dimensions of the box we were looking for?"

"Actually," Thomas began sheepishly, "I stole something myself, something of yours. I was feeling left out of your plans. I knew you four were up to something, so I decided to take Mother's suggestion to read that book she likes so much—the one she has read several times."

"The Susan Warner story?" asked Lillian. *The Hills of the Shatemuc?*

"Yes, the one you were reading and left in Priscilla's room on her nightstand. I noticed Luke and Garrett weren't in bed, and I couldn't sleep anyway. So I snuck the book out with the intention of reading it straight through the night. But I stopped at page twenty."

"Didn't you like the story?"

"The story is fine. But, Lillian, it wasn't too smart of you to leave Captain Steele's note as your bookmarker."

Lillian's face turned red with embarrassment. Ordinarily, she would have been upset over Thomas's brilliance and her inexcusable oversight. *Love feels no anger.*

"So I read the note," Thomas explained, "memorized the details, and figured out exactly what you four were up to. Then as you know, I met you that night down at the ship to help you search."

Lillian's newfound love for her smart sibling made her feel proud. *God made Thomas the way he is. Why should I be envious?*

Meanwhile, Mrs. DePere had a business deal on her mind. She glanced down at her purse, its drawstrings wound around her wrist. She bit her lip in apprehension as she approached Captain Steele, fumbling for a name to call him.

"Why, Captain . . . ? Captain . . . ?" Mrs. DePere searched for a name.

"Steele, ma'am. Captain Samuel Steele."

"They know 'im as 'Roaring Sam' in Milwaukee," Charley spit out, but only the children heard.

Mrs. DePere was far too intent to make an offer than to listen to Charley's chatter. "Captain Steele, about that third painting you have left over. We haven't discussed a price. You are so kind in offering to ship those cobblestones to my sister. Why don't I take that racehorse painting off your hands for, say, five hundred dollars?"

"Sold!" roared Captain Sam as he slapped his knee. And with a wink, he added, "And if I see that pirate ship, that *Silly Tompkins*, wandering around, I'll notify the authorities so that its devious captain can get his due."

"You are a delightful man, Captain Steele, unlike that disrespectful captain of the, the—*Sadie Thompson*, not *Silly Tompkins*, good captain. You must get the name straight if you are to go looking for it. As I was saying, maybe that disreputable captain can learn a thing or two from you should you chance a meeting with him."

"Oh, I'll bet Captain Steele *could* learn him a thing or two," Charley blurted out with a raucous yelp, but this time, it was Ross Clow's hand that clamped over Charley's mouth.

Mrs. DePere left for home with the precious purchase under her arm, happy beyond words to show off how she could pay for a famous painting in cash, on the spot—never mind that the five hundred dollars dislodged from her purse was supposed to go for something else entirely. In her excitement at the moment, she had consciously and completely put the real reason she and Lucinda had come to the lighthouse out of her mind. She would take up *that* matter at a different time. Securing an original Degas was, by far, more important.

Muttering wonderful things about racehorse pictures, Milwaukee rose gardens, and lake-smoothed rocks satisfied her thoughts completely. What's more, the haughty look on her face as she began her upward ascent to the lighthouse betrayed her worldly premise that everything works out for those who are clever, influential, and rich. She had to drag Lucinda up the long flight of steps as Lucinda dawdled, straining to gaze at the high cliff walls as if in search of something or someone.

Back at the lakefront, Luke was also curious about something. He approached Ross Clow with a burning question. "Mr. Clow," he began, "sir, I was wondering about something." Luke hesitated.

"What is it, sonny? Spit it out."

"When Father was talking about Debouteville's gas engine at the supper table a couple of nights ago, you threw Charley a look that made Lillian and me think you were hiding what we thought was a stolen gas engine aboard your ship."

"Yes," interrupted Lillian as she recalled the incident. "What was that about? We thought surely you were trying to keep Charley quiet by the look you gave him."

"Oh, don't even bring that topic up, kiddies, or Charley here will never give me any peace," began Ross.

"Gas engine?" blurted Charley.

"Here we go!" exclaimed Ross. "Charley's all fixed on modernizing our ship here. He's been badgering Captain Steele for weeks to look into gas power."

"And you didn't want him to dominate the discussion that night?" questioned Luke.

"Want you to know sumpin' about gas engines? I can learn you a thing or two about engine-powered rigs," Charley encouraged.

"No!" both Captain Steele's and Ross Clow's hands slammed against Charley's mouth to quiet him for the third time.

And that ended all talk about gas engines, at least for the time being.

Not to be shut down completely, Charley broke away from his mates and walked over to where Gabriel and Madelaine stood in complete fascination. Charley reached into a pocket and pulled out something white. He smoothed out the wrinkles by pressing it against his chest. Dainty lace edges, tatted delicately, betrayed recent wear by the gray of its color.

"I believe this be yourn, little miss." Charley smiled, pressing his lips tightly together to mask the black hole in his mouth. He did not want to frighten the beautiful young girl.

"My handkerchief from Mrs. Tivvy," Madelaine gasped. "You found it!" And without so much as a second's thought, she threw her arms around the big guy's neck and planted a thankful kiss upon his rough cheek. "Mrs. Tivvy from town gave this hanky to me for helping her son, Bennie."

Charley could have died happy that moment. He had known kindness from two lovely ladies in one week. A grown woman, artist Violet Wrede of Berrie's Island, and this beautiful little miss had recognized the depth of his soul without casting judgment on his appearance.

His heart having melted, he reached out and lifted lovely little Madelaine into the air at arm's length and flashed his ghastly toothless grin. To his utter and complete amazement, he found that Madelaine had neither shuddered nor screamed. She simply flashed back a sincere smile in return.

Chapter 28

Love Conquers

Saturday evening at Cobblestone Lighthouse

"Kari!" shouted Lillian in total surprise as she met her best friend on the lighthouse trail. It was the evening of the fourth day since the shipwreck of *Sadie Thompson.* Four dry, hot, breezy days in a row. "What are you doing here?"

"Miss Tourmalina and I . . ." said Kari, somewhat startled as she turned to her right.

"What's wrong?" Lillian noted her confusion. "What's the matter?"

"Why, I . . . Miss Tourmalina and I . . . She . . . Why, where did she go?"

"Who, Kari? What are you talking about?"

"Miss Tourmalina was here with me, but where did she go? She was here a minute ago."

"I saw all three not long ago on the cliff in front of the lighthouse. They were leaning on the new fence. I thought they would have come down to the lake, but they must have walked up here just to take in the beautiful view today. They never mingle much—with crowds, you know," replied Lillian. "They probably went home."

"Miss Tourmalina was with me a moment ago!" said Kari as she glanced over her shoulder in search of her missing companion.

"She was?"

"Yes, I have been so worried about your brother, Lillian. Father let me cross over from Washburn Island when I told him what you had told me about Thomas being missing. Father said I could stay for the night. I have been dying to know if you found Thomas or not. When I was halfway through my climb to the lighthouse, I met the Three on the trail. The other two kept walking, but Miss Tourmalina asked if I'd deliver a poem she has written for you."

"A poem . . . for me?"

Still confused, Kari turned around to search the forest pathway behind her. "Yes, from Miss Tourmalina . . . who, must have . . . must have, as you say, caught up with the other two and gone back home."

"Kari, you know Miss Tourmalina never strays far from Parakaleó. That's why I was so surprised to see her a while ago with the other two. But do tell me . . . she wrote a poem *for me*?"

"For you, Lillian Bates. C'mon, let's walk to the bluff cliff and watch the sun set. I can tell by how you are acting that Thomas is no longer in danger. I want you to tell me everything that has happened. And do not leave out any of the details."

Hand in hand, the girls walked to the spot where Lillian had seen her three friends on the bluff earlier that day.

The setting sun threw soft strawberry pink, apricot orange–colored ribbons of light across the teal-tinted lake. The two leaned against the newly built fence.

Lillian bubbled over with excitement, telling how Thomas had been found. Kari's teary eyes reflected genuine happiness for her best friend's good fortune. She was not a bit envious that she had not been as fortunate with her own brother. Still, she felt emotional. Kari listened with amazement as Lillian explained how Mrs. DePere and Lucinda had visited

Cobblestone Lighthouse and had made friends with Roaring Sam, the supposed pirate captain of *Sadie Thompson* or *Wanderer*.

Lillian retold Kari the whole story, this time in greater detail: the mix-up about the stolen gas engine, the Edgar "Duh-gah" paintings, her plunge into chilly Lake Michigan, the "missing" *Sadie Thompson*, and the change in Lucinda DePere. Lillian explained to Kari that neither she nor Julia nor the boys were quite sure whether Roaring Sam had acquired those famous French originals legitimately to sell or if he had pirated them through a meeting of ships on the lake. The true facts were anyone's guess.

Lillian and Kari agreed that Harry Hannibal, posing as Perry Hannah of Traverse City, was the real thief who had pirated away at least two of the valuable paintings. The girls could only wonder what Mr. Hannah would do when he found out that his paintings had been sold to someone else, to Harry Hannibal, whoever he was. They decided that whatever happened, the week had provided them with enough excitement to satisfy their cravings for adventure—at least for a while.

"Kari," Lillian felt close to her understanding friend, "I almost told my mother how we went snooping in Captain Steele's schooner that night—to find the gas engine but only found that box of paintings. But I couldn't. All I could think about was how Thomas was gone."

"Sure."

"And well"—Lillian smiled—"I should tell Mother and Father the whole story, I suppose, but all I can think about now is how happy I am that Thomas is back again. Right now, going aboard the ship that night doesn't seem to matter."

"Maybe someday you will know when to tell them."

"Yes, I suppose so." Lillian smiled because Kari really did understand.

Lillian and Kari sniffled and giggled in celebration of their close friendship. As the evening darkened, they saw that Lillian's father had lit the lighthouse lamp. The light's beam shot across the waves, and the two enjoyed a moment of silence. Finally, Kari unfolded the piece of paper she had tucked away in one hand, the poem that

Miss Tourmalina had written for Lillian. Feeling this moment as the perfect time to share, she led Lillian to sit on the nearby stone bench.

The evening continued to darken, and the fixed light from above illuminated the handwriting on Miss Tourmalina's note as Kari handed Lillian the poem. Lillian's voice softened to a whisper as she read the words out loud:

To Lillian—

When days are filled with wants and needs,
When pleasing self-instructs our deeds,
We look inside to satisfy;
We fill our hearts with what we eye.

How lonely such a life we lead,
How self-absorbed our wants we feed.
We grapple, struggle, kick each day;
We never cease to want our way.

So thoughtless is this daily creed,
So vile to plant such worthless seed.
We seek a straighter way to go;
We strive a richer boat to row.

In First John four the words we read,
In simple style our souls are freed.
We love another more than we;
We know that Jesus is the key.

Lillian slowed in her reading of the final stanza. Her voice was barely audible.

Now love your brother, this He pleads,
Now pull out deep and thoughtless weeds.
We cannot on our own this do;
We leave the work to Him—not you.

Understanding the pointed personal intent, Lillian repeated the last two words, "not you."

Kari rested her head on her best friend's shoulder, reading at an angle, wondering why Miss Tourmalina had chosen such words. What seemed like the passing of minutes was actually a mere moment. Neither spoke.

Lillian closed her eyes and pondered the words, *not you.* She understood. Her thoughts filled with the wonder of grace known and grace shared.

She glanced at the poem again, this time reading between the lines:

> *Not me.*
> *I have felt great longing. Longing to satisfy myself.*
> *I have been self-absorbed and lonely. I have kicked*
> *my poor Thomas.*
> *I have planted vile seeds. I have steered my life's boat*
> *in a dangerous direction. Then Love found*
> *me. Love set me free.*
> *Thomas is my brother, and I love him. I never real-*
> *ized it until now.*
> *Without Jesus, no one is my brother. I cannot love—*
> *on my own.*

"Kari?"

Kari raised her head.

"Kari, when I jumped off Captain Driver's fishing yawl . . ."

"Yes?"

"I had a real longing to swim. I couldn't resist the urge."

"I know."

"And when I did swim, I loved it."

"I know."

"The longing is still there."

"Okay."

"But something has changed. You see, I never felt quite right about why I wanted to swim at first. But now I feel different. I feel it's all right now." Kari studied Lillian, intently serious, entirely sincere. "And I think Miss Garnet has been trying to help me understand the importance of knowing the difference."

"The difference?"

"The difference between why I wanted to swim a week ago, which wasn't a good reason at all—and Miss Garnet somehow knew it wasn't a good reason, and realizing that if I thought about it deeply enough, I might discover a better reason to swim, which I have, and, and . . . Am I making any sense, Kari?" As Lillian searched for words, she saw Kari's face bathed in the dusky light of evening and was thankful for the uniqueness of their friendship.

Oh, Kari, how can I explain to you that I wanted to be like the children of Galena? Will you understand how I felt? The children of Galena have things I don't have. They do things I don't do. A week ago, all of that mattered to me. A week ago, my desire to swim was a desire to be like them. But now that I've tried it, my wanting to swim has nothing to do with an evil intention to imitate them—I am special, a Child of the Light, Kari. And you are too.

Now I want to swim simply to swim. It was a longing I've had for a long time, but the reason behind the longing is different now. This change is a wonderful gift. I feel . . . free!

Lillian struggled for words because trying to explain herself was not coming easily. "At first, I wanted to swim because I, because, um . . . but now I realize my reason is different because . . ." Lillian's intensity, her sincerity, her searching for words astonished Kari. Lillian seemed to have so much to say but seemed to have so little power to express her thoughts, even to her best friend Kari.

Lillian took a deep breath. *Dare I say this?* "You see," she continued, "almost losing Thomas . . ."—*Will Kari understand?*—"made me understand . . ."

"Yes?" Kari understood.

You loved Soren and then lost him. I hated Thomas but did not lose him. Oh, Kari, it doesn't seem fair at all for you. I don't want this to be painful for you.

"We can't judge the fairness of God. This thing with almost losing Thomas made me understand . . ." *Oh, Kari, I hope you know that you have always understood what is important, and that is why losing Soren is so hard. But you also understand God's will—and I didn't until now.*

"What I mean is almost losing Thomas made me understand what's important, and that has changed my reason for wanting to swim. Miss Garnet told me that understanding *why* we do things is important. Now I know *why* I want to swim. Why I *really* want to swim. Why I'm not afraid to because I had thought it might be wrong. Knowing sets me free."

Kari said nothing. She noticed a slight smile edge onto Lillian's face and wondered what she was thinking. She remained silent, offering Lillian time to collect her thoughts. She knew Lillian would share when she was ready to.

"Kari," Lillian began, "I still can't believe that my mother let our family swim at Galena's beach this week, alone. I've been bothering her about swimming a lot lately, and Mother has been quite firm about not letting me go. She seemed more cautious than ever, especially since Soren's accident." *Oh, why did I say that?* "Kari, I'm sorry. This is the second time I've brought up what happened to your brother at the lake. Oh, Kari, I'm . . . I'm . . ."

"That's okay." Kari lowered her head. She thought about the attention Lillian had offered when her brother Soren had died. Lillian's heartfelt sorrow then—when Kari needed someone to grieve with her—comforted her a lot. And Kari actually liked people bringing up Soren's name. But most wouldn't or couldn't. Bringing up Soren's name meant that he had not been forgotten.

"Mother isn't a worrier," Lillian continued, proceeding with caution. "But she hasn't been too excited about my wanting to swim. I can just sense that she doesn't want me—or any of us—to be in danger. I told her I feel strange that our family doesn't swim. I mean, everybody in Galena does, Kari. We're not *that* busy that we can't swim once in a while. I think I hurt Mother's feelings when I said that to her."

Lillian looked at Kari to determine whether speaking openly had now hurt *her* feelings. She only saw in Kari's face a look of true concern, so she persisted. "Ever since what happened to your brother,

Mother has been more protective than ever. Then when she actually *told* us to swim, she seemed suddenly okay with the whole idea. It's odd, Kari. It's like she personally asked for guardian angels to come to the beach with us or something." She sighed at the incredible idea.

"Maybe she did, Lillie. Maybe she did pray for angels to watch over you."

Lillian's sigh faded into seriousness. "Yes, well . . . I just know I feel right about swimming now—and that, for whatever reason, it's okay with Mother now too." Lillian turned to look at her friend directly. She continued with great passion, "Kari, I feel I can really *love* swimming now."

Kari said nothing.

"And love other things too."

"Things?"

"Well, people."

"Oh?"

Lillian let go of Kari's hands. She smiled with the satisfaction of understanding her own heart. Lillian chose not to explain her newfound feelings for Thomas. *I think Kari knows how I feel about Thomas now*, she decided.

But Kari could never know that a new thought suddenly swept through Lillian's mind, an idea even Lillian couldn't fully comprehend. In a burst of passion characteristic of a spontaneous personality that so easily acts on impulse, Lillian made up her mind. She would do something unbelievable—get to know storekeeper Mr. Scarsley. Soon. Maybe tomorrow or whenever the chance would come up. To understand him like she learned to understand Thomas.

As the sun sank below the horizon, Lillian looked through the dusk at the distant water, quiet and peaceful. She thought of Captain Steele. *Why does he treat his crew with such anger?* Her thoughts drifted toward Lucinda DePere in her perfect store-bought clothes but less than perfect attitude toward those outside her tight circle of friends. *Why does she scorn everyone not like her?*

Lillian considered the recent events of her adventure with the wandering pirate ship, the ship that pirated both a load of cobblestones meant for Milwaukee, then three paintings meant for Traverse

City. A light of empathy toward Lucinda and the captain filled her heart.

She smiled, thinking of her snug bed in the lighthouse. *I will pray tonight that the light of love fill Lucinda's, the captain's, and Mr. Scarsley's hearts as it has filled mine.* Lillian sighed as she harbored these thoughts with childlike faith. She had begun to understand love—to cherish it in her heart and to learn how to give it away. She also felt a sudden urge to share these thoughts with her sister.

"Let's look for Julia," Lillian suggested.

"I think she has read your mind," countered Kari. "Look, here she comes!"

Lillian turned around to see Julia bounding toward them.

"Mother was wondering where you two were," Julia called out. "It's late. You should come in."

I think you are the one who wonders where we have been, Julia. Lillian smiled. Without wishing to keep anything from her sister, Lillian grabbed Kari's hand and pulled her off the bench to meet approaching Julia. Together, the three girls climbed the outside steps leading into the side door to the lighthouse dwelling.

"It will be the three of us in our cozy bed tonight. Kari can stay over," Lillian explained. "And boy, do we have things to talk about!" She held up Miss Tourmalina's letter. "We have a poem to share with you, Julia."

The last one to step into the lighthouse, Kari walked straight toward a flower vase that Iona Bates had moved from the kitchen table into the front entrance foyer. The vase sat atop the lighthouse tender's newly delivered library box of books. Transfixed, Kari stared at the familiar but fresh blossoms. "Those aren't the flowers we picked in our meadow, are they?" she asked. Sure enough, the week-old wildflowers stood as straight and fresh as the day the girls had picked them.

USLH LIB

"I don't know. I guess they are," Lillian sounded casual. "C'mon upstairs. We have so much to talk about tonight. Things even more important than the wildflowers we picked for Mother last Sunday."

Kari's brows arched as high as the clouds, her eyes still staring incredulously at the flowers. On her way toward the climb upstairs, Julia also paused to study the contents of the vase.

Lillian had lost no time clamoring upward, her heart brimming full of expectation. "C'mon," she called down to the two lagging behind as they pondered the lifespans of lobelia and asphodel. "Let's go. We need to talk."

Kari turned around to glance at Julia whose eyes were fastened on the vase. They looked at each other, at the flowers, and then back at each other, instantly recognizing their simultaneous exchange of insight.

"Yes, Lillie, I think we have an awful lot to talk about tonight!" Julia smiled as she grabbed Kari's hand and pulled her up the stairs.

As the girls tumbled into bed, they bubbled with excitement, their eager chatter centered on the events of the week.

Mesmerized by the contents of Miss Tourmalina's poem, Julia led Kari into a discussion about the entrancing wildflowers, that somehow their mysterious ability to stay fresh had something to do with their visits to Cottage Parakaleó.

As Julia and Kari hammered out various theories and ideas about the flowers, Lillian's thoughts drifted off in a different direction. Less concerned with the transformation of flowers, Lillian concentrated on the transformation within herself. Her heart harbored more love than she ever dreamed possible, and she knew Miss Garnet, Miss Ruby, and Miss Tourmalina had much to do with this important new feeling.

Soon, Kari and Julia's chatter died down. Resting comfortably on her pillow, Lillian pulled the covers up to her chin. She closed her eyes. *This quilt still smells like Captain Steele.* She smiled. *What a week this has been . . . I'm so thankful for Thomas . . .*

Lillian drifted off to sleep with thoughts of a happy future, a future she felt certain would turn out well as long as her heart was enlightened with love.

To God be the glory

Holy Spirit, Light Divine
Shine upon this heart of mine;
Chase the gloom of night away;
Turn the darkness into day.

Epilogue

Two weeks later, Sunday evening, June 29, at Cobblestone Lighthouse on Lake Michigan, Lakeshore County, Wisconsin, 1884

In her nightgown, Lillian stood in the hallway just outside the kitchen, eavesdropping on her parents' conversation. From Luke and Garrett, the couple had indeed heard all the details about Captain Steele, "Harry Hannibal," and Mrs. DePere's big artistic purchase. They chose to say nothing yet frequently glanced at each other, offering a knowing wink or producing a wry smile suggesting they would not tell all they knew, especially to Gwendolyn DePere. It hadn't seemed to matter. Holding the latest edition of *The Lakeshore Advocate*, Curtis Bates read to his wife out loud a brief obscure article that had caught his eye:

> Lawsuit Filed
>
> Well-known Perry Hannah of Traverse City, Michigan, has filed a lawsuit against art expert Henry Hannibal of Elk Rapids. There appears to be unclarity concerning the value of three artworks by Edgar Degas, two of which have turned up at the East Side Picture Show art gallery of Traverse City. The whereabouts of the missing third work, heretofore recognized as an original, unverified, is unknown.

Perry Hannah. Lillian couldn't believe what she had just heard. *Perry Hannah found out about Harry Hannibal.*

"I had been wondering all along, Curtis," Iona commented, "why that Hannibal fellow had only taken two of the paintings. Being an 'art expert,' he must have known the third one was likely a fake."

"I imagine he did recognize the two originals," her husband said, "bought them cheap from Captain Steele, and then sold them for a profit to the East Side Picture Show. But who do you suppose this Perry Hannah fellow is?"

Should I tell them the whole story? Lillian wondered, still listening from the hallway.

"I don't know, dear," answered Iona, "but I'm guessing he is the man who was actually supposed to receive the paintings, for a more reasonable price than that Michigan art gallery charges."

How does Mother know these things? Lillian was incredulous.

"In any case, I don't want to be around Gwendolyn DePere if she reads this item and suspects she may have been swindled into buying fraudulent artwork," continued Iona. "*Her lawsuit* would not be hidden on an inside page. She would make sure *her lawsuit* would be front-page headlines."

Ha, Mrs. DePere paid all that money for a possible fake. Lillian smiled with satisfaction. Then because she was a Child of the Light, she was moved to hope that Mrs. DePere would somehow never see or hear this piece of news.

I do love my brother Thomas, Lillian admitted to herself. *Now I've actually learned how to love Mrs. DePere, which is nothing short of a miracle.*

At Cottage Parakaleó—three women, one studying at a writing desk, one baking in the kitchen, and one creating poetry in a loft—paused from their tasks to simultaneously ponder what they had recently tried to teach Lillian, first throughout her weeks of recovery and then throughout her weeks of freedom that followed. Red reflections created streaks of light that danced across the walls and ceilings as one woman fingered her ruby brooch, one touched her garnet necklace, and one flashed her tourmaline ring. The room transformed into a ruddy glow.

From the hallway, Lillian watched as her mother flipped through the family Bible that lay open on the kitchen table. Iona sat alone because her husband had gone upstairs to the lantern room. "Now where is that psalm?" Lillian heard her mother ask herself. "Is it thirty-two or thirty-three? Ah, here it is—Psalm thirty-four, verse seven. 'The angel of the LORD encampeth round about them that fear him and delivereth them.'" As Iona Bates closed the Book with a thankful smile, Lillian also smiled as she tiptoed away from the kitchen to climb upstairs.

Soon, Lillian lay nestled next to Julia in their cozy bed. Had her sister not been enjoying a deep slumber, Lillian would have awakened her to point out the beautiful flashes of light that darted about the room.

These are crazy reflections, no doubt from the lighthouse—although I've never seen these colors before. And they kind of look like hearts . . . and . . . they are red. But Cobblestone Lighthouse throws out a fixed white light. She let out a slow yawn. *Remnants of the sunset, I guess . . .* A second yawn.

I am very happy, Lillian concluded as she watched the lights, the brilliant rhythms hypnotizing her. She felt at peace with the world. *Thank you, God,* she began her nighttime prayer, *for brothers and sisters, for my parents, and for Kari.*

The softening lights began to lull her to sleep. *Thank you for my three special friends at Cottage Parakaleó who have helped me . . .* She paused as her mouth opened into a third yawn. "Who have helped me . . ." she continued out loud although halted by yet another yawn. "Who have helped me . . ." Lillian's voice trailed into nothingness as the unusual hovering russet glows found a resting spot over her pillow.

The lights lit upon Lillian and enveloped her much like the sudden mysterious warmth in the cold waters of Lake Michigan had

strengthened her body and spirit when she had struggled to save Thomas in the rickety dinghy.

Lillian's lips parted slowly as they formed a compassionate smile. She continued her broken prayers, this time out loud, "Thank you for my three special friends who have helped me gain a new understanding of . . ." Lillian had fallen asleep, bathed in happiness knowing she was a Child of the Light who without outwardly admitting had finally come to a closer understanding of love.

Read about more adventures featuring "The Children of the Light" in Book 2, *Moon Glow and Twisted Brew*.

Historic Note from the Author

Did pirates exist on the Great Lakes? "Roaring Dan" Seavey did. Although at times a courteous gentleman, Captain Seavey's fame came from his image as a rough and tough "pirate." And he was arrested as one. A *Milwaukee Journal* article, date unknown, entitled "Two Fisted 'Pirate' Is Lake Port Legend," states that on June 11, 1908, Seavey was actually taken to court and tried for pirating the lumber schooner *Nellie Johnson*.

Seavey and two crewmen had taken the sailing vessel out of a Michigan port and set themselves on a course bound for Chicago. The United States revenue cutter *Tuscarora* went after them and eventually captured the thieves. Seavey had made it to Chicago, but not according to his plan. Tried there as a pirate, the court eventually acquitted him, giving him the title ever after as the "old pirate."

Two sisters, Jeri-Lynn Betts and Lori Betts Lawrenz, heard from relatives that their great-grandmother Emily Rohn Betts had housed and fed a Great Lakes pirate. Emily did this on small Rock Island in Door County, Wisconsin, where she raised nine children and assisted her husband as a lighthouse keeper. Could Emily's pirate guest have been "Roaring Dan"? Does the newspaper clipping about Dan found in a Betts family scrapbook provide the proof?

History proves a Great Lakes pirate did exist. Although fiction, *The Wandering Pirate Ship* builds on this historical fact. Pottawatomie Lighthouse on Rock Island where William C. Betts kept the light for over sixteen years provides authentic background. His original lighthouse log from 1872 to 1886, newspaper articles about his island adventures, personal excerpts from the Betts family scrapbook, and

Rohn family letters add historical authenticity to these "Children of the Light" stories.

May the adventures continue.

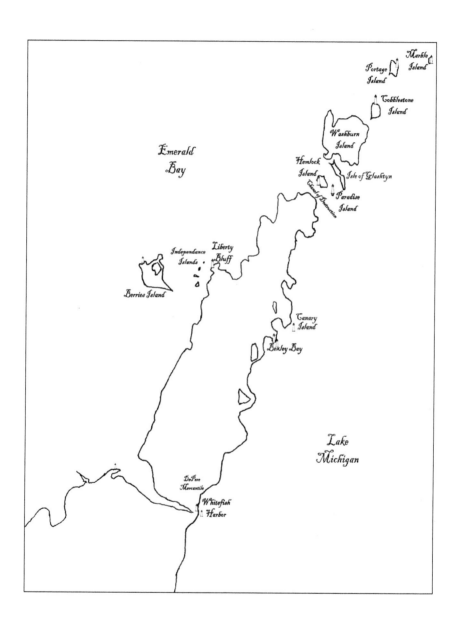

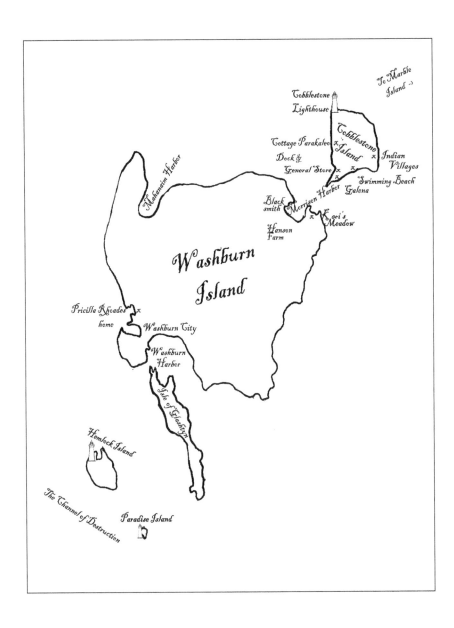

To Marble
Island

Cobblestone
Lighthouse

Cottage Parakaleo x
Dock &
General Store x

Cobblestone
Island

x
x x
x

Indian
Villages

Swimming Beach
Galena

Mahawatni Harbor

Black
smith
Merrison Harbor

Kari's
Meadow

Hanson
Farm

Washburn
Island

Pricilla Rhoades
home

Washburn City

Washburn
Harbor

Isle of Glashyn

Hemlock Island

The Channel of Destruction

Paradise Island

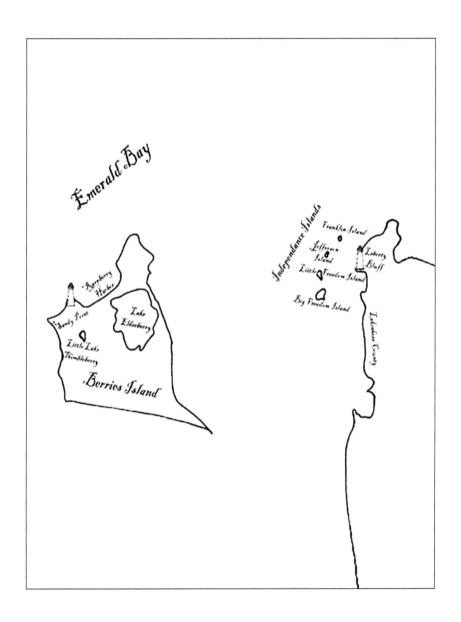

About the Author

Mary I. Schmal has taught students in Kindergarten through college. She holds both a Bachelor's and Master's Degree in education. In her teaching, she enjoys the opportunity to develop her students' creativity and a love of learning. Mary especially enjoys presenting workshops for teachers and students in creative writing. To this end, Mary designed, wrote, and produced *Rainbow Class* and *Pot of Gold,* two supplementary creative writing courses for middle grades. The courses encourage both creativity and proper writing skills. All of Mary's experiences have been directed toward a common goal: to stimulate motivation for her students to realize their God-given potential in becoming the unique children of God that he created them to be. Now, as author of the *Children of the Light* series, it is her hope that the books in this series will create a desire to dig deeply into God's Word. Her prayer is that through the characters in the stories, readers know and embrace the free gifts known as the Fruit of the Spirit: love, joy, peace, patience, gentleness, goodness, kindness, self-control, and faithfulness. *Nine kids. Nine gifts. Nine blessed.* When Mary isn't teaching, reading, or writing, she enjoys singing, performing in or attending the theatre, visiting lighthouses, studying astronomy, and most of all, spending time with family and friends. She also enjoys vacationing in Door County, Wisconsin. Door County is home to many lighthouses and was inspirational in the creation of the *Children of the Light* series. Mary is married to her husband Dan, and they have two married children and three young granddaughters—all who light her life with great joy.

Mary@cotlb.email

About the Illustrator

Leanne R. Ross holds a Bachelor's in Education from Martin Luther College (New Ulm, MN). She studied art at Inver Hills Community College and the University of Minnesota at Mankato and Minneapolis. She has taught many art courses for children through adult levels including calligraphy, drawing, painting, ceramics, mixed media, fiber arts, and graphic design. She has taught speech communication, drawing, ceramics, and graphic communications at Wisconsin Lutheran High School (Milwaukee, WI) and has served as artistic and general editor and advisor of the high school yearbook staff. For her it has been a wonderful adventure to create illustrations for the *Children of the Light* series. Leanne is married to David, and they have been blessed with six children and seven grandchildren.

Leanne@cotlb.email

CPSIA information can be obtained
at www.ICGtesting.com
Printed in the USA
FFHW02n1342130818
47715529-51373FF